# RUNNING Mates

A NOVEL

# RUNNING Mates

## A NOVEL

## EMILY LOCKER

Bancroft Press

bancroft
press

Cover Art & Interior Design by Anita Dugan-Moore, cyber-bytz.com

978-1-61088-622-2 (HC)
978-1-61088-623-9 (PB)
978-1-61088-624-6 (Ebook)
978-1-61088-625-3 (PDF)
978-1-61088-626-0 (Audiobook)

Published by Bancroft Press
"Books that Enlighten"
410-627-0608
4527 Glenwood Ave.
La Crescenta, CA 91214
www.bancroftpress.com

Printed in the U.S.A.

*To my extraordinary parents, Roger and Pauline, thank
you for all the love and support. You let me believe there were no
limits if I tried hard enough. I hope to be half the parent, spouse,
grandparent, and person you modeled so well. With all my love
and gratitude, this is for you.*

# CHAPTER 1

"Annabelle, try to hustle. The world isn't going to save it-self," Mom calls to me from somewhere downstairs. "The Bahars will be here in fifteen minutes!"

*Ugh!* How could I forget? My hands pause on the laces of my running sneakers.

"An-na-belle!" Mom calls again, impatience growing with each syllable.

"Coming!" I quickly finish tying my shoes and dash down the stairs, pulling my unruly curls into a ponytail as I try to remember what we're protesting today. Factory farming? No, that was last week. Restrictions on reproductive rights? No, that's every third Saturday of the month. It's hard to keep track.

After all, there's just so much wrong with the world. And no, I do not find it at all problematic that I can't remember what we're protesting (or that we were protesting at all today). Just because I'm not always as well-informed as my best friends, Del and Mason, or Mason's dreadful girlfriend, Zoe, doesn't mean I care any less.

Saving the Greenway! I finally remember as I hit the landing and turn into the sun-filled kitchen at full speed. Mimi (my other mom) smiles at me as she pours coffee into a plum-colored ceramic mug. "I see the protest has you all fired up." She tosses me an apple. At five-foot-three, she's shorter than Mom or me, but despite her petite frame, she's the strongest person I know.

"Well," I bite my lip guiltily, catching the apple in midair. "For sure it does, but also, Ms. Adler just emailed me that my book order came in." I carefully omit the title, not sure *Reforming a Rake* would exactly resonate with Mimi. I am absolutely, not-at-all ashamed I secretly read romance novels. It's just that I know how it makes me look—especially to my two uber-educated moms and my highbrow friends.

Mimi looks at her watch, then pushes her blonde hair behind her ear. "Do you really have time to go to Bookcourt before the protest?"

"Hey, I'm a fast runner," I remind Mimi. I may not have the same academic chops as my nearest and dearest, but I'm one of the stars of Edgartown High's cross country team. "And Bookcourt is on the way to the Greenway. Just tell Mom to tell Ms. Bahar to meet me on Main Street after they pick up Mason."

"Okay," Mimi relents. "I guess they'll be driving right by it." Her sky-blue eyes hold a warning. "Just hurry. You know how your mom is about time."

"I heard that!" Mom sweeps into the kitchen, glamorous in her silk green shirt and jeans. Her auburn hair is swept into a perfect low ponytail, and tiny gold studs spark at her ears. Her porcelain skin looks flawless and dewy.

"I was just telling our daughter how I so admire your commitment to punctuality." Mimi kisses Mom's cheeks and winks at me. "I wish I could come with you two! Hate to miss this one."

"You're too busy saving actual lives," I assure her as I inch quietly toward the door. Mimi is dressed in her teal scrubs, about to head to the OR to perform surgery.

"We're saving lives too, sweetie," Mom reminds me as she turns to fill her coffee mug, thankfully not noting that I'm trying to leave the house. "We just don't get covered in blood while doing it."

I put my hand on the doorknob.

Mimi nods in bemused agreement. "It's a good thing, too, because I don't think that silk shirt would convey the same 'woman about town' look with blood splotches on it."

I stifle a laugh before turning quickly toward Mom. "Mom,

I'm running to Bookcourt first. Pick me up there. Mimi will explain!" I say as fast as humanly possible and practically leap out onto the flagstone steps leading from our backyard to the front. I take a half-second to enjoy the changing colors and smell the crisp fall leaves from a beech tree overhead. Then I pop my earbuds in, press play on my favorite romance novel-themed podcast, "Fated Mates," and sprint toward town.

* * * *

Sarah and Jen, the podcast co-hosts, are discussing grand gestures in romance novels, as I continue my grueling pace down my understated yet tasteful Eastside neighborhood of Edgartown, North Carolina, where we (and anyone we like in Edgartown) live. Whizzing past the tree-lined streets, espresso bars, community gardens, and yoga studios, I turn onto Cranberry Road, one of the rare residential streets that borders both sides of town. On the Northside, gas-guzzling SUVs sit parked in front of McMansions, with impeccable, pesticide-treated lawns that are environmental nightmares, but look straight out of *Better Homes and Gardens*. On the Eastside, Craftsman houses with hybrid cars and virtue-signaling LEED plaques seem to compete for the "I care about the earth the most" award.

I start to imagine what it would be like to be on the receiving end of a romantic gesture. Would I even like it? Sounds kind of intense, I think as I finally hit Cranberry and Main Street, where the Northside and the Eastside collide. I push a sweaty curl off my face as I wait for the light to change. To my right, on the Eastside of Main, are the local yarn shop, specialty cheese store, and Bookcourt, my destination. To my left, the Northside of Main, Vineyard Vines, Starbucks, Restoration Hardware, and other upscale chain stores reside. Mimi says the Northside lacks imagination, but Mom disagrees—she thinks it lacks taste.

The traffic light changes and my heart rate ticks up. Not just because I'm racing down the street again, but because the podcast hosts instruct, "Earphones in," meaning they're going to say something *really* juicy. My vocabulary has been wildly expanded since I started listening to "Fated Mates." And I do mean *wildly*.

As Jen and Sarah start ranking the sexiest beach scenes they've ever read, I am about six feet from Bookcourt when BOOM!

I slam into what feels like a wall of bricks, my earphones fall out, and my traitorous iPhone starts blaring, *"And she had FOUR, that is right, FOUR, orgasms in two pages. Now THAT is impressive."* I scramble to get my phone and turn off the sound. My cheeks are on fire as I hope against hope that no one overheard.

"That really is quite impressive," a voice from above me says, followed by a low, masculine chuckle.

I close my eyes briefly, remaining crouched down, filled with all the cringiest feelings. I force myself to slowly stand up and open my eyes. I want to slam them shut again when I find myself face to face with Gabe Freaking Delgado, quintessential Northside boy. I don't know him well, but, because of his father, everyone knows who he is.

I rub my shoulder, which is stinging from where it slammed into Gabe's splendid chest (not that I'm noticing, of course).

Like me, Gabe is dressed in running gear. He's wearing a white Edgartown lacrosse team t-shirt and navy shorts. I try hard not to notice how toned his arms are as he lifts his shoulder and rotates it as if working out a kink, probably from where I barreled into him. And then I try even harder not to notice how chiseled his cheekbones are as he tilts his head to smile at me and says, "Is your shoulder okay? Sorry about that."

He actually looks concerned and is genuinely apologizing even though I'm ninety nine percent sure we collided because I looked down to turn up the volume on my phone. I find this all super annoying—Gabe Delgado acting like Mr. Nice Guy. Please. Northern guys are many things, but nice is not one of them.

"Yeah, it's fine. I wasn't looking where I was going."

"Well, I can't say I blame you." He shoots me a half-smile. "You were listening to some pretty enlightening stuff there." Gabe gestures toward my phone and laughs when my face flames again. "I'm just kidding," he assures me, apparently softening his teasing tone when he sees how embarrassed I am.

Before I can decide how to reply—my top options being: 1) claim I'm flushed only because of my high running speed or 2) cheekily tell him I hope I gave him something to aspire to—Ms. Adler, the owner of Bookcourt and one of my favorite people, appears, holding my book. Unfortunately, due to the recent paperless policy at the store, there's no bag, just the naked book…bodice-ripping cover and all.

"Honey, here you go!" Ms. Adler says in her soft sing-song voice. Her gray hair is in a neat, low bun and her warm brown eyes crinkle. Her face is lightly weathered due to age and her lifelong love of the beach. Per usual, she smells lightly of lavender. "Your mom is across the street and looks like she wants you to hurry so I thought I'd run this out to you." Ms. Adler hands me my book.

My head whips across the street, where I see Ms. Bahar's Volvo pulled over. Mom is in the passenger side, window down, motioning for me to hurry. My best friends Delasa (Del) Bahar and Mason Brent are in the back seat looking at me slightly agog, likely wondering why on earth I was standing next to Gabe Delgado on Main Street.

"Hi, Ms. Adler," Gabe says pleasantly. If I weren't so aware of Gabe looking at the cover of my book, biting his lip to prevent himself from full-on laughing, I'd have wondered about Gabe's familiarity with the Bookcourt owner. I never saw many Northsiders in the bookstore.

"Annabelle, let's get going!" my mom calls from the car.

"Coming!" I yell back.

"Thanks, Ms. Adler," I say as she heads back into the store.

Gabe pops his own earphones back in and apologizes again for the run-in.

"Not as sorry as I am," I reply through gritted teeth.

Gabe laughs again. "Enjoy the book," he says as he resumes his steady jogging pace down the street, athleticism evident in each stride.

I shake my head and run across the street, dodging cars. I slide in the back seat next to Del and Mason.

Mom throws me a disapproving look, presumably of my time-management skills, and hands me a granola bar. "Mimi was worried you didn't eat breakfast."

I take it, suddenly realizing how hungry I am, and bite into it, sliding low into my seat as Del and Mason turn to look at me inquisitively.

With Ms. Bahar steering the Volvo back onto the road, Del, in the middle seat, pokes me in the rib. "You okay? You look a little flushed."

I turn and look at my bestie. She's removing a hipster beanie, her thick, wavy (but never frizzy) hair spilling from it. Meanwhile, my own ponytail seemingly triples in size as I wait for the Bahars' AC to cool me off.

"Why is he so perfect muscley?" I whisper, barely resisting the urge to symbolically fan myself. "I mean really. Sure, I have no doubt that all good-looking lacrosse players are probably at least mildly misogynistic, but I mean, wow."

Del rolls her eyes at me. *"Perfect muscley?"*

"Like not big, creepy, and steroidy—because gross—but not so small that he looks like the underfed vegans we hang out with," I elaborate.

"Hey!" Mason objects, glaring at me. Mason's wearing jeans and a plaid button-down along with his trademark red scarf.

"Don't worry, you pull off the anemic look better than most. Being pale makes the gray flecks in your eyes pop."

Del and Mason laugh, but I catch Mason scrutinizing his reflection in the mirror. He still feels like the scrawny little kid getting picked on by the guys who'd won the puberty race. By fourth grade, Mason had shot up like a weed, but he officially made the jump from "'nerd" to "cool" in fifth grade when he first picked up the guitar. Ever since, he's been *quite* popular with Eastside girls. His red scarf even has its own entire Instagram account, thanks to some precocious Eastside freshmen last year.

"Anna thinks Gabe is hot," Del complains to Mason.

"*Shh.* Remember, sore subject." I elbow her.

"It's fine." Mason crosses his arms. "If Annabelle wants to

lust after Gabe — not just my personal enemy, but the enemy of the left—that's on her. Should I ask your mom what she thinks about it, Anna Banana?" He winks at me.

Horrified, I swing my head toward the front seat to make sure my mom hasn't heard. Lilly Morningstar, darling TV pundit of the liberal elite, would be displeased, to say the least, to hear that her daughter thinks Gabe Delgado, the son of Republican Senator Oscar Delgado, is a total hottie. Which, for the record, he is. With wavy dark brown hair and large, piercing eyes, Gabe is the very definition of tall, dark, and handsome.

But we put our talk of preppy lacrosse players on hold as we pull into the driveway of the community center. We gather Del's hand-crafted signs, tighten our shoelaces, and prepare to march to save the Greenway.

# CHAPTER 2

I'm in a terrible mood and not for any of the reasons I should be—like the fact I knew the "vegan" burger I ordered for dinner last night was the real thing, but it tasted so good I didn't send it back.

I'm in the middle of meeting with Ms. Thatcher, the school's college counselor. I like Ms. Thatcher—she's kind and reasonably competent at her job, and her office isn't dreary or sterile like those of the other school counselors. That said, she doesn't really get me. She overly associates me with my chic mom ("She always looks so great on TV!") *and* is oddly too sympathetic about my learning "issues."

"Ok, Annabelle, the good news is you're doing quite well academically. Impressive, given your challenges."

I grimace. It's annoying how learning disabilities can be so misunderstood. "Um, thanks. Yeah, it's been a good year so far."

"Especially for history! Getting placed in honors…I'm sure having moms as brilliant as yours helps."

I force a smile.

She looks down at her folder. "And your SAT scores are coming up nicely. We were worried there for a bit."

My affection for Ms. Thatcher wanes. "Yeah, that was embarrassing. At least they're only kind of bad now and not terrible."

"No, sweetie, that's not what I meant at all. I'm just saying you're really turning things around."

"Enough to consider Yale?" I ask hopefully.

Ms. Thatcher's expression drops a little. "I'm afraid that would be a huge leap, even with your legacy status."

"Oh." My face crumbles. "Even with all my extracurriculars? I'm in the Young Democrats, Liberal Liaisons, and Eating Vegan. I write that monthly op-ed on politics for *The Red and Blue*. And I'm the star of the cross-country team... or at least one of the most enthusiastic runners. And I volunteer for Planned Parenthood and NARAL."

Ms. Thatcher glances at my file. "You certainly do have a lot of activities. But this is the age of Greta Thunberg. You can't just show you care about changing the world. You have to actually change it."

"No pressure or anything," I joke, but I feel tears well up in my eyes. I don't know what's wrong with me. I knew getting into Yale was unlikely. But why does hearing it aloud, from my counselor, make me feel so terrible?

Ms. Thatcher looks sympathetic and hands me a box of tissues.

"There's nothing I can do?" I look at her imploringly. "I'd really be happy with any of the top, like, say thirty-five schools." I link my fingers together nervously. "You see, it's just that Del and Mason are definitely going Ivy. Between that and my moms... well, I don't want to be totally left out!"

Ms. Thatcher nudges the tissues closer to me. "Sweetie, a lot of very successful people don't go to those types of schools. I'm worried you're placing too much importance on it. You're a smart, charming young woman. There is so much you can do with your life no matter where you go to college."

I feel shocked. *Too much importance?* After how hard I've worked for years to make the cut—studying for endless hours, throwing myself into activities with abandon—and I still fall short?

"Everything okay, Annabelle?" Ms. Thatcher asks encouragingly.

I nod glumly. "Too bad college admissions don't place more

value on self-awareness. I've had more therapy than all my friends combined! You can't put a grade on knowing yourself."

Ms. Thatcher uses her mug to hide what appears to be a smile. "I'm sorry, Anna. Maybe self-awareness will be a quantifiable admissions credential one day, but for now I think we need to focus on more realistic options."

"Right, right, I know." I wipe my tears away, feeling like a baby and a spoiled brat. Most people don't get to go to elite schools. But I guess most people aren't surrounded by people who have.

Ms. Thatcher hands me her list of more "realistic" colleges, which I find depressing, but promise to consider.

Just as I'm sure my life is over, Ms. Thatcher looks at my folder again. "Well, this could be a long shot, so please don't get too excited, but—"

I shoot out of my chair with anticipation. "What?"

"You're quite an accomplished runner. It seems your long run is just one minute shy of recruitment level."

My excitement fades. "One minute isn't really small potatoes," I say.

"No, it isn't." She pauses, tilting her head. "But, as you just pointed out, maybe you're over-committed with all your extracurriculars. Perhaps with a little more focus on cross country, you could shave off enough time."

"Ms. T, this is a little Sophie's Choice here," I say, my shoulders jerking back in alarm. "Are you suggesting I cut down on social justice activities to get into a better college?"

"I'm not suggesting that at all, Annabelle. I think being well-rounded is priceless. However, if going to a top school is that important to you, this is a potential path to pursue." She raises a finger in the air as if an idea just hit her. "Do you know Gabe Delgado? He's in your year. He's organized a weekly Monday conditioning session for student-athletes who are serious contenders for college recruitment. Apparently, he has a pretty big-deal coach—a Coach Farmer, I believe—leading it."

My jaw drops and my stomach swirls with excitement. Coach Farmer is the track and field coach at Edgartown College, He was

11

a star runner at Stanford. How did Gabe manage that? "All of a sudden, I can't escape Gabe Freaking Delgado?" I grumble, not sure why hearing about this irritates me.

"Excuse me?" Ms. Thatcher squints her eyes in confusion.

*Oops*, did I say that aloud? "Uh, I meant, I thought we weren't allowed to use gym facilities on Mondays?"

"Gabe got the school to make an exception."

I roll my eyes. "Of course he did."

Ms. Thatcher narrows her eyes. "So you do know Gabe?"

"Not really. I mean, I ran into him Saturday," I unconsciously rub my shoulder. "Like, literally. The whole thing was kind of embarrassing actually."

Ms. Thatcher squints again and purses her lips in confusion. "Well, he's a lovely young man, and he told me he's concerned no women have signed up for the conditioning program yet."

"He cares about gender equality?" I ask doubtfully.

"Apparently so." Ms. Thatcher looks at her watch. "Okay, Anna, I need to take my next appointment. Why don't you look over that list and make an appointment with me in two weeks so we can further discuss this?"

I nod, my ears ringing.

Running out of Ms. Thatcher's office, I feel her list of colleges burning a hole in my bag. I look left and right, wanting to dodge run-ins with anyone while my mind is spinning out of control.

# CHAPTER

## 3

Over and over, I grapple with my choice—join a training program with a legendary coach or keep my spot on the Liberal Liaison executive team. Then the final bell rips me from my stupor. Or rather, it's not a bell, but Edgartown High's version of a bell, which is actually the first three notes of Beethoven's Ninth playing through the loudspeakers. Honestly, his Fifth symphony would be more appropriate for the foul mood I'm in. *Dun, dun, dun, dun!* indeed.

My head pounds. A buzz from my coat pocket grabs my attention. I swipe open the notification and sigh. It's Zoe Dart with a text alert instructing all us Liberal Liaisons to meet at Orange Street and Hicks at 4 p.m.

Another buzz. Now, it's Del asking me and Mason to meet for pre-Liaison "activism fuel"—aka coffee.

I rush down the hall, pushing past some idling freshmen, anxious to find my friends and tell them about my dilemma when I hear "Anna, wait up!"

I turn to find Gabe, a friendly smile on his face. In fact, his smile is so winning, I find myself grinning back for no reason. But then I remind myself that I'm beaming at a Northsider, and I force my smile down a few decibels. "Um, can I help you?"

Gabe nods sheepishly. "Yeah, you can, actually." He straightens his shoulders. "Don't mean to put you on the spot, but Ms. Thatcher said you might be interested in joining the conditioning club on Mondays."

Taken aback that Ms. Thatcher had already talked to Gabe, I struggle to formulate a response. "I might be," I hesitate.

"It's going to be awesome, especially if we nail down Coach Farmer." Gabe's expression dims. "But he won't do it without a girl."

I narrow my eyes. "So that's why you need a girl. I knew Ms. Thatcher was confused."

Gabe tilts his head to the side. "I'm going to dodge that bullet since I have no idea what you're talking about. But listen, if you're serious about running in college, this is a great way to qualify."

My frown deepens as his grin widens. He makes it sound so easy. "I'm very serious about it," I start assertively, before hesitation kicks back in. "Or at least I've been serious about it since Ms. Thatcher mentioned it three hours ago. But it's really not that simple."

Gabe's lips twitch with amusement. "How is something you've been contemplating for three whole hours not simple?"

I want to throw my hands over my head in exasperation, but I remain still. Why am I explaining myself to Gabe Flipping Delgado? I really need to talk to Mason and Del. But since Gabe is looking at me expectantly, I answer: "If I agree to do it, I'll miss the Liberal Liaison meetings, which is a problem. You can't be on the executive committee if you miss more than two meetings, and all my friends are on it." To my horror, I feel tears beginning to burn in the corner of my eyes.

Gabe looks alarmed, but there's nothing I can do to stop myself. As my tears start to fall, he reaches over and pats my shoulder awkwardly.

"Sorry," I mutter. "This isn't like me. It's been a really, really rough day."

"It's okay. We all have them," Gabe attempts to sound reassuring, but he's looking at me like I'm completely unstable.

Before I can think about how it sounds, I blurt out, "I just found out I'm most definitely not getting into an Ivy unless I shave a minute off my long run. So, basically, everything I've been working for has been for nothing." I cringe. "I know there are bigger problems in the world than where I go to college, and I'm sure I'll be totally fine by like 6 p.m. tops, but it's hitting me pretty hard right now."

Gabe gives me a skeptical look. "Really? By 6:00 p.m.? Totally fine?"

"Yup, I will be," I insist.

"I'll take your word for it, but it sounds like the Monday training sessions are just what you need."

I bite my lip. "How many other people have signed up?"

Gabe's expression falters. "Only two of us so far, but you know how seriously everyone here takes their extracurricular Mondays."

I laugh a little. "I sure do." To make sure students participate actively (and I mean actively) in other extracurriculars, Mondays are a devoted no-sports practice day at our school. "So who is this other person?" I ask.

"Sam Price. Do you know him? He's on the lacrosse team with me. Awesome guy."

I sigh. Sam is basically the blond-haired version of Gabe. "You should have chosen soccer," I say. "Lacrosse just reeks of toxic male energy and privilege. Don't you think?"

"What?" Gabe wrinkles his brows in confusion. "Is that a joke?"

"Eh, never mind. So, I have to choose between saving the world with my friends or running sprints with two Northside lax bros?"

"I wouldn't put it quite that way," Gabe says.

My phone buzzes a third time, then a fourth. It's Mason saying he and Del are waiting. Through my iPhone, I can sense Mason's annoyance.

"I've got to run, but I'll think this over and get back to you tomorrow if that's okay?" I grab the straps of my backpack. "Although heads up, I'm leaning toward not doing it."

15

Gabe nods. "Look, do whatever you have to do, but I promise training will be rewarding. Sam and I plan to leave it all out there."

I lift an eyebrow. "As rewarding as saving the world?"

"No," Gabe sighs. "But I don't think you Liberal Liaison people—or whatever you call yourselves—are doing that anyway."

"Hey!"

"I'm just saying, I know your run time will improve if you do this. The other outcome —the world-saving outcome—is harder to predict."

We look at each other for another moment, me with annoyance, he with steady calm, which only annoys me more.

Finally, I excuse myself to go find Del and Mason.

"Think it over," Gabe says one more time before waving and heading the opposite way down the hall.

# CHAPTER

4

$A$t my insistence, Del, Mason, and I walk the scenic way from school to our Liberal Liaisons meeting, which takes twice as long but optimizes what I love most about Edgartown: winding, magnolia-lined side streets, brick Georgian-style homes, and picture windows spilling over with hydrangeas and tulips. We're sipping iced coffees, which we bought from The Bookery, the café attached to Bookcourt. Del and Mason always complain that the coffee is better at Reveiller, the trendy espresso bar downtown, but I am steadfast in my loyalty.

"What do you know about Sam Price?" I ask, trying to sound disinterested.

Del stops to brush dirt off her new pink high tops. "Blond, tall Northsider. Seems friendly…for a Northsider." She's wearing black faux leather pants and a fuzzy green sweater. She looks awesome.

"He's good friends with Scott." Mason finally looks up from the stupor he's been in for the last twenty minutes. "How nice could he be?"

"True," Del and I agree in unison. Scott is the worst. He's also good friends with Gabe. Gross.

"Everything okay there, Mase?" I tuck an errant curl behind my ear as I examine Mason. He's been tugging on the bottom of his scarf for the last ten minutes and seems to barely be listening to me or Del.

"What? Yeah, I'm fine," Mason practically snaps.

Del and I exchange a look.

We round the next corner, just a block from Zoe's. Mason falls back into his silence and scarf-tugging.

I gesture to Del to do something.

"I think what Anna is getting at is you're being unusually quiet."

"And shockingly non-judgmental," I add. I was sure he'd read me the riot act for even considering giving up my spot on the exec team to train. Mason doesn't really appreciate sports. Like at all.

"Um," he sputters as some of the blood drains from his face.

Del looks startled. "What's wrong?"

Mason shows intense interest in his scarf strings once again. "It's, well, maybe we should just wait to discuss this after the meeting. I promised Zoe I wouldn't tell you guys."

I roll my eyes to the high heavens. Zoe is such a pot stirrer.

Stopping directly in front of Mason, I block his path. "Spill it, Brent."

Del laughs at my antics and stands at my side, adding to the barrier. "Yeah, you have to tell now, having admitted there was *something* to tell."

Mason bites his lip, clearly troubled.

"Chicks over dicks," I proclaim.

Now it's their turn to look at me, bewildered.

I roll my eyes. Why are smart people always so literal? It's annoying. "You know what I mean. Friends over chicks."

Del laughs again. "What she said."

"Okay, but don't shoot the messenger." He pauses dramatically.

Del snaps her fingers. "Out with it!"

Mason takes a deep breath. "Zoe wants us to boycott Bookcourt."

"W-what?" I say, telling myself there's no way I heard him correctly.

Del closes her eyes and rocks back on her heels. "I was afraid of this." She looks more resigned than upset.

"What are you talking about?" I ask. "Why would anyone boycott a small, independent bookstore?"

"Ms. Adler is really reluctant to let her employees unionize," Del says carefully, looking at me concerned. We all love Bookcourt, but they both know how much it means to me in particular.

I blink again, not sure I can be hearing this right. "Zoe can't be serious. Where does she want people to buy books…Amazon?"

Mason shifts uncomfortably. "Of course not, but we can't just ignore workers' rights."

"Oh my god! Don't tell me you agree with her," I seethe. I turn to Del, my eyes flashing. "He's been brainwashed by her."

Del frowns slightly. "It's a complicated issue."

I open my mouth and snap it closed. They cannot be serious. For the second time today, I feel tears fill my eyes.

Mason grabs my hand. Del puts her arm around me.

"We all love the store," she says quietly. "This is hard."

As tears spill down my cheek, she reaches into her bag to pull out a tissue while Mason continues to grip my hand.

Zoe appears seemingly out of nowhere. It's not until then that I realize we're standing in front of her house. She's looking at me and Mason with clear displeasure. "Always so touchy-feely, you two."

Del raises an eyebrow, while Mason and I look at each other a bit startled.

"Zoe," I manage to bite out. In that moment, a red haze takes over my vision.

She looks at me and turns to Mason. "You told her!" she accuses. "I wanted to present it properly."

Zoe's baggy overalls showcase her thin frame. Her hair is in a loose topknot. She has large blue eyes that are startling against her otherwise darker features. Most of our classmates think she'll likely be the next AOC. She's the president of the Liberal Liaisons and the Environmental Justice League, another club Del and I are in, too. She's basically the queen of the Eastside.

Zoe lets out a frustrated breath. "Come on back. Let's start the meeting and I can give you my whole presentation."

Del and Mason move to follow her. But I find myself stuck

in place. The thought of sitting through a meeting criticizing Ms. Adler and Bookcourt is unbearable.

Zoe, Mason, and Del turn to look at me, realizing I'm not following.

"Uh, Zoe, there's actually something I wanted to talk to you about. Um, I won't be able to attend a bunch of upcoming meetings because of cross country training."

Zoe rolls her eyes. "We know, Anna. You'll come Mondays and Fridays. That's fine, just like the rest of our athlete activists."

"Eh, well, I actually wanted to mention that I'm being recruited for college now, so I just committed to this super intense, but absolutely necessary, training program on Mondays."

Zoe looks at me, startled, while Del and Mason muffle their reactions to my *somewhat* exaggerated claim.

"What? Like every Monday? But that's our main meeting, and it's required if you want to stay on the executive committee."

"I know. Super big bummer. But, like, I had zero choice. You know how it goes."

Zoe's eyes round. "No, I really don't. Are you sure about this, Anna? You'll be off the executive team and, if you want to join again, you'll have to be re-elected."

Del makes eye contact with me. I can tell she's asking if I know what I'm doing. A spot on the Liberal Liaisons is a real accomplishment.

I shrug at her.

Mason is looking at me completely horrified.

I feel filled with doubt, uncertainty, and panic, so I open my mouth and say, "Yup, I'm hundred percent sure." My voice cracks with each word.

"Why don't you sleep on it?" Del suggests.

"She sounds pretty sure to me," Zoe counters and I swear I hear some glee in her voice. Even though we're supposed to be friends, I always have the sense she doesn't really like me and can't understand why people as cool as Del and Mason are close to me. It bothers me more than I'm proud to admit.

The rest of the Liaisons start to trickle in, giving us odd looks, reading the tension on our faces.

We finally follow Zoe to the back of her house, through a stone entryway under a white arbor with colorful plants and vines embellishing the arch.

Zoe holds Mason's hand possessively and tugs him along. Del follows them, and I trail her.

Del turns to me, concerned. I squeeze her hand to let her know I'm okay, but internally I am freaking out. What am I doing?

\* \* \* \*

After sitting through Zoe's forty-five-minute plan to boycott Bookcourt, the meeting is all but over. Then Zoe announces that I am stepping down from the board, but will remain actively involved in the club. The announcement causes a bit of a stir. I can tell Mason is pissed she's declaring it in public so soon. As we gather our stuff to leave, I hear Zoe hiss at Mason that he's always defending me. Mason sees people looking at them and pulls Zoe to a far corner, his face rigid.

Del links her arm with mine. "Come on, let's go get some ice cream."

I smile, relieved to have her by my side. "That sounds amazing."

"It's probably a double scoop kind of night." Del's expression sours as she eyes Zoe and Mason huddled in the corner, still in a heated exchange.

"A double scoop, chocolate sauce kind of night," I say gently. Del has had unrequited romantic feelings for Mason for years. She usually hides them well, but I know it hurts her.

We smile at each other and our arms remain linked as we head out of Zoe's backyard.

"You'll see, Del. I'll still come to as many meetings as possible. It won't be that different!" In that moment, arm-to-arm with my best friend about to get ice cream, I truly believe it.

# CHAPTER

## 5

On the first Monday of training, I nervously jog up to the Edgartown High's athletic fields and spot Gabe and Sam already warming up.

Sam sees me first. "Hey, Anna," he salutes me with a grin and a friendly wave.

Hearing Sam's greeting, Gabe turns and acknowledges me with an easy but more controlled smile. He exhales audibly, which causes me to suspect he doubted I would show up.

"Hey, guys," I say, realizing that outside of my two run-ins with Gabe last week, this may be the most I've spoken to either of them since sixth grade. Northsiders and Eastsiders don't really hang out, like, ever.

"Are you all ready for this?" Sam asks, looking a little nervous. "I've heard Coach Farmer is killer."

Gabe's eyes sparkle a little. "Yeah, it should be intense."

"You look happy about that," I say.

Sam laughs. "Gabe loves a chance to improve. It's really annoying to be around someone so consistently hardworking. I hope you're not like that too."

"I wish. I'm definitely the slug of my friend group."

"Phew," Sam says, pretending to wipe his brow.

"He's here." Gabe's spine straightens as he points to a large male figure approaching us. Coach Farmer's stride is long and efficient. His eyes are shadowed by a baseball cap, but his lips are pressed together in a firm, humorless expression. A silver whistle glints from his neck and a clipboard is tucked under his slim arm.

"Should we do some sort of cheer to pump us up? You know, like Ted Lasso style?" I ask, my stomach suddenly fluttering with nerves. What have I gotten myself into? Gabe and Sam are both all-star athletes. I'm a solid runner, but of the three of us, I have the most work to do to be college-considered.

"'Leave it all out there' … on three?" Gabe suggests.

I squish my nose in distaste. "Let's try to find a catchier cheer than that, but for now, sure," I agree.

Gabe gives me a half-amused, half-exasperated look.

We put our hands on top of each other and shout, "Leave it all out there!"

Gabe frowns. "You're right. That does sound kind of awkward."

* * * *

I'm doubled over, my stomach heaving against my ribcage as if about to upend itself. Finally, I give in and collapse on the grass like a rag doll. I lie there, not willing to move, even to get my water bottle, which I'm dying for.

When a shadow falls over my face, I reluctantly open one eye. Slowly, I open the other and blink away drops of sweat. I find myself looking at Gabe's face, the sun highlighting his form, making him appear like the archangel I'm sure he's named for.

Gabe laughs softly at my appearance. "Good practice." He offers a hand, which I limply accept, and he pulls me up with no effort, like he hasn't spent the last two hours in pure misery. To my surprise, he uncaps a Gatorade and hands it to me. Generally speaking, Eastsiders shun chivalry if it encroaches on women's independence, but in this case, I appreciate not having to take one extra step to grab and chug the electrolyte-filled liquid.

I hold up a hand as I continue to down the sports drink. Finally, I stop and say, "Thanks. You too," I say before letting out a small burp. "Whoops, that's embarrassing."

Gabe chuckles, rocking back and forth on his heels. "What's a burp here or there between teammates?" I try not to notice how well-toned his legs and arms are, or how amazing his skin looks slick with sweat. I direct my gaze to the grassy field.

Sam joins us and lets out a loud fart. "Heard Anna burp and didn't want to miss all the fun."

"Gross," I laugh, shoving him playfully.

Gabe shakes his head and smiles. "I see I'm surrounded by free spirits."

"I take it you're not one?"

"Not really. I'm more of a 'play it close to the vest' kind of guy."

"He's a politician's son after all," Sam adds, running a hand through his blond, sweat-dampened hair.

"Because of the whole fishbowl mentality?" I ask.

Gabe shifts his weight and looks uncomfortable. "Something like that."

I look at him sympathetically. "That must be totally awful."

"Not really," he shrugs.

Sam laughs. "I mean, you could use a little lightening up now and again."

"Hey," Gabe says, "I'm pretty light."

"Yeah, light as a pound of steel," Sam says under his breath.

Gabe gives him a disapproving look.

"I have an idea!" I exclaim. "It's actually something we do weekly at Liaison meetings, and I think it could really help."

They both groan.

I ignore them and continue. "We start the meeting with free expression."

"What the hell does that mean?" Gabe asks, crossing his arms at his chest.

"So, Barry sometimes starts with an original poem. Or Mason will break out some freestyle guitar ballads."

"Like a talent show?" a dubious-sounding Sam asks, starting to stretch out his quads.

"No, it's more like a forum to say whatever comes to your mind. Sometimes people bring in a picture that inspires them. I personally like to just start talking and see what falls out."

"That sounds like my personal nightmare," Gabe says with alarm.

"I thought you said you wanted to be a free spirit."

"I said I was surrounded by them, not that I strive to be one."

"Why not?"

"I'm just not comfortable with it."

I make a mental note to press him on this subject later and turn to Sam. "What do you think?"

"I think it sounds like it might not totally fit in with conditioning training, but I'm all for doing it for fun one day." Sam looks down at his phone and notes the time. "Guys, where are we doing our post-mortem meal? Gabe, you ran the fastest today, but Anna definitely left the least out there."

"The most sweat at least," Gabe jokes.

"Hey!"

"Well, it's kind of true. I thought you weren't going to make it through that last sprint." Sam barely suppresses a smile.

I decide to ignore them and ask, "What's the post-mortem meal?"

"We basically stuff our faces with milkshakes and fries or whatever the practice winner chooses," Sam explains. "So, that would be you."

My eyes light up. "A milkshake!" I clear my throat remembering my pledge to be a little more adherent to my vegan diet. "Eh, an oat-based milkshake sounds amazing right now."

"Okay, Anna, I'll give the torch to you. Where to?"

"Floppies!" I say without missing a beat.

\* \* \* \*

Floppies is very on-brand with Edgartown's college town vibe. It's a play on an old-time diner but with the hipness, and locally sourced eggs, required for any restaurant to stay in business on this side of town. The back of the diner has an "alive wall," lined with green plants that appear to sprout from every inch, and in the front, there are plastic booths and 50s-style jukeboxes. I'm always comforted by the white lights and Christmas decorations (forgive me, Jewish soul) that grace the diner 365 days a year.

A college student with the name tag "Maddie" seats us. She gives Sam and Gabe a once-over and looks at me as if to say, "Aren't you one lucky lady?"

I smile weakly, trying to respond to her unasked question with a look that says, *They're my teammates, not my lovers.*

Gabe looks at me strangely. He waits for Maddie to give us menus and water. After she leaves, he asks, "Why do I get the sense you were trying to non-verbally communicate with our waitress?"

"Oh, I was, but she started it." I lean forward to gulp down some ice water. Will my pH balance ever return to normal?

Sam chuckles. "You're pretty funny, Morningstar. Glad to have you aboard."

I don't want to feel thrilled by his approval, but I am.

"So, what did she say?" Gabe asks.

"She was like, 'You hang with some good-looking boys. Sure, they smell, but they sure are cute."

Sam looks shocked. "She said that to you?"

"No, dummy. Anna thinks she's telepathic." Gabe sits back and stretches his arm behind his chair. "But I guess what this really means is Anna thinks we're hot."

"Hell yeah, bro," says Sam, who gives Gabe a high-five.

I roll my eyes. "Whatever, I ... let's say, communicated ... to Maddie over there, it's complicated."

"Complicated to be around such gosh darn handsome guys?" Gabe jokes.

"No, it's complicated because you are Northsiders, and so I should either find you unattractive or not notice you at all."

"Please, no politics," Gabe groans. "The perk of doing this on a Monday is supposed to be that we don't have to discuss anything other than sports."

I look at him, surprised. "Wait," I say. "So, you're not upset about missing your Young Republican meetings?"

"Not at all."

"Me neither," Sam says. "What a snoozefest."

My face brightens. "So you're both secret liberals!"

Gabe and Sam look at each other and crack up.

"Not in the slightest," Gabe states, and his smile widens when my face falls.

"You're not political then?" I ask, careful to keep the judgment—and the hope—out of my voice.

"True for me," Sam says, "but Gabe here is more of a mystery."

I turn to look at Gabe. "Interesting! Tell me more."

"It's not mysterious or interesting. I can't stand those meetings because any time I'm to the right or left of my dad's positions, everyone makes a huge deal out of it. So, I basically say nothing and try to deflect any questions directed at me."

Before I can inquire further, Maddie returns. She seems to have reapplied her lipstick, I note. "Ready to order?"

Sam puts in an astoundingly large order for chocolate chip pancakes.

"Are those all for you, or are we sharing?"

"All for me."

Gabe smiles and orders a large but slightly more manageable load than Sam.

Maddie turns to me. I don't want to the be the classic girl who eats less than the boys, but I'm literally not sure I'm capable of eating that quantity of pancakes.

"And for you?" Maddie nudges me.

"I'll have the petite four stack, but with extra chocolate chips, and a scoop of the Vegan vanilla on the side." Take that, boys.

"Oh, that sounds good. I'll have mine à la mode too," Gabe says.

"Make mine a double scoop," I one-up him.

Maddie doesn't crack a smile, and when she walks off, I whisper to the boys, "I never trust people who don't have a sense of humor."

"Okay… noted," Gabe says.

I roll my eyes. "I'm talking about Maddie."

"The waitress? Maddie?"

"How do you know she doesn't have a sense of humor?" Sam asks.

"I just know. I'm an excellent judge of character," I inform them.

"And modest, too, I see," Gabe observes.

"Hey!" I object, but then relax my shoulders. I guess that's a fair statement.

I'm enjoying myself more than I care to admit, and by the time the pancakes come and we're stuffing our mouths, I feel super relaxed. It hits me that this is the first time I've felt unstressed since beginning my hiatus from the Liaison meetings. I excuse myself to go to the bathroom, leaving my phone on the table. Feeling a little guilty for saying anything snide about Maddie, I shoot her a huge grin as I pass her on the way to the restroom.

I walk back to the table, prepared to suggest we order a round of hot chocolates next, when I see Zoe, Lizzy, and Barry (a fellow Liaison, who is shamelessly in love with Zoe, and hates Mason as a result) walk into Floppies.

Automatically, I step back, not wanting them to spot me. The last thing I need is for Zoe to catch me hanging out with Sam and Gabe on a Monday night. I'll look like a total traitor.

Please, *please* let them be picking up a to-go order, I think as I crouch behind the booth closest to the bathroom.

You've got to be freaking kidding me. I watch as my pal Maddie seats them in the booth directly next to Sam and Gabe. Barry sends the boys a disdainful glance, but neither Sam nor Gabe seems to notice the animosity.

Frozen in my spot, I consider my options. One, I can do the mature thing and return to my seat, greet Barry and Zoe, and face the music. Or two, I can run for the door.

I choose option two.

# CHAPTER

6

An hour later, I am sitting down to dinner (although I am pretty full after all those pancakes and ice cream) with my moms, sneaking under-the-table looks at my phone. Mimi has a strict no-phone policy at family meals, but I am desperately waiting for Gabe and Sam to respond to my text... well, technically texts...as in multiple un-responded-to texts.

For the tenth time, I re-read my earlier messages to the boys.

Me: Sorry I had to bolt, guys! Major stomach issues. Great practice! Can't wait for the next one.

Three minutes after that...

Me: Go us!

Seven minutes later...

Me: Ugh, I've tried Eastside Wellness and You, and the two Northside CVSes, and no one has any Tums. Does all of Edgartown have upset stomachs or something???"

Crickets

I'm trying to remember if giving too many details or too few makes you look more like you're lying, when Mimi exclaims, "No phones at dinner!"

Mom and I both jump and say, "Sorry!" Then we look back and forth between each other and Mimi to figure out which of us she caught.

Mimi narrows her eyes toward Mom.

I sit back smugly, happy to be the one not in trouble.

Mom gives Mimi a sheepish look. "Mind if I snap one picture? It's just you've outdone yourself with this meal, love, and Hen says I need to post more family moments." She gestures to the farro salad and lemon sage tempeh, beautifully presented on the table.

"Fine, just make it quick," Mimi agrees.

Mom claps her hands together. "Great." She furrows her brow. "Mimi, look like you're laughing at something Anna says," she instructs.

Mimi dutifully plays along but winks at me with good humor, while Mom snaps some photos.

"I see that look, you two!" Mom wags her finger. "I know it's annoying, but Hen is the best publicist in the business, and I'm *this* close to getting the 9 p.m. slot."

"We know, honey, and we're proud of you. Ignore us."

I roll my eyes, Mimi is such a pushover. I take a sip of seltzer water and sneak another glance at my phone. Still nothing. I sigh. "Mom, we'll keep taking all the pictures you want, but we definitely get to make fun of you for becoming a celebrity monster."

Mom laughs and loads her fork up with salad. "Fair point. And I do love hearing you say 'celebrity'!"

Mimi and I laugh.

"Speaking of Hen, for my show tomorrow, she booked three Bookcourt employees fighting to unionize, Mom says, clearly satisfied, as she sips her wine.

My head snaps up and I forget about my phone for the first time since ditching Sam and Gabe at the diner.

A look of hesitation flits into Mimi's eyes, but she leans forward and asks, "Which ones?"

"Billy, Brenda, and someone named Tom. Do you know him?"

"Isn't that the new guy who oversees non-fiction? The annoying graduate student?" I say sharply, not believing my ears. What does some brand-new hire know about anything?

32

"Ah, yes," Mom says, snapping her fingers.

"Won't this interview be bad for Ms. Adler?"

Mom frowns. "Unfortunately, yes. I just wish she had consulted me before kiboshing the idea of a union."

"How could you do this to her, Mom? After everything she's done for me?" A memory pops into my mind of sitting next to Ms. Adler when I was nine, feeling so frustrated and behind in reading. I recall her calming presence as she helped me sound out word after word of *Matilda*.

Mom sighs. "I care for Ms. Adler deeply, honey, and will always be grateful for how she helped you. But this is a complicated, thorny issue. When it comes to stuff involving our friends, it's not always easy to do the right thing, but it's necessary in this case."

"Come on, Mom," I object, annoyed she sounds so clinical about something so personal. "Isn't it unusual for small stores like Bookcourt to have unionized employees? Maybe she can't afford it or something?"

"Probably," Mom acknowledges. "But I think this could be an important model for other small businesses. After all, workers should be protected whether they're working at a company of millions or tens."

I want to say more, but notice that Mimi looks upset. Maybe I should let it go for the night. But my stomach swirls with anxiety. What am I missing? How can everyone I care about see this so differently than I do?

Despite my moms' best efforts to engage me in conversation, I eat in relative silence for the rest of the meal, only perking up when the boys finally write me back, assuring me that my sudden, unannounced departure caused them no problems, and refusing my attempts to Venmo them for my portion of the bill.

\* \* \* \*

After dinner, I sit on our front porch swing, sipping my hot cocoa and staring at the stars. I let my foot send the swing into a big dipping motion when, to my surprise, I see Gabe Delgado walking by, his face briefly illuminated by street lanterns. He stops in front

33

of my house, and I feel my stomach flutter as I admire his handsome face and broad shoulders.

"I'm on my way to see a friend and wanted to stop by to check on you and give you this." He smiles sweetly and holds up a plastic bag.

I accept the bag and look in it to find Tums, Pepto Bismol, and a bottle of ginger ale.

"Wow. This is super nice of you," I finally manage, shame coating my stomach.

Gabe peers down at my drink and then tilts his head questioningly. "I didn't know hot cocoa was good for stomach aches?"

I cover my face with my hands and mutter, "Busted."

Gabe shakes his head in disbelief, but his expression is filled with humor. "What was that, Annabelle? Couldn't quite hear you with your hands covering your mouth."

I part my fingers and peer through them, looking at Gabe with guilt. "I lied. I totally suck. I'm sorry."

Gabe shakes his head again in mock outrage and then smiles. He pulls out his phone.

I squint, trying to see what he's doing.

He playfully nudges me away. "I've never met anyone with less shame."

"Hey!" I object, but then reconsider. "Unless that's a compliment?"

Gabe throws his head back and full-on laughs. The sound is deep and lovely.

Wait, did I just describe the sound of a guy's laughter as lovely? I'm officially losing it.

"I was just texting Sam to tell him that I owe him twenty."

"Why?" I gesture next to me on the swing, inviting him to sit.

He checks his watch, and then sits next to me. We're only about an inch apart on the swing. The cool air swirls around us, and I take in the faint smell of mint and soap that seems to be coming from him. I grip my hands around my mug, feeling a little too aware of my body.

"Why do you owe Sam twenty?" I repeat.

Gabe doesn't respond right away and I grow more agitated.

Clearly enjoying my curiosity, he continues to delay his response.

He peers into my cup and lifts his eyes teasingly to mine. "How about you give me some hot cocoa and I'll tell you how you made me lose a bet?"

I grin instantly. "Deal."

Hastily, I go to the kitchen to get him hot chocolate. I glance upstairs, listening for my moms, who went up thirty minutes ago and are likely reading or watching TV or some combination thereof. I quickly pour Gabe a mug from the steaming pot and go back out front with a sigh of relief that went unnoticed. After everything else today, I don't really feel like having a "Why is Gabe Delgado here?" convo with them.

I sit back down and hand Gabe his mug, trying not to notice when our fingers brush, or the tingle in my spine when they do. "So?" I prompt.

"Sam bet me that the reason you Irish-exited was because Zoe Dart sat down next to us. I said no way would you be willing to make up having diarrhea to avoid being seen with us."

"I never said diarrhea."

"It was strongly implied."

"I guess it was."

Gabe and I both grin stupidly at each other.

He looks down at his hands. "It's that big of a deal to be seen with us?"

I wince. Gabe and Sam are practically gods on the Northside. "I just couldn't deal with it after everything else," I say. I tell him about how conflicted and confused I feel over the Bookcourt drama, finding myself with such a divergent opinion from my friends and mom.

He nods sympathetically. "It's really hard to realize you think differently from the people you love the most."

I look at him curiously. "I feel like you really get this."

"I do." He sighs and sends the swing into another big swoop. "I've been in your spot more than once. It's tough. I love my dad. He's really the best father. And I'm so proud that he's one of the only Cuban-American senators, and most of the time I do agree with him..."

35

"But when you don't?"

He sighs. "It's been awkward."

"So what do you do then?"

He smiles sadly. "I usually go along with what I think is best for him."

"Do you regret it?"

"I haven't, at least not in any significant way."

"Really?" I press, not sure I buy it.

He looks at me and then down at his mug. "Well, I guess I do wonder if I should hold true more, but I'm just not sure it's worth it."

"How can it not be worth it to stand up for what you believe in?"

"There will be a lot of time for me to figure out and express my beliefs. I'm only sixteen after all. But this is really his time."

I nod slowly because that kind of makes sense, but I almost feel like it shouldn't.

Gabe's phone buzzes, and he glances at his watch again. "Better get going."

"Who are you meeting this late?" It's only 9 p.m., but, still, it's a school night.

His face turns a little pink. "Caroline Loran."

"I thought you broke up?"

He raises a brow. "Glad to hear Northside gossip gets to the Eastside. Must mean I'm pretty important," he teases.

I laugh and roll my eyes, but since I feel strangely interested in what's happening between him and Caroline, I forge on. "So, you all are back together or something?"

"Or something," he says.

"Pretty vague."

Gabe laughs at my frustrated tone. "Hard not to be vague about a vague situation."

"Is that why you smell so good? Because it's a maybe-date?"

Gabe tilts his head. "You think I smell good?"

I turn a deep shade of scarlet, which has Gabe cracking up.

"Well, considering how awful you smell at practice, it's hard not to notice a marked improvement!"

"Hey," he protests, chuckling. His phone buzzes again and he frowns. "She doesn't like to be kept waiting."

I respond with a non-committal grunt because I strongly dislike Caroline Loran.

Another beat passes, and then he stands and gives me a friendly smile. "See you at school, Anna."

He hands me his mug.

"Thanks for checking on me, and I again apologize for faking an illness. It means a lot." I smile up at him.

He turns to leave after one final wave.

I watch him go off to Caroline's to do God knows what, and an unfamiliar pit settles uncomfortably in my stomach.

# CHAPTER 7

"I cannot believe I let you drag me here." Del pulls on her oversized sunglasses as we sit in the stands to cheer for the Edgartown Blueberries. You heard me right. *Blueberries.* I watch as Blub, our team mascot, dances around the sidelines in a fuzzy purplish-blue uniform. The mascot changed from something far more offensive (at least to Eastsiders) in 2005, and in a clear "F-you" to the Northside, several Eastside families voted on the most peaceful representative of Edgartown they could agree upon …hence the Blueberries, a fruit that thrives in temperate North Carolina weather.

Mason slumps down next to me. He has a baseball cap on, which he never wears, and no scarf, which he always wears. As he pulls the brim lower over his forehead, I realize he doesn't want to be seen.

I sling an arm around my best friends. "Guys, this is a true test of friendship, going to a lacrosse game with me." I was still feeling bad about ditching Gabe and Sam at Floppies, so this was my peace offering of sorts. Well, that and I was kind of curious to see them in action.

Del shakes her head with mirth. "Never thought the three of us would be doing *this* on a Sunday afternoon."

Mason grumbles. "That's for sure."

Del and I laugh at his misery. Mason can be theatrical, which is both endearing and annoying. He'd reluctantly agreed to come, after I begged Del and Mason not to let me go to a Northside hotspot alone.

As we wait for the team to come out, we talk about everything we want to happen to us in college. Me: to lose my virginity in a terribly romantic fashion. Del: to uncover a major scandal and break it in the college newspaper, landing her a job at *The New York Times*. And Mason: to find true contentment through an awesome, politically active music group.

The ridiculously talented Edgartown orchestra starts playing the theme from *Chariots of Fire* and the team runs out onto the field, a sea of white and blue. Despite the helmets and shoulder pads, I easily spot Gabe's tall, athletic frame. He follows a senior, Jake Webie. They both have "C's" on their arm. Sam follows and glances into the stands, waving a thumbs up when he spots me. I wave back, grinning widely at my buddy.

Mason and Del watch the exchange, both looking startled at the level of chumminess.

I shrug. "We spend a lot of time together now." I hug my sweater closer to my body as a gust of wind blows through the stadium. I hand Del the popcorn I was munching on.

My eyes trail back to the field and land on Gabe as he warms up. I watch as Gabe cradles the ball expertly, whipping it to his teammate, who catches it and throws it back. My gaze lands on the "C" on his uniform once again.

"I didn't realize he was captain," I mutter to myself.

Mason and Del turn to me, making me realize I was speaking louder than I intended.

Mason shoots me another look, this one harder to decipher. "Well, you haven't always been a fan of his. This is a charming new development."

"So glad you're charmed," I bite back.

"Children," Del chides. "Play nice." She turns to me. "Yes, Gabe was voted captain at the start of the year. It was a bit unprecedented." It pays to have your best friend be editor-in-chief of the school newspaper *The Red and Blue*—so she's always in the know.

I turn to her, stealing some more popcorn from her lap. "Really? But why?"

"I think just because it's the lacrosse team's tradition that only seniors are captains," Del explains and looks back to the field. She clearly doesn't find this as fascinating as I do.

"So how did Gabe get the spot?"

I feel a tap at my shoulder and turn around to face a sophomore Northside girl I barely know. She's wearing a mini skirt and a polo shirt and her hair is ironed straight to within an inch of its life. "Want to know why Gabe was voted captain as a junior?"

I flush, embarrassed someone overhead.

"Because he's hot as hell, talented as hell, and nice as hell. It's not that complicated." She rolls her eyes. "You Eastsiders are always looking for a story where there is none."

I feel like I should be insulted, but as I watch Del bite her lip to keep from laughing, I just say to the girl, "Thanks for the intel," and turn back to the game. Does this sophomore have a point?

I turn back to Del and Mason, "What do you think of what she said?

Mason eyes me. "You sound a little obsessed, Anna."

"I do not!"

"Maybe a little," Del agrees.

I roll my eyes. "You guys are so dramatic."

Del bursts out laughing.

"I assure you that, of our little trio, I am not the dramatic one." She looks at Mason, then me, and then laughs again.

"What?" Mason objects. "I am not that dramatic."

This statement has both me and Del doubling over in mirth. Mason is the most dramatic person I know. He regularly lies down on the ground—literally—when he hears upsetting news of any sort. It's completely ridiculous.

"I'm not," he insists.

The referee blows the whistle and the game starts. I watch as Gabe takes his position on the field and Sam takes his in the goal.

Watching Gabe race up and down the field, expertly cradling the ball, not to mention passing and faking out the defense, is quite a sight. He's somehow graceful, determined, tough, generous, and competitive all at once. When the other team calls a time out and he takes his helmet off, revealing dark, sweat-slicked hair and his handsome face, I gulp. He really is hot as hell.

* * * *

"I did *not* know this sport was so violent," I say from under my shirt, where I have been hiding on and off for the first half. After watching Sam take a violent blow and Gabe crash into more players than I can count, I have reached my wincing capacity for the day.

"It doesn't bother me so much. I just think it's kind of dumb," Del says, earning a loud grumble from the sophomore behind us.

Mason, who has stretched out his legs in front of him with a copy of *The New Yorker*, seems bored. "Yeah, I don't get the appeal," he agrees without looking up from the article he's engrossed in.

I risk peeking out from my shirt just in time to see Gabe take a lacrosse stick dangerously close to his eye. I loudly gasp as I watch blood spill from his cheek. The whistle sounds, indicating the end of the half.

"Have we had enough of this?" Mason asks, unmoved.

"Uh ...." I kind of want to stay for the whole thing.

Del looks at me understandingly. "You know, I should probably stay myself. We have a new freshman covering the game and I need to make sure he doesn't miss anything."

I smile, grateful to her, and she shakes her head at me in a cross between disbelief and humor.

* * * *

I have broken into a full sweat by the time the game ends with a win for the Edgartown Blueberries. Gabe scored one goal and assisted on the second. Sam was also pretty amazing, barely letting a shot elude him at goal.

Del and I walk down to congratulate them. Del is in full reporter mode, noting the dynamics of the fans on both sides.

"Morningstar! You came!" Sam rushes over to me and, with an enthusiastic whoop, lifts me on off my feet in a sweaty bear hug. The boys had been highly skeptical when I'd texted them this morning saying I'd be at the game, claiming "they'd believe it when they see it."

"Gross," I laugh, pushing him away, but then give him another quick hug. "You all were awesome! Hated every minute of it, but it was a nail biter."

"Hated every minute?"

I whirl to find Gabe behind me, a smile ghosting his face.

"I didn't like seeing you all get so beat up! It was so physical!"

"She hid under her shirt for most of the game," Del tattles.

Sam shifts to look at Del, an appreciative gleam in his eye. "And you brought a cute friend."

Del laughs at his boldness and gives him a "keep dreaming, buddy" glance.

But I blank out as Gabe turns toward them and I see the huge gash on his cheek. Without thinking, I step toward him, my hand going to his face. "Oh god, that looks awful."

Gabe freezes and stares at me. Heat creeps onto my cheeks as I realize I'm touching him rather tenderly right below the cut. Our eyes lock, and the unfamiliar feeling rushes back, making the hairs on my arms stand at attention. I swiftly remove my hand.

"Gabe-y!" a voice calls.

Sam, Del, and I turn to see Caroline Loran glaring at our four-some. Her chin is on the pointy side, and she's dressed to the nines, as always.

Is it my imagination or does Gabe look a little annoyed at be-ing beckoned? I guess not, as a moment later he says goodbye and thanks us for coming. He heads over to Caroline, who gives him a close and lengthy hug.

I look away and turn my attention back to Del. Sam is accost-ed by some Northside fans and Del and I start heading out.

We don't make it farther than the parking lot when Mason, who left the game at halftime, runs over to us. He's out of breath as he exclaims, "Major development. Bookcourt hired Brenson Oakes to stop the employees from unionizing. Zoe is already out there, protesting with the Liaisons."

My mouth falls open. Brenson Oakes is one of the biggest conservative law firms in the South. They always seem to represent the most extreme clients and are a regular target of my mom's TV specials.

"What? It's crazy that such a big firm would get involved in this," I say.

Del looks pensive. "I'm not sure it's that surprising. Brenson Oakes prides themselves on union-busting."

"I'm heading over to Bookcourt now," Mason says. "You guys want a ride?"

My feet feel glued to the ground. As much as this news unsettles me, it's still Ms. Adler, one of the kindest people I've known. I've personally seen her go above and beyond for her staff over and over again. Something doesn't feel right here.

"Yes, I'll meet you over there. I want to grab some supplies first," Del says, referring to the school's newspaper office.

I remain silent and still

Mason and Del look at me.

"It's okay if you're not ready," Mason finally says, laying a kind hand on my shoulder, but I recognize the disappointment flickering in his green eyes.

"Thanks for understanding," I say quietly, giving him and Del a hug.

Five minutes later, I find myself alone in the parking lot as a pit the size of California settles in my stomach.

# CHAPTER

— 8 —

It's now a month into "Conditioning Mondays." Today, I'm warming up before practice starts, or at least pretending to, when in reality I'm sneaking peeks at Gabe and trying to think of a non-obvious way to ask about his relationship with Caroline. I've noticed some confusing interactions between them at school and am semi-dying (note: only semi-dying, not stalker-level dying) to ask Gabe what's up. What did that lingering look across the courtyard really mean? When did Gabe's Patagonia fleece become Caroline's new uniform? I'm about to shout this across the track when Sam does it for me.

"So, buddy, what exactly is happening with you and Caroline? Are you back together for… what is it now?... the tenth time?"

I bend down to re-tie my shoes, feigning indifference.

Gabe playfully throws a towel at Sam. "No, it's the third time. Or fourth if you count spring break last year."

"Why would you be with someone you've already broken up with four times?" I chime in, pushing myself up and brushing invisible dirt off my shorts. Gabe looks somewhat startled by my presence, as if he hadn't realized I was there.

"Well, three, but yeah, it's a bit excessive, I admit."

"So why?" I can't help but push. "And if you're going to break up with someone so many times, shouldn't they be more interesting than Caroline Loran?"

"Harsh," Sam says, but his eyes round in amusement.

"You agree with me," I exclaim, delighted.

"You do?" Gabe turns toward Sam.

Sam raises his hands in a fake surrender. "There's often more than one truth in a situation," he deflects.

I stifle my grin, pretending to yawn when Gabe looks at me. "Well, that's super philosophical, *friend*." Gabe emphasizes *friend* like he's sending Sam a not-so-subtle reminder.

"We just did the mindfulness segment in P.E. class." Sam taps his temple.

"Right," I nod. "I remember that, but I was too distracted to listen to what Mr. Hall was saying."

For some reason, Gabe and Sam seem to find that hysterical. I wait until they finish laughing before I continue talking.

"I think I get it, Sam. You're saying there are two truths to every situation. Yes, Caroline is a mean, social-climbing girl, but she's also Gabe's first girlfriend, so it's complicated?"

Sam laughs. "Something like that."

Gabe raises an unamused eyebrow. "Who said she was my first girlfriend?"

Raising an eyebrow of my own, I ask, "Well, isn't she?"

"I mean, my first serious one, but what does that have to do with it?"

"People often confuse their first with something more meaningful." Catching myself, I clarify, "Not that I have actually ever had a boyfriend, but I do read a lot of romance novels, so I kind of know about this stuff."

All Caroline-induced tension evaporates from the air, and Sam and Gabe burst into laughter again. I don't understand why, but I can't help but join them.

"I'm a little insulted by your reaction, guys, but also sorta get it, so I'll let it go."

"Okay, this is getting a little too real for a pre-sprint talk. Can we hold it till after?" Gabe requests.

I nod, and Sam shrugs. In the ensuing silence, I take a moment to look at my two strapping Monday partners, and it hits me.

"Wow, guys, we're becoming real friends. That's wild, isn't it?"

Sam and Gabe look blankly at me.

Gabe tilts his head, a mocking expression on his face. "I don't know if I'd really use the word 'wild'?"

"Yeah," Sam says, mirroring Gabe's puzzled expression. "Maybe if we were streaking across Main Street every Monday, that would be 'wild,' but I'm not sure training for college recruitment qualifies." Unable to maintain his serious expression, Sam grins at Gabe, a twinkle in his cornflower-blue eyes.

I roll my eyes, pretending not to be amused by their theatrics. "Very funny, but you know what I mean! Like Eastside/Northside friendship. It's kind of radical?"

This time, Gabe and Sam look at me even more blankly than they had thirty seconds ago.

"Aren't you friends with Mary Sue?" Gabe asks me.

"Hmm, yeah, but that's totally different."

"How?" Gabe pushes.

"Well, she's my track teammate." I pause, realizing it's not so different.

The boys smirk at their logical victory.

"Anyway, I wouldn't really say it's revolutionary to be friends with someone who has different political views than you or your family. But, then again, I'm not some radicalized lib like you," Gabe teases.

"Burn!" Sam gloats. He holds up a hand for me to high-five, but I leave him hanging. Gabe's jab suddenly reminds me of what I'm giving up for Monday training—the sacrifices I've made to hang out with these guys instead of my usual group. My hands feel clammy as I start to panic a little. "Guys, seriously, what does it mean that I enjoy spending time with you?" I swallow a newly formed lump in my throat. "Like, will I just wake up one day and stop caring about the environment and women's rights?"

Sam and Gabe roll their eyes hard.

"I think it means you have great taste," Sam quips.

"Who do we call to fix this? Is there a liberal crisis line that only Eastsiders know about?"

A snort of laughter escapes my body, releasing all my anxiety into the open air. I lunge for my water bottle and spray it toward Gabe, barely missing him. He and Sam take off in different directions as I chase after them.

By the time Coach Farmer arrives, the three of us are drenched from our water fight, but we quickly fall silent, all dreading what's in store for us today. I swig what's left in my water bottle and prepare to focus for the next hour and a half.

# CHAPTER

## 9

Tonight the dinner table is unusually tense. Hen, my mom's publicist, had just left after sharing social media feedback that shows Mom's friendship with Ms. Adler has made her audience question her impartiality and trustworthiness. After all, the posts claim, Ms. Adler hosted, just last year, the launch party for Mom's debut book about the vulnerable state of American democracy. A small ripple of bad press is slowly cresting into a wave.

I listlessly nod as my moms talk about the blowback. I feel numb. The whole situation isn't sitting right with me. Zoe and the Liaisons have been protesting in front of Bookcourt every night. It all feels like too much. I told Mason and Del that even though I I'm not ready to actively protest outside Bookcourt yet, I won't buy any books until they drop Brenson Oakes as their lawyers. I've kept my promise, mostly…the new Tessa Baily book I pre-ordered hasn't come in yet, so that doesn't count, right?

How can I cut Bookcourt out of my life just like that? It has always been my refuge from the rest of the world. A place where, without judgment, I could dive into the endlessly pleasurable world of romance novels, where I could try and sound out words in the reading corner as a kid without feeling stupid or overwhelmed by my language processing disorder.

And don't we owe more to Ms. Adler than an outright rejection of the store we know she puts her blood, sweat, and tears into? She's not some corporate giant. She's a kind senior citizen whose entire life is this small store. The protest seems off-scale, out of whack.

"How was Coach Farmer today?" Mimi asks, noting that I'd fallen silent. "Must be pretty intense with just three of you there."

"It was good. Hard, but good. And Sam, Gabe, and I went to Mooburger after, which was really fun, although I wonder if pigging out after practice is undoing our training." I shrug and dig into the beautifully prepared cedar-planked salmon and broccolini that Mimi somehow managed to "whip up" after a full day in the OR.

"You seem to be spending a lot of time with Sam and Gabe Delgado." Mom always calls Gabe by his full name and lingers over his last name as if she's forcing it out of her mouth.

"Mom, just say it."

"Say what?" she replies, all innocence, taking a sip of white wine.

"You don't like that I'm hanging out with two Northside boys."

"Please, sweetie, as long as your friends are nice and kind, I'm happy. It does give me pause that they have such conservative politics at such a young age, but who am I to judge?"

I almost snort my water. "Mom, come on. You'd rather I hang out with crystal meth addicts than Gabe and Sam."

Mom laughs. "That's my Anna, always with a flair for the dramatic."

"Come on, Mimi. Back me up here."

Mimi cuts a piece of her salmon and chews it before responding. "I think what Mom is trying to say, honey, is that we don't want you to feel pressured over college admissions. We know how much you love the Liberal Liaisons, and we're a little surprised that you're so nonchalant about missing meetings and not being on the executive committee anymore."

I open my mouth to respond to Mimi but realize she's right. I haven't given it much thought. Sure, Del and Mason always give me a play-by-play of what I miss on Mondays, and I've joined all the recent protests except for Bookcourt, but why haven't I felt more regret about missing meetings? Is it because I'm having so much fun with Gabe and Sam? Is it because my running times are improving so much? Or am I just escaping the confusing feelings that the Bookcourt boycott creates in me?

"I don't know," I put my fork down on my plate. "I guess hanging out with Sam and Gabe and running feels a lot easier than having it out with Zoe Dart over Bookcourt. I just read on the *Edgartown Eagle*'s Twitter account that sales have plummeted, and I can't imagine they have huge margins to begin with." My heart clenches nervously.

"No one wants to see Bookcourt fail." Mimi looks down at her plate. "Hopefully, this will push Ms. Adler and Alfred to do the right thing."

"Alfred?" I say. "Who's Alfred?"

"Alfred is Ms. Adler's son. He oversees the store's day-to-day operations," Mom says, taking over for Mimi.

"Well, I've never met him." I feel suddenly defensive; I thought I knew all the employees of Bookcourt.

"Anyway, hopefully this will be over quickly. It would be in their best interest to end this anyway."

I suddenly feel angry with my mom. "Have you forgotten what it took for Ms. Adler, right after her husband died, to open the store in the first place? How you can be so uncaring?"

Mom holds her wine glass in one hand, taking a measured sip. "Honey, I do care…about the *workers*."

"Ms. Adler has always treated all her employees like gold!"

"Except right now, which I suspect has more to do with Alfred." She and Mimi exchange a knowing glance, and I can't help but wonder what they're not saying.

"What's that supposed to mean?" I ask.

"I just wonder if this is his influence."

"Why do you sound so detached?" I bunch my napkin and throw it onto the table, pushing my chair out suddenly so it scratches the floor. "We used to spend every Sunday at Bookcourt."

Every Sunday, until I was in high school and started wanting

51

to see my friends more on the weekends, my moms and I would go on a Greenway hike, followed by a pancake feast at Floppies. Then we'd cap the afternoon off with a trip to Bookcourt, where I'd bury myself in the romance section. It was our ritual, and it was sacred.

Mom turns to Mimi. "It's you who taught her to be so sentimental. So I'll let you take this one."

"We all care about Bookcourt and Ms. Adler, Lilly. Including you." Mimi's tone is softer than both of ours.

"Of course we do," Mom replies. "But we can't prioritize our personal feelings towards someone over our moral values."

"And that is my failure?" Mimi's voice is clipped.

My gut starts churning again at double speed. "Stop, guys," I finally say. "Don't get mad at each other. This is my fault." I feel suddenly deflated. "I'm just not seeing this the way you are, which feels so weird."

With guilty glances at each other, they inch their chairs closer to me.

"Honey, you know we love each other and you so much. But families argue and disagree, and that's okay," Mimi comforts me.

Mom looks at Mimi. "I'm sorry, my love. My tone was awful."

Mimi smiles lovingly back at Mom. "It's okay. I know you have a lot of strong feelings about a variety of topics."

We all laugh. I take a deep breath.

Mimi changes the subject, but my mind is stuck on Bookcourt. Memories of being in fourth grade, sobbing in a store corner after failing a history test, not because I didn't know the answers, but because I spelled all the answers wrong. I felt so small and dumb. Terry, the head of the children's section, found me and brought me to Ms. Adler. She sat me down at the cafe, gave me a apple cider and a scone, and explained to me that truly creative people never spell a word the same way twice.

She then brought over a book she thought I might love— *Anne of Green Gables*. We sat there and started reading it together. I was so entranced that the usual frustration I felt when I didn't know specific words fell away. It was the first time I fell in love with a book. It was the first time I fell in love at all. Thoughts of Gilbert and Anne consumed my imagination for the rest of the summer.

I think of the smell of the store, some odd mix of lemon cleaner and sweet pastries, and even now, it soothes me.

I know I'm not thinking clearly about how all of this impacts workers' rights. Is there a legitimate reason smaller businesses don't unionize? Or is it—as my mom and Zoe claim—just plain wrong? And isn't the bookselling industry in more than a bit of trouble these days? I think of the Barnes & Noble and Better Books that are now a Nike store and a movie theater downtown. I think of the simple joys of wandering through aisles and aisles of books.

I sink into my chair, confused. Why is everything so hard?

# CHAPTER

## 10

"Do you guys think I've been checked out lately?" I ask, thinking of my recent conversation with my moms. It's Wednesday morning, and we're at Reveiller for our weekly Coffee Wednesday. We've been meeting Wednesday mornings before school since we were freshmen and only drank non-caffeinated beverages.

"In what ways?" Del straightens her long cardigan over her black halter top and adjusts her camo pants. Her hair is piled dramatically on her head, looking fashionable as always.

"Like not as involved with the Liaisons as I should be? Even though I am off the executive team?"

You've been a notable "MIA," Mason states plainly.

"Oh," I reply to Mason and frown at my coffee.

Mason notes my disappointment. "Didn't you ask partly because you knew that would be our answer?"

"It's annoying to be such a know-it-all, Mason," I reply.

"Even more annoying when he does it on a Glasses Day," Del adds, trying to break the tension.

I give in and laugh lightly. "Too true. Glasses Day makes him so much worse."

"Hey!" Mason says. "You two helped me pick out these glasses. I thought you said they were cool and personified the geek-sexy look."

"Hmm, I don't recall saying that?" Del glances at me.

I really laugh this time. "I definitely don't remember saying it."

We snicker as Mason tries to catch his reflection in the coffee shop's mirrored door.

"You look like a cutie, Mase. We're just teasing," Del reassures him.

"Yeah, you're a hottie. I wouldn't say a geeky one, more like a troubled poet one. Tall, thin, and tortured."

Del snaps her fingers. "He totally is. Good call."

Mason's face turns such a deep shade of scarlet that Del and I can't help but belly-laugh.

"Weren't we talking about how Anna is such a total sellout?" Mason reminds us.

Now it's my turn to say, "Hey!"

"Well, it's kind of true. But what girl could resist hanging around a sweaty, sometimes shirtless Gabe Delgado and Sam Price?" Del's eyes twinkle.

Mason looks a little startled.

I look at Del. "I feel like you would resist."

"Yeah, that's true. They aren't really my type."

"They're Northsiders," Mason sneers. "They shouldn't be anyone's type." Then he turns to me. "And they aren't yours either, right, Anna?"

"Of course not!" I say, but my stomach turns in a funny little circle. I look at my friends uncomfortably and pause. "Actually, Gabe and Sam are kind of my friends now."

Mason and Del exchange glances.

"Guys! Don't do that."

"Do what?"

"Give judge-y looks."

"Okay, okay. Just as long as you're still you."

"Of course I'm still me."

Just then our phones ding.

It's a protest alert from Zoe. I let out a sigh of relief when I see it's about climate change, a cause I'm unreservedly passionate about.

"Great. Just to prove how much I am me, just watch and see who shouts the loudest today."

# CHAPTER
11

As the fall weather turns colder, our Monday workouts continue. I'll never admit it to Del and Mason, but Monday afternoons have become the highlight of my week. Not only because Gabe and Sam are kick-ass athletes who inspire me to push myself harder, and not only because we pig out afterward, but also because our camaraderie makes each hangout sparkle with fun.

The biggest surprise of these Mondays, however, is realizing how nice Gabe is. He's always trying to make things extra special, creating fun playlists for our workouts or proposing silly challenges on days Coach Farmer pushes us especially hard, although afterward, when I post one of his dopier challenges on Instagram, he gets flustered and asks me not to.

He also does random thoughtful things all the time. One day he notices how much my hair is getting in my eyes during training, and the next week, as if it is nothing, he buys and gives me a new Lululemon workout headband. Sam smiles at my reaction. "That's Gabe for you. He's always doing stuff like that for his friends."

But it's not only how he interacts with his friends. I notice how he gets along with everyone, from Coach Farmer to waiters and teachers—he treats people with a care and respect that's unusual. Last Monday, at Floppies, Sam was regaling us with a wild tale from his Saturday night (funnily enough, it sounded like he was at a gay bar and didn't realize it), when suddenly Gabe popped up to help an elderly woman two tables down get to her feet. I hadn't even noticed her struggling, but he seems to have a sixth sense for people in need. He walked her all the way to her car before coming back.

These thoughts swirl in my head today as I watch Gabe complete a cool-down lap around the track. He strips off his blue Nike workout shirt, putting his sculpted abs on full display. I gulp, feeling a weird pressure all over my body. I shake my head to clear it. This feels like a crush. But it's not a real one, I remind myself. After all, he's a Northsider, he's a Delgado, he has zero interest in me that way, and he's dating Caroline … or at least I think he is. I complete my own cool-down and start stretching, pushing these ridiculous notions from my mind.

Later, we're at Mooburger (and I'm pretty jealous of the amazing aroma coming off the boys' meals compared to my Impossible Burger) when Gabe announces he broke up with Caroline the day before.

"Oh, wow! Are you okay?" I say, offering him some of my sweet potato fries as a consolation.

"Yeah, I think I'm fine, which is weird." Gabe winces, then smiles as he takes a fry.

"Not that surprised you're fine, man. I never really got it, to be honest." Sam looks hesitant, as if he's said too much. He turns to me. "Did you?"

I look at Sam, delighted. "Wow, this is a great convo, guys. I really feel like part of the gang."

Sam shakes his head and ruffles my hair, and I don't even mind that he's touching my gross post-workout hair. "Morningstar, you're weird, but I like you."

Gabe rolls his eyes. "Glad my broken heart is making you so giddy."

"You just said you're definitely not broken-hearted," I point out.

"True." Gabe looks a little troubled.

"Everything okay over there?" Sam inquires. He takes a loud

sip of his drink waiting for Gabe to answer. I admire how Sam asks gently, without intruding.

"I don't get why I'm so fine." Gabe's brows furrow. "I was so bummed after our last breakup, but then, after we got back together, it was so, so…."

"Dreadful? Awful? Terrible?" I suggest.

"Not helpful, Morningstar," Sam admonishes me.

"Right, sorry, but she really is a mean girl."

Sam shakes his head at me.

Gabe ignores me. "I guess I was bored with her."

I'm thrilled to hear this. To my way of thinking, calling someone boring is the ultimate insult. "Why did you like her in the first place?"

Gabe looks directly at me. I squirm, trying not to be affected by his beautiful eyes. "I don't know. I thought we had a special connection, but now I'm questioning it because the last three weeks were just … " he pauses, raking a hand through his hair, "nothing."

Sam practically spits out his milkshake. We turn to look at him. "Gabe, are you joking, bro? You lost your virginity to her. That's what this is all about."

Gabe looks a bit startled, but then a slow smile spreads across his face. He looks relieved. "I think you're right, Sam."

I lean forward, fascinated. "Have you both had sex? Like a lot of times?"

Gabe blushes, and Sam suppresses a grin.

"Gentlemen don't discuss such matters in front of ladies," Gabe says. "Especially virginal ones."

"Hey! How did you know I'm a virgin?" I pout. "I thought I gave off a confident, worldly vibe."

Gabe doubles over with laughter as Sam tries to hide his snorting behind a handful of waffle fries.

I roll my eyes and bite into my burger. "It's not that funny, guys."

"It really is." Gabe picks up his buzzing phone and smiles. "Nice. Party Friday. My parents are going to be out of town."

"Awesome! You going to come, Anna?" Sam asks.

"A Northside party. Can you handle it?" Gabe teases. "But, seriously, you should come. I throw the best parties. You can bring Del and *Mase*." Gabe's tone is mocking as he uses my moniker for Mason.

"Didn't know you were on a nickname basis with him," I comment dryly. "I'm actually supposed to have dinner with Mase—Mason— on Friday, but maybe after…" I trail off, worried about how much it could set back my relationship with Mason if I suggest going to a Northside party. "I'll have to play it by ear."

"Don't sound so enthusiastic. It'll go to my head." Gabe smiles at me.

I look down, a little embarrassed.

"Do you think Del or Mason might come?" Sam asks hopefully.

I laugh. "You want them there?"

"Yeah, they're both hot."

I look at Sam, curious. "I mean, I agree, but I'm a little surprised to hear you say Mason is hot. Don't Northside jocks usually deny their homoerotic tendencies?"

Sam shrugs and pops a fry into his mouth. "Not me. I not only acknowledge it, but I act on it."

My jaw drops and my eyes sparkle. "Wow, Sam, how evolved of you. Is this, like, public knowledge?"

"Not really. Like you said, some Northsiders aren't so evolved."

"So, I guess that makes *you* evolved?" I turn to Gabe, who is calmly listening.

He chuckles. "I guess it does."

Sam sighs. "Not evolved enough to let me kiss you."

"I'm pretty sure you did get one kiss in before I kiboshed it. Though I should thank you for allowing me to clearly identify my spot on the Kinsey scale."

Now my jaw practically hits the floor.

"You two made out?"

They both lean back into the booth, howling with laughter.

"I wouldn't really call it a make-out," Gabe chokes out between laughs.

"Too bad for me," Sam adds.

I blink, trying to digest this news. "I don't get it," I start. "Sam, if you're into men and women, and Gabe, if you're so okay with it, how can you stand Senator Delgado's homophobic legislation?"

Gabe takes a sip of water. "He's my dad. And it's not a matter of standing it. I just accept it."

"And Senator Delgado doesn't write that legislation," Sam adds in Gabe's defense.

"He just votes for it?" I realize my voice is getting higher and squeakier. I take a frustrated breath before turning back to Gabe. "And you have no desire to do anything about it?"

"Not really." He picks up his burger, then puts it down without taking a bite. "When I'm older, maybe I will, but not now."

"Well, that's not entirely true," Sam counters.

Gabe glares at him. My eyes flit back and forth between their two faces trying to read the subtext.

"Why are you upset?" I ask Gabe.

"I'm just reminding Sam not to speak for me."

Sam flops back onto the vinyl seat. "Gabe is weirdly private about some things."

"Yeah, I've seen his Insta. It's more like an L.L. Bean ad than the reflection of an actual person."

"Well, I've seen your Insta, and it makes you seem legit nuts. A lot of oversharing. That bit with you at your therapist's office?"

"It's the waiting room, and it's inspirational!"

"It's certainly exhibitionist."

"Being open about mental health is how we de-stigmatize it," I shoot back.

Sam laughs, and we both whip our heads in his direction. He grins cheekily, stuffing fries in his mouth before he speaks. "Sounds like y'all have been spending a lot of time creeping on each other's social media."

Gabe and I suddenly take an intense interest in our milkshakes.

I swallow and look at Gabe, determined to get to the truth. "So what then did Sam mean by 'that's not entirely true'?"

Sam looks at Gabe for permission. Gabe sighs in resignation

and motions for him to continue.

"Gabe doesn't give a crap about who people want to kiss or who they want to be. He's totally cool with it. Doesn't faze him."

"Okay, so doesn't it bother you when other people do care?" I turn to Gabe.

"Yeah, those people are dicks."

"Like your dad?"

"Hey, watch it." Gabe's expression goes stone cold.

"Sorry, I just don't understand how you can reconcile your views and his."

"You're not going to like it."

"Go on."

"I think eventually society will catch up and accept people for whoever they are." Gabe pauses.

"Okay?" I press.

He sighs. "But I don't think we'll recover from a trillion-dollar deficit, high inflation, and stunted job growth or, most importantly, inept leadership. My dad is awesome at his job, and that helps people in a substantial way."

"So you're saying money matters more than the right to be who you are?" I sit up straight, my spine rigid.

"No, I'm not saying that at all." For the first time, Gabe looks entirely flustered. "I'm just saying my father can't ignore his base. What he says to voters and what he believes personally aren't always the same."

"So your father does believe in gay marriage?"

"I wouldn't go that far, but I'm saying my dad can't ignore the very people who got him elected."

I look at Gabe. I'm beyond disappointed at Gabe's apathy. Sam seems to want to change the subject. As I lean down to take a sip of my vegan milkshake, I'm reminded of just how different I am from the boys sitting in front of me.

# CHAPTER

## 12

Later that night, I'm curled up on the front porch swing, my back on the new yellow pillow Mimi added to the already colorful collection, reading (okay, re-reading) *The Playboy Prince*, one of my favorite Nora Roberts novels. I hear the sound of leaves crunching under footsteps and look up to once again spot a streetlamp-illuminated Gabe Delgado approaching the stone steps to our porch.

"You again?" I joke clumsily, still tense from this afternoon.

"I was really craving some more of that hot cocoa."

I grin.

"No, seriously. It was super good."

"Mimi mixes in some chocolate chips."

I hand him my cup, which is untouched beside me.

"Thanks." He grips the mug as his eyes fall on my book.

I try to quickly hide the title, but it's too late.

He lifts a brow.

I blush. "Busted."

Gabe sits beside me and takes a sip of the hot chocolate. He smiles boyishly. "It really is good."

I smile back. "I'll pass along the rave reviews to Mimi."

We fall into a compatible silence, swinging next to each other, the cool air breezing gently around us.

"So, the reason I really stopped by is…" He pauses as if unsure of himself and takes another sip.

"Yes…?"

"I wanted to know…" he pauses again.

My heartbeat ticks up a notch.

"If I could borrow *The Playboy Prince* sometime? I've been dying to read it." He breaks into a grin.

"Ha ha! Very funny." I swat his arm with the book in question.

"Seriously, though, I felt a little weird about our conversation at Mooburger and just wanted to make sure we're okay."

A warmth spreads in my chest. I sit up straighter and face him on the swing. "I was feeling the same way. To tell you the truth, I've been feeling a bit off since leaving the restaurant."

Gabe looks into my eyes. He swings around to mirror my cross-legged position. "I've been enjoying our Mondays so much," he says. "It's not always easy for me to feel relaxed, but with you and Sam … I don't know … I can really breathe. I don't want any of this other stuff to mess that up."

I nod emphatically. "I know what you mean. Mondays rock."

"Even though you're spending them with a walking L.L. Bean ad?"

"Hit a nerve, did I?"

He laughs. "Yeah, I never know what to put on my dumb Insta."

"You have a bajillion followers, so you know more than I do. But maybe no one wants to follow a legit wacko like myself."

Gabe winces. "I don't think that's quite what I said."

"Close enough."

"Look, the truth is I admire your boldness when posting about … What did you call it? Your 'neurotic, but charming, but still pretty freaking neurotic thought process' for all of the world to see."

I laugh. "You really have been creeping on my account."

"It's certainly not like the other ones I follow."

Our smiles linger, and another silence follows.

The upward turn of my mouth falters for a moment. Part of me wants to press him, to ask him if he realizes that not voicing his concerns to his dad implicitly condones the darkest parts of society. But something stops me. Maybe I am a coward who doesn't want to know more about someone whom I consider a friend?

Finally, Gabe says, "Well, I should get going. School night and all, and I know you have to get back to your important reading." He stands and hands me back the mug. "Thanks for the drink."

"Thanks for coming by and clearing the air, Gabe. I feel a lot lighter." And in that moment, I realize why I held my tongue. The tension between us since our ill-fated debate at Mooburger felt intolerable.

Gabe nods, a gentle expression on his face. "Yeah, me too."

# CHAPTER

## 13

Two days later, I run to catch up with Del and Mason at the end of the school day.

I'm breathless when I finally catch them. "Weren't you all going to wait for me to walk to the meeting?"

"Eh, sorry, Anna. It's not really a given that you're coming anymore," Mason says.

"What do you mean?"

"Well, you've missed two of the last three meetings," he retorts.

I cross my arms defensively. "Yeah, but it's hardly my fault Coach Farmer called that random Wednesday session last week. I'd never miss one otherwise. Just look at my shirt!" I point to the "It's a Woman's Right to Change Her Mind" slogan.

Del laughs and swings an arm over my shoulders. "You can't argue that point. Let's get going."

We start walking, but Mason can't help himself. "Anna, people really are talking about how absent you've been lately."

"People? You mean like your pot-stirring girlfriend?"

He stops walking, and a crowd of sophomores push around us—we're blocking the stairs. "You're making her sound like a gossip."

"She is." I step off to the side.

Mason remains frozen on the steps. "She'd do anything to help people she feels have been wronged. I think it's her best trait."

"It's maybe her most annoying trait," I immaturely reply, though the truth is I am a little jealous of Zoe's moral purity.

"Del, back me up here," Mason pleads.

Del shakes her head. "You're both right. Zoe is an impressive advocate, but she seems to have it out for Anna." She shrugs as if to say, "That much is obvious."

Mason turns a little red, then toes the ground with his sneaker.

Del observes Mason with a grim expression. "What's happening over there, Mase?"

"Uh, well, I think maybe you're on to something."

I scoff. "I've been saying that all year! Why do you suddenly buy it?"

Mason practically turns purple. His Adam's apple twitches.

Del and I exchange pointed glances.

"Mase," I say. "What?"

"Well, eh, I think Zoe was acting out, kind of."

"Acting out about what?"

"Well, she has it in her head that there's something going on between me and you."

My jaw drops. "What?!"

Del shifts her weight. "Interesting."

I glance at Del. She seems upset, but she has to know how absurd that is.

"Well, didn't you dismiss that as ridiculous?"

"Of course I did!" Mason defends himself.

"And?"

"She doesn't believe me."

I throw my hands up in the air. "All of this because you have a jealous girlfriend? Are you kidding me?" I take an enraged step towards my oldest friend.

Del swiftly moves in between us. "Guys, let's calm down here. Yes, Zoe sucks."

"Hey! She's still my girlfriend!"

Anger seeps into my bones. "Have you noticed that, all of a

sudden, she's made a lot of things 'executive team only'?"

Del considers this. "You know what? You're right."

"Come on, guys. She might be a tad jealous, but she wouldn't purposely exclude Anna."

Del and I give him twin "you-got-to-be-kidding-me" looks.

Mason snaps his finger. "Actually, she mentioned that Anna ignored a text from her," he says triumphantly, as if that proved Zoe wasn't trying to exclude me.

I roll my eyes. "It's not like it was a friendly 'let's hang' text, Mase. She asked if I'd heard the rumor that Terry was fired from Bookcourt right before the idea of the union was proposed."

"Is that true?" Del asks, taken aback.

"No," I say emphatically. "No way. Everyone loves Terry, especially Ms. Adler."

"You know it's not true, or you think it isn't?" Mason says.

"I know there's no way that could have happened," I insist, glaring at Mason.

He gives me a condescending look. "So you think."

"Whatever, Mason. Can we talk about something else, please?"

An unusually long pause settles over our group.

Finally, Mason shifts the conversation to his French quiz tomorrow.

By the time we meet the Liberal Liaisons on the corner of Cranberry and Orange, the awkwardness has drifted away, and we are back to conversing full-volume as best friends.

* * * *

We arrive to find Zoe holding court on the curb. Barry dutifully hands out signs that say "You Can't Legislate a Woman's Body" and "My Body, My Choice" to the eight Liberal Liaison members already there. My heart starts to pump faster as the excitement of standing up for my rights takes hold. I'm going to scream until my voice is hoarse and stomp my feet until the pavement shakes.

"Oh good, you're here." Zoe nods at us and gives Mason a gentle smile.

Del and I exchange a glance. It's rare to see a soft side of Zoe, but Mason brings it out in her.

"Our plan is simple. We'll go to the door of the enemy. We will demand justice. And we will prevail!"

The Liaisons cheer. I clap wildly myself. Even though I find Zoe insufferable, she does inspire me.

Zoe continues, "We'll march ten blocks down Cranberry and go to the mouth of the beast and let him know what we think of his recent vote to restrict choice even more."

*The mouth of the beast?* What does that mean? Ten blocks down? And then it dawns on me. Uh oh.

"Senator Delgado's house will have security. If they approach us, link arms and hold your ground."

A chill falls over my body. Is Gabe home? Will he see me yelling outside his house? Will he understand?

"Let's start marching."

I nervously fall in line.

Del looks over at me. "Are you okay?"

"I'm not sure." I struggle to walk. My sign is bumping into my calves, so I raise it onto my shoulder, where it digs into my skin.

"What's wrong?"

I lower my voice so the other Liaisons can't hear. "Well, I'm kind of friends with Gabe now. I feel weird going to his house like this."

Mason looks over at us. "What's going on?"

Del starts to explain, "Anna is worried—"

I cut her off. "I'm worried I have a cold coming on, and that I won't be able to yell loud enough." I fake-cough.

"You seemed fine earlier." Mason scans my face for signs of illness. "You feeling okay?"

I nod guiltily and assure him I am. Luckily, Zoe calls him over, and he walks ahead to catch up with her.

"What was that about?"

I shrug. "He's already so up my you-know-what about loyalty to the Liberal Liaisons. I didn't want to give him any extra fodder."

"Okay," Del says. "But it's not like you to lie to Mason. If anything, you're usually overly antagonistic." Now we're in front of

Gabe's McMansion. The Liaisons start chanting, and I mouth the words with them.

Del nudges me, and I finally answer, "I can only take so much anxiety in one day. And right now my main focus is hoping Gabe doesn't look at out his window and see me throwing tomatoes at his house!"

"Tomatoes?"

"Yes," I gulp. "Look!" I point to where Lizzy and Mason have started chucking tomatoes at the mansion. Red spots splatter across the pristine driveway. Barry manages to land one to the side of the front door and looks to Zoe for approval. I'm relieved when we finally run out of produce and we link arms. I hear the faint wail of sirens in the background. I remind myself why I'm doing this, and how very much I hold this cause dear. I also try to push all thoughts of Gabe out of my head.

# CHAPTER
## 14

Gabe has barely said a word to me for over four miles. I stare into the clear sky and smell the fresh, woodsy scent of the Blue Ridge Mountains. Our training today involves trekking across the six-mile, super-steep loop of the famed Greenway range. I love hiking, but this is the hardest route on the Greenway and my calves are already screaming.

"So, I take it by your icy silence that you saw me at your house?" I wipe my brow and look at Gabe's stoic profile. Of course Sam had to twist his ankle over the weekend and miss the bonus Sunday hike Coach Farmer assigned us.

In stillness, I take in the misty mountain range. Having such beauty just an hour from Edgartown is one of the many things that makes our area such a magical place to live. I look back at Gabe. He still hasn't responded.

"Look, I feel really crappy about all this, but I was stuck between a rock and a hard place. I didn't know what to do. So I stayed with the Liaisons. I really care about a woman's right to choose, now more than ever."

Gabe stops and turns to me. "You threw things at my house."

I cringe. "Well, yeah, but I truly didn't realize we were going to your house till the last second."

"And then when you were there and realized it—you were like, oh well, let me throw a tomato?"

Now we are fully stopped and facing each other in the middle of the trail. Tall pine trees flank us.

"I swear I didn't throw any fruit!" When Gabe looks at me unmoved, I add, "Or veggies!"

"Is that supposed to be funny?" Gabe starts walking quickly ahead. "Never mind."

He looks genuinely hurt, and I begin feeling guilty again. I basically have to start jogging (on an incline!) to keep up with him. "Hey! I'm not six feet tall like you!" Nor are my legs as perfectly sculpted, I think, but decide to keep that to myself.

"I'm six-two," he shoots back.

I roll my eyes. "That's just bragging." I finally catch up to him.

He starts to smile, but then stops. "I'm still mad at you."

I bite my lip. "Look, it felt super suck-y to go to your house like that. I'm genuinely sorry about that part." I hold my hand up in a peace offering. "I've never felt as distant from the Liaisons as I have this last month, and I just knew if I didn't stick with them for a pro-choice rally, then I'd really be lost somehow."

"I get that friend dynamics can be awkward. And I get that you really care about being pro-choice, but I don't see how going to my house and screaming helps bring back *Roe vs Wade* or whatever you all were trying to accomplish." He pauses. "I thought we were buds."

I smile at "buds." "We are, but I also think your dad's vote to restrict abortion at such an early stage is outrageous."

"Okay, but couldn't you express that somewhere else? It's where I live."

I sigh, thinking over his words. "This is really hard."

He stops again, and his eyes, looking more tired than normal, meet mine. "Yeah, it is." He puts his hands in his pockets. "Look, I admire how much you stand up for things. I do. You and your friends are really, really, really..." his voice tinges on outright sarcasm by the third *really*. I arch a brow.

"Really passionate. But, look, our views differ, though I doubt they differ as much as our parents' views differ."

"What's that supposed to mean? And, by the way, what are

your views on abortion?"

"Are you asking as a friend who's honestly interested in hearing what I have to say? Or as someone who's going to start throwing stuff at me if she doesn't like what she hears?"

"Well, I guess that depends on what you're going to say."

He gives me a pointed look.

"Okay, okay," I assure him. "I promise no throwing."

"I don't think anyone should be governing anyone else's body."

I start grinning from ear to ear.

"Don't look so happy. I also don't think people should be governing much of anything."

I open my mouth to ask for clarification, but decide not to push my luck... at least today. "Okay, at least you don't agree with your dad on everything."

"Just for the record, I may not agree with him, but I do understand where he's coming from. And, Anna, I need you to hear this. I admire my dad a lot. If you and I are going to be friends, I'd like you to try to understand that. By the same token, I'm sure that you and your mom are not totally alike."

"I'm not that different from my mom, though."

"Then why was she at the Bookcourt protest three days straight last month, and you were nowhere to be seen?"

"That's not the same."

"Why?"

I frown. "I don't know why, but trust me, it isn't."

Gabe laughs. "Okay. Being in the middle is now, somehow, a bad thing. And it seems like everyone has to be so extreme. I don't know how I'd feel about any of this if my life was different, if I wasn't a senator's son. And, if you weren't a liberal journalist's daughter, I don't think you would know either. We're both too close to it."

And yet, I've never felt further away from it. "But shouldn't we at least try to?" I say. "Isn't that the whole point?"

Gabe looks at me, his face unusually intense. "I guess it is, but for me, my family comes first. At least for now."

"I guess that gives you a center."

"Yeah, it does. I don't think it's so different for you."

I think about that… about what I hold dearest. "I guess you're right." I look down, feeling a little ashamed of one thing. "I'm sorry if I was rude about your dad. He's accomplished impressive things. Plus he raised someone like you, and that says a lot about him."

Gabe smiles, and I can tell I'm forgiven.

I notice I'm a little winded. "Hey, we're almost at the top!"

Gabe grins. "I barely noticed. Usually this is the hardest part."

"We should fight more during conditioning. It really makes me forget that my thighs are screaming at me."

When Gabe laughs, it's as if a weight left his shoulders. "Deal."

We ascend the final few steps and both let out whooshes of breath. I stare at the beautiful vista, the far-off mountain ranges, and the small dots of the towns. I look up at the sky and then at Gabe and I smile.

# CHAPTER

## 15

"So explain to me what made you think this was a winnable challenge?" Del huffs a little from the incline.

I smile. The weekend after Gabe and I completed the trail, Del and I are on the longer but less steep loop of the Greenway. Sam (who has mostly recovered) and Gabe are a good bit ahead of us, but I'm not worried. I challenged them to a partner race after Sam said something asinine about boys having more athletic stamina than girls.

Then to make it even more fun, we agreed the loser had to donate to whatever cause the winner wants (me/Del: ActBlue, Gabe/Sam: The Heritage Foundation). They thought it was hysterical that I agreed to the bet, but they didn't know about my foolproof, unbeatable plan!

Del lifts a brow. "Why are you gloating?"

"Because you're out of breath and I'm not!"

"Thanks, friend." Her voice drips with sarcasm.

I shrug, unbothered, and retaining a pep in my step. "I gotta take my wins where I can. It's not always easy having besties like you and Mason. You're both pretty, in a Brooklyn hipster kind of way. You're also cool with great taste, and freakishly good test takers—"

"Is this about the SATs?"

I ignore her and continue with my monologue, "—and good at everything you both do."

"Except for hiking apparently."

"Exactly." I give her another gloating smile.

"Remind me why I'm friends with you?" She tightens the hair bun on top of her head.

"Because I'm irresistible."

"That must be it." Del looks around nervously.

"What's wrong?"

"I thought I heard something."

"We aren't going to see any bears or cougars or whatever else Dr. Bahar told you we might see," I assure her again. Del's parents are on the nervous side. They think there's danger everywhere.

"At least I have this cute hiking outfit."

I glance at her. She does look totally chic, in brown hiking boots, a gray semi-haltered workout top, and black and gray yoga pants. "You look awesome."

"Apparently not awesome enough."

I look over at her. "What are you talking about?"

She shakes her head. "Ignore me. I'm wallowing. This Mason and Zoe stuff is getting to me."

I swing an arm around her shoulders. "He's an idiot. You're the best and the hottest."

"I don't get what he even sees in her."

"She's a zealot. He's into that. It calms his nerves to know he's with someone who cares *even more* about the world than he does."

"True." She checks her watch. "Speaking of which, if we want to give you a shot of winning this bet..."

"The shortcut is foolproof."

"I hope so, because I don't know how you're going to explain to anyone why you've donated to The Heritage Foundation."

My mom has done about two dozen segments on how the Heritage Foundation's conservative policies are threatening democracy as we know it.

"Lilly might go into cardiac arrest," Del continues.

"Good thing we know some good cardiologists!" We both break out in big grins.

Del looks ahead of the trail. "I have to say—and don't repeat this—Gabe is super attractive."

"Ah-ha! So you think so, too!"

She smiles. "It's hard not to admire his, uh, form in that black tank top."

"The bandana sent me over the edge," I admit with a giggle. My stomach warms at the image.

Del looks at me. "Watch out, Anna, you're blushing."

"You just said he was good-looking too!"

"But I'm not having the same visceral reaction as you."

I frown. "Tell me the truth. Am I anti-feminist for being attracted to Senator Delgado's son? I mean, Gabe is such a Northsider."

She shrugs. "What's the harm of looking? As long as you stay just friends …although it does seem like you're getting kind of close."

"We are." I smile a little.

"Uh oh," Del intones.

I laugh. "Please! If anything, I'm closer to Sam."

"Who is also hot, but you seem to notice that less, which is making me really wonder."

I roll my eyes. "Look, it's honestly really fun hanging with them. They're so different from our friends."

"I get that."

"And it feels like my own thing, my own special Monday world. Besides, I think they're good people." I know I'm rambling, but I can't help but tell her how sweet Gabe is with his little sister Bea, how loyal he is to Sam and the select few he considers his real friends, and how he helps everyone, from the old lady at the diner to the stray kitten who wanders onto the school's athletic fields. "He even picks up random litter, which I don't even do, and I give some of my allowance to Greenpeace."

"He's practically Mother Theresa."

"Ha, ha. I know he takes a lot of problematic positions on important issues."

Del smiles a bit. "Just wanted to make sure you remember that, but I get it. I do. He sounds like a good guy in a lot of ways. So does Sam."

I nod, glad she understands. "What do you think the chances are that Mason will ever see that?"

"Zero?"

I sigh. That sounds about right. "Okay, the turnoff for the shortcut is right here," I say, but hesitate. Why does this look different from the last time I did it with my moms?

Del eyes me. "Anna, you have to be sure. We can't fool around with this."

I swallow my doubt. "I'm sure." I adjust the rim of my green "There is No Planet B" hat, shoving stray curls under the brim. "Let's win this thing!"

Del sighs and takes a more than ample sip from her water bottle. "Let's beat those preppy lacrosse players once and for all."

I smile. "They won't know what hit 'em!"

\* \* \* \*

"Anna, are you *sure* this is right?"

After a mile of walking, my shortcut seems less like a timesaver and more like an unmarked path in the woods. We have scratches on our legs from scrambling over thorny branches, and our feet are damp from slipping on rocks in a shallow creek. "I am mostly sure."

"Anna!" Del stops and looks sternly at me.

I swallow nervously. Del rarely gets mad. I give her my best *I'm sorry* smile.

"We need to backtrack. We could get really lost." Del looks around anxiously. I can tell the thought of bears is going through her head right now.

"We can't go back! Then we will definitely lose the bet." I panic. "And I'll have to post on Instagram about my donation to The Heritage Foundation."

Del looks incredulously at me. "I think that's better than dying!"

I roll my eyes. And "I thought I was the dramatic one."

"I'm putting my foot down. This is the canoe trip all over again."

"Will you ever let that go?"

"We were stranded on that rock for an hour and a half while waves crashed over us, so no!"

I harrumph. Looking into the forest behind Del, I hear something rustling in the bushes. It sounds suspiciously large. Suddenly, scary images from every lost-in-the-mountains movie I've seen start to rush through my head. Maybe Del is right and we should turn back. "Okay, fine," I say, my shoulders slumping. "I could have sworn that was the right turnoff." I look at the downward slope of the mountain. "What if we just go down?" I suggest. A new hope alights in me.

Del full-on glares at me. "One side is Tennessee, Anna."

"Oh, right." My shoulders slump even lower.

Del takes the lead, carefully retracing our steps. When we approach the dreaded creek again, she sighs with relief. On the other side, there's a clear path back to the blue markers of the proper trail. "Let's look for some more stable rocks," she suggests.

"Look who's becoming a mountaineer," I say. Del is a quick study, a trait I highly recommend in a bestie.

But just as I am about to follow her to the rocks on the far left, I freeze. "Del," I whisper. "Don't move."

"What?" She turns around to see what I'm looking at.

I cringe. Her sudden movement has the large black bear on the other side of the creek growling and looking over at us.

Del starts muttering in Hindi, her eyes large and shaking. I cautiously grab her hand.

"Listen, we need to slowly back away."

Del manages to nod, though she looks like she's in shock.

"Del, I need to confess something."

"Does it really have to be right now?" Del panic-whispers.

"To support Ms. Adler, I've been buying books at Bookcourt this whole time. And every time I go to return one, I just find another one I want. And I even had to hide in there for an hour the other day when I saw Zoe, Mason, and Barry outside handing out flyers."

"I really hope this lame confession isn't the last thing I ever hear."

Again, we both freeze in terror as the bear emits an even more forceful growl.

I tell her to go first. This is my fault, after all. And Del is too smart and fashionable to be mauled by a bear at such a young age.

"Whatever you do, be as still and as slow as possible," I instruct her as softly as possible, remembering Mimi's safety lessons on all my hikes growing up.

Del lets out a gasp, blood draining from her face. My throat freezes, suppressing a scream. Two more bears have joined our first friend. They all look at us.

"Screw this!" Del says. "We've got to get out of here. Run!"

It really does feel like the only thing to do, so I follow her lead, and we start booking it straight down the mountain.

The bears growl. I look over my shoulder. Fuck. Now on all fours, they start to cross the creek at an alarming speed. I take my backpack and throw it as hard as I can into the bushes uphill. And then throw some sticks for good measure. Miraculously, this seems to distract the bears, and they shuffle toward the backpack. Del and I barrel full force down the mountain, terror leading us fast and far.

Gold rays of sunshine stream through the huge trees as we hop over rocks and branches, falling and helping one another up as we race down. Finally, the trees break into smaller bushes, and we hear the sounds of people talking. We look at each other hopefully. Could it be? A trail? With gasping relief, we race toward the voices.

As we stumble through the thick of bushes onto the trail, I slam into a stunned Gabe.

Del lands panting beside me. Sam goes to her side, offering her water and looking concerned about her bleeding legs. Gabe grabs my shoulders to steady me, his face a little pale.

I look down and wipe blood from my own cuts. Then I pull a twig from my hair.

Gabe looks at us with alarm. "What happened to you two?" he asks. His voice sounds tight with nerves as he scans every inch of my body like he's making sure I'm still intact. He relaxes his hold on my shoulders once he sees I'm okay.

"Bears," says Del, finally managing to catch her breath.

"What? You saw a bear on the trail?"

Del glares at me.

I shrug. "We weren't exactly on the trail."

Gabe throws back his head and laughs. The color returns to his face. His sexy bandana is holding back his dark hair, and between that and the sweat, he looks even hotter, which sours my mood even more. "So you tried to cheat."

"No, it was supposed to be a respectable shortcut."

*"A respectable shortcut?"* Gabe laughs even harder. "Nice try. I say you're disqualified."

"No! The rules are that the winner is whoever's first up and down the mountain. We did go all the way up."

Gabe arches his brow. "As you recently told me, we're supposed to follow the spirit of the law, not the letter."

"That was about the constitution. Not about this."

Del looks at me like I should give it up.

I sigh, not sure what to do. My stomach drops. Oy. I'm going to donate to The Heritage Foundation. But then it occurs to me: We are about one hundred feet from the end of the trail.

"Oh my god!" I yell, calling on my best acting skills. "They're back! Bears!"

Del lets out a petrified scream, and Sam and Gabe whip around.

As soon as their eyes lock onto the mountain, I take off at full speed toward the trail marker, years of sprints at track practice propelling me quickly forward.

From behind me, Gabe yells, "Hey!" Then Del shouts, "Anna, I am going to kill you!"

I hear the sound of what must be Gabe's footsteps behind me, and they're getting closer. I push myself to go faster. *Don't look back*, I urge myself forward, refusing to relent for even a second. My conditioning training has paid off; I'm moving faster than I knew possible. I can see the path giving way to the pavement of the parking lot in front of me. The footsteps behind me grow louder. I peek back, unable to control myself.

"Hey!" I yelp as I feel myself not so gently tugged back.

My look back allows Gabe to catch up with me. Damn my impulsivity!

He races ahead and wins, then raises his sculpted arms in victory. I throw my arms down in frustration.

"Great. Once Zoe gets wind that I've donated to The Heritage Foundation, I'll be lucky if any of the Liaisons ever speak to me again."

From behind us, we hear an exhausted Del panting as she jogged alongside Sam. "Are you really going to make her do it, bro?" Sam asks.

"That depends." Gabe turns to Del. "Do you think she'd have made me do it if we lost?"

"For sure," Del answers with a laugh.

"Not helping! Please, Gabe, please don't make me. I'll do anything."

"Anything? This is getting kinky," Sam jokes.

"Gross." Del scrunches her nose.

Gabe looks at my desperate face and shrugs. "Fine. But you're buying lunch."

My eyes widen. Am I really getting off that easily? "Okay!"

"But you're not getting off that easily."

My expression falls. "Fine. Then what is it?"

"For now it's an IOU." Gabe smiles, apparently pleased with himself.

"Whatever," I say with a wave of my hands. "As long as I don't have to donate to that freakin' foundation, I'm happy."

As we walk down a small sloping dirt path to the parking lot, all of us chug water like we've been left for dead on a deserted island.

"So the plan is still the Tavern Inn for lunch?" Gabe asks.

"Yup," I confirm. The Tavern Inn is a small, rustic restaurant sandwiched between town and the mountains that's become a popular post-hike lunch spot.

"Mason is still coming?"

I check my phone. "He just confirmed."

"This shouldn't be at all awkward," Sam says sarcastically. "Hope we don't end up in one of his songs after this."

I roll my eyes. "Very funny," I say sarcastically and then force a smile. My plan to unite my friends, which had seemed like a good idea at its inception, is beginning to feel as practical as my mountain shortcut. "Guys, lunch is going to be really fun. I can feel it."

Both Del and Gabe look doubtful, and I swallow, wondering if the bears are going to be the least of my problems today.

# CHAPTER

## 16

On the way to lunch, we hit zero traffic and manage to beat Mason to the Tavern Inn. Seated in a booth at the back of the restaurant, Sam flirts with Del semi-outrageously while she rebuffs his attempts with humor and ease.

"You know," Sam says with a good-natured sigh. "You make rejection feel not-so-bad, and that just makes you even cooler. Guess we just aren't meant to be."

Del laughs. "I guess not."

"We aren't the ones with the will-they-or-won't-they vibes at this table anyway," Sam adds.

I look at him blankly, then at Gabe, who has developed a sudden interest in his phone.

"Who has those vibes?"

We all look up at Mason. His cheeks are pink from the wind, and he adjusts his glasses as he stares at the table. His eyes fall to me and his Adam's apple seems to pulse. I follow his line of vision and suddenly become very aware of my posture. I'm slouched back in our horseshoe corner booth, exhausted from the hike, and Gabe is stretched out, his arm over the cushion where I'm seated. I lean forward, folding my arms on the table.

"Hey, Mase," Gabe says.

Del looks at me and mouths, "Mase?"

I shrug. I wonder if Gabe is deliberately provoking him, even though that seems out of character.

Mason meets Gabe's glance. "What up, G?"

Sam laughs. "Glad we're already onto the nickname phase of this meal." The waiter arrives and places baskets of fries on the table.

"Did you guys already order?" Mason asks in an annoyed tone.

Sam and Gabe exchange looks and I cringe.

"No, silly," Del reassures him calmly, "we were just craving some fries." She nonetheless shoots me a glance. This is going about as well as expected, which is to say, not well at all.

We all scoot down and make room for Mason, who is standing at one end of the curved booth next to Sam.

"Yeah, and since Anna is buying, we decided to make this a multi-course meal."

"Why are you buying?" Mason asks as he sits down awkwardly. I haven't seen Mason look this socially out of place since elementary school.

"Anna lost a bet on the hike," Del explains.

I can tell she's trying to help Mason relax.

"Oh, ha, well, Anna's never really been great at winning bets," Mason jokes, finally sounding like himself.

"Yeah, remember when she bet Caroline Loran she could recite every line of any Broadway show Caroline could name?" Del recalls.

Mason starts laughing. "Yeah, that was hysterical."

"How was I supposed to know Caroline knew anything about Broadway? She doesn't strike me as the musical theater type."

Del turns to Gabe and Sam. "Anna had to belt out all the king's lines from *Hamilton* every day before first period for a week."

"It was brutal."

Gabe laughs. "Not sure how I missed that, but I guess I'm glad I did. I mean, I've heard you sing enough to know how painful that must have been for everyone."

Mason looks startled. "How often have you heard Anna sing?"

Sam groans. "*So many* times. Let's toast to never again." Sam raises his water glass.

"We can't all have the voice of an angel like my pal Mason here," I say.

"Yeah, man, seems like you're super talented," Sam offers.

Gabe nods. "I admire your skills. I was never any good at guitar, even after begging my parents for lessons in fifth grade."

I look at Gabe in wonder. "I'm shocked, twice."

"She's shocked." Sam mimics my tone.

"Twice!" Del piles on, and she and Sam laugh.

"Yes, twice! First that Gabe ever wanted to play guitar, and second that he was actually bad at it."

Sam hoots. "There's a first for everything."

Sam and I high-five and do a little boogie together at the table.

Gabe rolls his eyes and turns to Del and Mason good-naturedly. "Great friends I've got, right?"

Del smiles back but looks a little sad. Mason's Adam's apple starts twitching again.

"Actually, I've always found Anna to be an exceptional friend," Mason says. "Loyal and funny."

I'm embarrassed Mason is taking this weirdly serious tone. Why can't he just act normal? I look at Del for help.

Gabe looks at Mason steadily. "Yeah, but no one is saying she isn't."

Sam, happy to lighten the mood, cuts in. "Personally, I'm only friends with Anna so I can follow her on social media."

Del laughs. "Totally. How else would we know all the reasons she believes she's her therapist's third-favorite patient."

Gabe chuckles. "I did enjoy that. Not everyone would have the balls to livestream it."

"You wouldn't. That's for sure, buddy," I tease. "All your posts are the same. Do we really need more evidence that you're good at sports and school, *and* that you can wear a button-down and denim like it's nobody's business? We get it. You're kind of perfect. Boring!" I say theatrically.

Sam and Del laugh.

Gabe shrugs, looks down at me, and smiles. "I guess you have a point. I could put myself out there more ...like you do."

I grin back at him.

"I've got to use the bathroom," Mason says suddenly, slamming his drink down on the table with enough force to make me jump. "If the waitress comes back during my absence, would you order me the veggie burger?" he asks Del.

"Sure."

Mason leaves, and the server comes to take our orders.

I bite my lip, wishing this weird mood would disperse.

While Del and Sam are ordering, Gabe turns to me again and asks, "Are you okay? You look a little worried."

"I just wish this was going a little better. I feel like Mason is acting weird, or maybe it's just me."

Gabe nods. "I don't think I'm helping."

"What do you mean?"

But Mason returns before he can answer.

Gabe shoots me a reassuring look before turning to the rest of the table. "I've actually been watching this really cool show. Not sure anyone has seen it? It's that Apple TV docuseries on the last fifty years of music. It's super thought-provoking."

Mason's face lights up a bit. "Yeah, I've been streaming that too. It's great."

Sam and Del, who apparently have also been watching this show, join in, and for the rest of meal, the conversation flows easily and naturally. I'm the only one who hasn't seen any of the shows (probably because every time I go to turn one on, I end up watching a made-for-Netflix rom-com instead. Whoops!). But as I witness all my friends debate the best episode, a feeling of contentment hits me. This is pretty awesome.

# CHAPTER

## 17

The Monday after our close bear encounter, we're finishing a round of grueling sprints. Coach Farmer left ten minutes ago, instructing us to complete three more rounds before we call it quits for the day. The only thing getting me through it is the knowledge that these training runs are my best hope of getting into an Ivy. As I force myself forward, I push my sweaty hair out of my eyes and glance at the sky. The sun sets earlier each Monday, and the sky glows as the yellow turns to orange and pink

Gabe is several paces ahead of me and just edging out Sam. I'm trying to focus and not stare at his graceful strides when Gabe lets out a groan, grabs the back of his leg, and stumbles to the ground.

I panic, heart in my throat, as I race to his side. Sam's there first, bending down to assess the situation. I throw myself on the other side of Gabe. His face is scrunched in pain. I place my hand on his shoulder, trying to soothe him. "Are you okay?" I ask, worried.

Gabe nods but winces again and rolls to his side, holding his thigh.

I look to Sam for reassurance.

"He just needs a minute. Gabe gets these really awful hamstring pulls, and he won't ever rest enough to let it really heal."

Gabe nods again, still writhing in pain and unable to speak.

Sam hurries off to get Gabe's water bottle.

Once Gabe's face relaxes a fraction, he looks up at me, a hint of a smile on his striking face. "Didn't mean to give you a scare there, Morningstar."

"Oh, I wasn't scared," I fib, my heart still racing.

"Glad to hear it," he says, a teasing look in his eye.

Sam comes back and hands Gabe his water bottle.

Gabe looks at me instead of taking it.

Confused, I ask, "What?"

"I kind of need my hand back," Gabe says.

"Oh," I say, flustered. I hadn't even realized I'd been clasping his hand. When I release my grip, the stiffness in my fingers lets me know just how tight my hold had been.

Gabe gives my hand a gentle squeeze before letting go and taking the water bottle.

He lets out another groan as Sam and I help him into a sitting position. He throws his head back and gulps down water.

Sam snaps a picture with his phone, then shows us the photo. "If that doesn't say 'leave it all out there,' I don't know what does."

I nod, taken by the picture. Gabe's head is tilted back as he drinks from the bottle, his beautiful features contorted in obvious pain. Sweat drips down his brow. He looks completely vulnerable, yet somehow (maybe it's his strong jawline) unbreakable.

"You should post that on Insta, Gabe," I say as he puts his water bottle down and looks at the picture.

"No way! I look awful, like I'm about to cry."

"You look human," Sam observes.

"Exactly," I agree. "I feel like people should see this. A chink in the armor."

Gabe looks skeptical. "I'll think about it."

Later that night, just as I'm finishing my math homework, Gabe texts me to look at Instagram. I quickly pull up the app and am pleased (and a little shocked) to see that Gabe has indeed posted Sam's photo. He's captioned it simply: "not my best practice."

I stare at the photo, moved. Gabe finally has posted something real.

# CHAPTER

18

On Tuesday, after our respective team practices, Sam, Gabe, and I gather on the athletic field to discuss when we should meet for the extra drills Coach Farmer assigned us. Gabe suggests the following morning at dawn so we can watch the sun rise over Edgartown, but Sam and I boo at the thought of cutting our beauty rest short. When Gabe counters with "Well, there's no time like the present," we again resist. My legs are already jelly.

We compromise by agreeing on Saturday morning, long after the sun has risen, but just in time for a short stack at Floppies. Just as we're about to head home, I spot Mason and Zoe walking near the bleachers, about to cut across the field to the parking lot. I dive behind a large pile of cones and a water cooler, trying to avoid being seen.

Sam and Gabe watch me, bemused.

"Hiding from your best friend? Is this the emotional 'wokeness' you're always preaching so loudly about?" asks Sam, a twinkle in his eye.

"So very loudly," Gabe drawls.

"Very funny," I respond dryly. "It's just that I told them we were meeting for an extra hour tonight, and I don't want them to see us packing up."

"Why'd you lie?" Sam asks.

"They're meeting to discuss more Bookcourt boycott strategy, and I can't handle that right now." I wait until Mason is completely out-of-sight before stepping out of my hiding spot.

"And you can't you just tell them that?" says Gabe with a shrug.

"I don't want to rock the boat any more than I have. They're already kind of pissed at me for not taking the Bookcourt stuff more seriously." I bite my lip. "And I'm really sick of feeling on the outs with my best friends."

Gabe looks at me intently. "Anna, on some stuff, it's okay to see things differently than your friends. You know that, right?"

"You just don't get it," I reply. "It's not that simple."

"I think it's pretty simple, but I'll let it go." Gabe frowns.

I frown back at him.

He holds up his hands. "Alright, enough about Bookcourt. You won't hear me utter the word 'union' for the rest of the week."

"Thank you," I say.

But then Gabe frowns again. "Speaking of unions—"

I groan.

"I thought we weren't using that word until Monday?" Sam laughs.

Gabe ignores us and continues. "Bookcourt has been open for a long time. So, why did the employees want to unionize now? Did something happen?"

I open my mouth to respond when I realize Gabe has a point. "Good question. Most of the employees have been there since the store opened." Bookcourt's staff always felt like a big, happy family. What changed? I look at Gabe and consider. "Well, there was a weird rumor going around about Terry... you know, the head of the children's section. People are saying he got fired right before the union stuff started, but I don't really buy it."

"Maybe you should find out?" Gabe suggests. "Might make you less likely to hide from your friends if you get some clarity on what actually went down over there."

I let his words sink in, realizing just how little any of us knew about the situation. Is it possible that no one, including the mighty

Zoe Dart, knows the whole truth? "Yeah, I think I will." I smile at Gabe. There's something unfamiliar but strangely comforting about being in the presence of someone who asks questions instead of giving answers.

Gabe looks smug. "So I guess I do get it."

"Maybe … but only a very tiny bit of it."

Sam and Gabe laugh at my response as my mind turns toward Bookcourt.

* * * *

An hour later, Sam and I walk into the bookstore, the entrance conveniently free of any Liaison protestors. Gabe had to go home because his family was entertaining some diplomat tonight, and I'm kind of glad it's just Sam and me. When Gabe is around, I'm too aware of myself, and this visit requires my full attention.

Pushing open the glass doors, I step onto the light oak floors as Sam trails behind me. I'm immediately struck by how much emptier the store is than usual.

"So, who are we looking for exactly? The owner?" Sam asks, looking a little dubious.

"Or one of the long-time employees," I answer hesitantly, realizing I don't quite have a plan. Investigative journalism has always been Del's thing. A twinge of guilt courses through me as I imagine how Del and Mason would view what I'm doing … and with whom. I shake my head to clear the thought. They'll understand once I have answers. I throw my shoulders back and, as much as possible, try to channel Del's confidence.

As I walk through the aisles, the eerie quietness of a warm, usually bustling store hits me again.

Finally, I see Shelly, one of Bookcourt's most senior managers, organizing books in the Mystery/Sci-Fi section. Shelly never seems to age. She's still wearing the big bottle-cap glasses she's worn since I was a kid, and her hair is tied in a tight, low bun. A thick gray streak stands out against her otherwise dark brown hair.

Happy to see a familiar face doing her usual thing at the store, I wave enthusiastically and call her name.

"Hey, Anna," Shelly intones, giving me a barely detectible smile. For Shelly, this is the equivalent of a beaming grin. Unsurprisingly, her gaze moves disinterestedly over to Sam. Shelly thinks people are far less interesting than books and dogs. I'm comforted to know some things never change.

"This is my friend Sam." I introduce him, stalling for a beat.

Sam grins and says hello.

"Anything either of you need help finding?" Shelly asks. She glances over her shoulder longingly at the Mystery/Sci-Fi section. It's clear she wants to get back to shelving.

"Well," I start, "I was wondering how things are around here? Seems kind of empty and dead."

Shelly sighs and adjusts her glasses. "Yeah, it's been pretty slow since everything went down."

"Have a lot of people quit?" I survey the store. Not only are there fewer customers, but the store is also noticeably devoid of workers. No one is manning the counter at the café, and a small sign reads: "Closed until further notice."

"No one has quit, but a lot of them are refusing to come in until the boss allows the union."

"But not you?"

Shelly shrugs. "Hey, I think a union would be great, but I'd never turn my back on Ms. Adler."

"Because she's a kickass boss?" Sam asks. He throws me a supportive thumbs up like we're on the verge of cracking the case.

"Sure." Shelly gives him a wary look. "Plus she co-signed my student loans when I went back to night school. Not many people would do that."

My heart swells. That's the Ms. Adler I know. Then I remember Del's monologues on the importance of impartiality in journalism, so I force my face into a neutral expression. "Was the union something people wanted for a long time? Or did something happen that suddenly made it feel necessary?" I try to ask as dispassionately as possible, which makes me sound like I'm fighting a yawn.

Shelly doesn't look moved by my line of questioning, so I try a more direct tactic. "Maybe something to do with Terry getting fired?"

A spark of recognition flares in Shelly's eyes. Before taking a step closer to us, she looks around to make sure no one's listening. "Don't tell anyone I told you this, but Terry was caught eating an edible in the kids' book section. It was almost closing time, and no kids were around, but Ms. Adler fired him on the spot."

Sam shoots me a puzzled look. "Doing drugs at work sounds like a problem, right? Or am I missing something?" He doesn't attempt the same journalistic tone I'm striving to achieve, but he looks between me and Shelly for clarification.

I roll my eyes knowing Sam expects us Eastsiders to have radical views on drugs. "I'm sure no one thought it was okay to have weed in the kids' section, Sam, but Terry has worked here for years. He's an institution."

"Yeah, Terry is awesome, but his judgment ..." Shelly trails off.

"So that's when the union idea started?" I ask, trying to refocus on the mission at hand.

"Kind of. We all wanted him to get a second chance. Ms. Adler was open to it if he went to counseling, but Alfred was worried he was a liability." Shelly does another sweep of the store. Once she's sure it's clear, she continues, "Then, while Ms. Adler and Alfred were going back and forth on the Terry stuff, Tom got everyone all worked up about the idea of being fired willy nilly and started emailing all of us about unions."

"Who's Tom?" Sam asks.

"He's a new guy, a graduate student at Edgartown College. Started a couple of months ago," Shelly clarifies. "He used to be kind of quiet, but now, not so much. Anyway, things got heated fast."

"What a mess."

"Sure is." Shelly looks back at the Sci-Fi section once again. "I need to get back to work."

"Okay, thanks so much, Shelly." I pause, wanting to offer something more. "Is there anything we can do to help?" I know Mason would call me a scab for crossing the picket line, but it sounds like Ms. Adler was backed into a corner.

"Well, if you're around the first Saturday of the month, we have our big shipment coming in. We could really use some help stocking books. It's been brutal with our skeleton staff." Shelly runs her hand over her gray patch of hair as if the stress of the protests is a direct cause for its existence.

I nod, happy there's something concrete I can do.

"We will be there!"

"*We* will?" Sam asks, uncertainly.

I elbow him. "We will. And we'll bring another friend too." I'm not sure how Gabe will feel about me volunteering his services, but it's only fair since this investigation was his idea.

Sam looks at me in acquiescence and shrugs. "I guess we will."

"Thanks, guys. That would be a huge help." Shelly gives us the closest thing to an actual, big smile I've ever seen from her. "We usually start around 8 a.m."

Sam winces at the early start, but, always the gentleman, says, "It was nice to meet you."

As we walk towards the front of the store, Sam turns to me and says, "Well, that was a weird story. Bet you twenty dollars that Tom kid has a super annoying major."

I laugh, glad Sam is here to break the tension.

# CHAPTER

## 19

My mood rides high all Monday morning. I feel victorious. I'd spent part of my weekend with Mason and Del, and the other part with Gabe and Sam. I love moments when everything clicks into place and just feels right. Even though I'd never have believed it if you told me this on the first day of school, being with Del, Mason, Sam, and Gabe makes me feel strangely whole and utterly in the moment. The lunch we shared was pretty successful. Now if only I could get them to all hang out together again.

Throughout the afternoon, I continue to feel practically giddy. I sail into my usual seat for History, my last class of the day, beaming at Lizzy and Zoe, who are seated to my right. Lizzy smiles back nervously, twining her stick-straight brown hair around her finger. Zoe gives me an odd look, confused why, after weeks of tension between us, I'm grinning so widely at her now. I take out my pen and notebook, ready to learn all there is to know about the Industrial Revolution.

A smiling Mr. Sullen walks in, as always rocking a bow tie, and today holding a stack of papers. My heart ticks up when I realize we're getting last week's tests back. It was a big one and I studied super hard until I was confident I'd get an A. I know how important it is to start getting better grades this year. I mean, how could Mr. Sullen not be at least mildly floored with my expansive knowledge of the Gilded Age?

My heart thuds louder as he approaches my row, placing each test face down. I watch as he gives Zoe and Lizzy their exams. They quickly flip them over and seem pleased with their scores. Finally, he reaches my desk. I barely wait for his hand to leave my paper before flipping it over. I open and shut my eyes, feeling gut-punched as the 78 stares back at me. How could this be?

I quickly slam the test booklet face-down so no one can see it. I blink back tears. I want to bolt from the classroom so badly, but pride keeps my butt rooted in my chair. The next fifty minutes painfully tick by. Despair sinks into my chest and panic races through my bloodstream. I look around the room at my peers and feel utterly like an outsider looking in.

\* \* \* \*

As soon as the bell rings, I throw the test into my backpack, escape out the door, and rush down the hall. I suck in my first breath of cool air and feel the tears start to unleash. I take off down the stairs at a full racing speed, not wanting anyone to see me cry.

I vaguely think I hear my name being called, but I ignore it, plunging towards the athletic fields and the woods behind them so I can hide.

I make it just past the outside gate of the fields when a strong hand closes over my arm.

"Anna, are you okay?" Gabe's soft voice asks.

I still myself completely, tears flooding my cheeks.

"Anna," he says, again gently pulling me around to face him.

I can't meet his eyes. My lips quiver as I feel his eyes studying my face. Wordlessly, he pulls me into his chest, wrapping his toned arms around me until I'm engulfed in his embrace. I breathe in his crisp, clean smell, bury my face in his solid chest, and start sobbing. Gabe holds me tighter, gently stroking my hair. His touch leaves me feeling comforted and safe. My sobs subside to tears. Gabe patiently waits me out, until I've managed to cry myself dry.

He steps back a half-inch and I immediately feel the loss of his closeness. I step back toward him, wanting to burrow my head again, but he stops me by placing a finger under my chin and lifting my head so I'm forced to look him in the eye.

I find myself staring into his depthless golden-brown eyes.

*Depthless?* Clearly, I'm reading way too many romance novels.

"What happened?" Gabe looks at me, concern etching his features. "Are you hurt?"

When I don't answer, Gabe starts to look panicked. He looks me up and down as if reassuring himself I'm fine. His eyes turn cold and angry, and I blink, confused by the rage I see on his face.

"Did someone do something to you?" he asks in a steely monotone.

I hiccup and blink. I've never seen protective Gabe before and I don't know what to make of it. A tingly feeling runs down my spine.

"No, no," I reassure him. "The only thing hurt is my pride."

Gabe lets out a relieved breath and squeezes my shoulders gently. He lets his hands fall to his side and we are no longer touching at all. I wrap my hands around my body and bite my lip so I can't ask him to hold me longer.

"What happened?" he asks again.

"I … I," my voice breaks. "I got a 78 on my history exam," I finally say and burst into a fresh wave of tears.

Gabe lets out a relieved breath. "That sucks, but it's just the first part of the year, and there's so much time to make it up. I can help. History is my thing."

I shake my head. "You don't get it. I knew the material. I really did."

"Okay," Gabe says slowly. "So what went wrong?"

I shrug, brushing a hand over my tear-stained face. "I don't know. This happens to me sometimes. I have a learning disorder and I've mostly grown out of the worst of it, but sometimes it still trips me up. I think that's what happened."

"You think or you know?"

"I haven't really looked at the test yet," I admit.

"Do you want to look together?"

I blush at the idea.

"What?" Gabe asks, noticing my red cheeks.

101

"I don't want you to think I'm dumb," I admit, feeling ashamed. "Because I'm not. It's just sometimes my brain works in a different way. And you're a straight A student." I heard Sam teasing him about his 4.0 last week. As if I needed any more perfect students in my life.

Gabe's jaw drops slightly.

"What?" I say nervously.

"I could never think you're dumb. You're one of the quickest, wittiest people I know. Your intelligence is so clear. You could get a 40 on a test and it wouldn't change my opinion of you."

My heart turns uncomfortably in my chest as his words wash over me. Then my heart travels north and lodges itself in the base of my throat. I breathe through the sensation until a calm takes over. I look at Gabe. My tears dry up and I smile at him.

He smiles back and lets out a shaky breath of his own. "Show me the test. Let's see what went wrong."

Some embarrassment creeps back in as I take out the test from my backpack.

We sit side by side, knees bent to our chests, against a huge oak tree. I hand the test to Gabe and watch it flap slightly in the wind. I try not to be too worried about my messy penmanship (fine motor skills are not my strength). Gabe carefully reads over my exam and essay.

When he's done, he looks at me and smiles. "I love your essay. It's actually fascinating."

I look at him skeptically, but his face is sincere. "Thanks," I say, pleased, but then I frown remembering the grade I got. "Why do you think Mr. Sullen doesn't agree with my assessment?"

Gabe smiles widens. 'I think it's mostly because you didn't actually answer the question."

"What do you mean?"

"He asked you to write about one of the key influences that the Gilded Age had on the Industrial Revolution."

"Yes, so?"

"The biggest influence is what he means. Not sure the Knickerbockers qualify as that," he says ruefully. "It kind of seems like you just wrote about the part of the Gilded Age you thought was the most interesting."

"Oh," I say, feeling blood rush to my brain as the explanation begins to click. "I completely skipped over the word 'key.'"

Gabe smile grows wider. "Anna, look at this."

He hands me back my test and points to a note from Mr. Sullen saying my essay was quite detailed and impressive; it just wasn't what was being tested. He offers me a chance to make it up by writing an essay and turning it in by Wednesday.

"I can help if you want," Gabe offers. "Not that you need it. You clearly know your stuff, but I'm a pretty good proofreader."

I stand on my tippy toes and brush my lips over Gabe's cheek in gratitude. Gabe looks stunned for a moment, and our gazes lock. I drop back down, my heart racing again. I press my tingling lips together and we stare at each other for another moment before walking side by side out of the woods and back towards the school to change for practice.

* * * *

Tuesday at 11 pm, I text Gabe to tell him my essay is done.

Gabe: Awesome! Want me to take a look?

Me: Only if you want! Both Mimi and Mason looked it over. I think I'm in good shape!

Three dots appear, then disappear and reappear. I fidget, wondering what he's going to say.

Gabe: Ah, well, you're clearly in good hands. Get some rest!

I look at my phone, expecting him to say more. Usually, Gabe and I zing texts back and forth for a pretty long time. Just last week, we had such a lengthy, nighttime text exchange that I fell asleep with my phone in my hand.

Me: You too! And thanks for everything. You really helped me yesterday.

Gabe: Sam and I are going to hit up Floppies before
school tomorrow. Want to join? We could celebrate
you turning your essay in.

I pause. I turn down so many of their invitations it makes me feel bad. But Wednesday before school is when Mason and Del and I observe one of our most important traditions: Coffee Wednesdays. *Hmm.* Would it really hurt to invite Sam and Gabe one time? We all had a good time last weekend, it is a major relief to turn in this essay, and would Del and Mason really care if just one time I invited them to join?

I almost laugh at my concern. Of course they won't care. I'm the one who always makes sure, come hell or high water, that we don't skip out on our Coffee Wednesdays. I shoot off a text to Gabe and Sam asking them to join.

I smile. It really is so satisfying to combine old and new friends!

# CHAPTER
## 20

The first sign that combining old and new friends might just be a fantasy is when neither Del nor Mason responds to this text:

Me: Guys! See you in an hour for Coffee Wednesday. Hope you don't mind but I invited Gabe and Sam to come just this one time!

Ten minutes later, after no response:

Me: Sorry if this is a last min plan change!!! Just they invited me to breakfast this morning and it felt kind of rude to not extend the invitation. You know how that goes!!

Me: It's just a one-time thing! Next week back to just us! Xoxoxoxoxoxox.

15 minutes later:

Del: Ok.

The second sign I'm indulging a mere pipe dream is when Gabe and Sam approach the entrance to Reveiller and Mason throws me an angry scowl. When I invited the guys to join our standing coffee hang, it seemed like a great idea, but the fury in Mason's eyes tells me that once again, I miscalculated. That seems to be a recurring theme of late.

"Anna, not cool." Mason crosses his flannel-clad arms. "This is our thing. Just because we all had lunch together one time, and it wasn't entirely terrible—"

"I thought we all had fun," I cut in.

"It doesn't make us some sort of 'group.' I know you love rom-coms, but we're not *The Breakfast Club*."

"I wouldn't call *The Breakfast Club* a rom-com exactly," I mumble.

"Besides, I thought she was going for more of a *Ten Things I Hate About You* vibe," Del jokes.

A blush creeps up my neck. "I am not!" I pull my sweater up to my chin.

Mason's face contorts in confusion. "You're into Sam?" he asks.

"What?" My eyes fly to the entrance of the coffee shop, and I'm relieved to see Gabe and Sam are still outside, looking at some sports highlight clip on Sam's phone with awe in their eyes.

"No!" I say a bit too loudly. "Of course I'm not into Sam."

"She's into Gabe!"

"Del!" I narrow my eyes at her, but she shrugs as if to say, *I'm calling it like I see it.*

"Even worse." Mason glares at me. "Makes sense. You two were all over each other at lunch the other day." His voice reeks of bitterness and judgment.

Now my blush has grown into a full-on rash. The neckline of my sweater feels suffocating. "What are you even talking about?" I manage to sputter out. "That's ridiculous!"

"You were cracking all these inside jokes! I thought that was our thing."

Del looks at Mason without blinking, her tone stilted. "Lots of people have inside jokes, Mason."

"You know what I mean." He has the decency to look flustered, but then his face hardens. "They seemed so intimate."

Something about the way he spits out this last word makes me finally snap. "You're being completely insane."

"I'm being insane?" Mason scoffs. "You're bright red! You

like him that much?" In all our years of friendship, I've never felt this level of animosity from Mason before.

Confused and wanting to end the conversation, I retort, "You're blowing this way out of proportion."

Del steps between us. "Look, we don't think he's into her."

For some reason, I find myself barely resisting the need to glare at Del, even though I agree.

"Plus her parents would disown her if they dated, so it's a non-issue," Del elaborates.

I nearly lose the full contents of my coffee when I slam my cup on the counter and exclaim, "I have no interest in Gabe Delgado!"

I grimace, embarrassed by my volume. Luckily, Gabe is still engrossed in the video Sam is showing him.

Lowering his voice, Mason says, "You flipped out when I asked if Zoe could join Coffee Wednesdays."

I grab some napkins and start sopping up the coffee puddle from my spill. "That's different."

"How so?" Mason's eyes narrow in the same way they do when he accidentally encounters a Fox News segment.

"It's totally different." To buy time so I can come up with a decent answer, I take a sip of my remaining coffee. "Because…" My mind is blank.

"Because she makes you uncomfortable?" His voice rises in volume again. "How did you so eloquently put it? Ah, yes, 'Coffee Wednesdays is a treat meant for friends you can show your ugly to, not virtual strangers.' How do you think I feel about Sam and Gabe?"

He's right. Just because I feel comfortable around Gabe and Sam doesn't mean Mason does. I tried to force a group dynamic without consulting my best friends. "I'm sorry. I wasn't thinking."

"Yeah, that seems to be a pattern with you lately, Anna. Do you know what I risked by going to that dumb lunch with you? By continuing to hang out with you after everything?"

I gasp. But the sting of rejection quickly turns to anger. "What is that supposed to mean?"

"It means I think Zoe is right!"

"About what?" I bark more than ask.

"That being close to Ms. Adler isn't an excuse to ignore what she's doing to her employees! And, when it comes to something personal, it sucks that you won't do the hard work."

"Mason," Del admonishes him. "You're upset. Don't say stuff you'll regret."

"Will I?" Mason's eyes flash, but I see a flicker of doubt.

"If that's what you think of me," I say, "why are you even here? Why don't you run to your AOC wannabe girlfriend and leave me alone?" I stare at our table, willing my eyes not to water.

"*AOC wannabe* isn't an insult, Annabelle. You used to know that."

I look up and find Gabe and Sam next to our table. Sam steps back, looking apologetic for intruding.

Gabe notices my tears and steps forward. "Are you okay?"

I don't answer. He looks at Del and Mason. "What happened?"

"Stay the fuck out of it," Mason snaps, storming away from the table and out of the shop.

Del's eyes dart between me and the door Mason just slammed behind him. "Should I go after him?"

I can tell she wants to. Probably doesn't feel right being with Gabe and Sam while Mason is hurting.

I nod, not wanting to hold her back.

She squeezes my arm. "It's going to be okay. You guys will talk it out when he calms down."

I know Del is right to check on him. I messed up by inviting anyone new (much less Sam and Gabe) to invade the sanctity of Coffee Wednesdays. Mason looked upset in a way I hadn't seen since 9th grade when Zoe opted to go to the freshman fling with Barry instead of him. But still… I feel a swift, overwhelming sense of loneliness without Del and Mason by my side.

Sam pats me on the arm sympathetically. "Coffee is on me." He eyes my empty cup and the pile of wet napkins beside me.

I smile weakly at him and give him my order. He confirms that Gabe wants his "usual," a flat white, one of those drinks I always see on menus but assumed no one actually ordered. Sam again smiles reassuringly at me before heading toward the counter. He really is so nice.

Gabe and I are now alone. The music in the store is humming behind us. "Are you okay?" He studies my face, reaching over to brush a tear off my cheek in a gesture so intimate my stomach swirls.

He drops his hand quickly and shoves it into his pocket, then looks at me.

It takes me a moment to realize he's waiting for me to respond.

"I'm really not sure. I keep messing up."

Gabe smiles. "Me too. Must be our age. My dad always calls this the 'mess-up age.'"

I laugh because it rings so true.

Sam comes back with our coffees, and we move outside to sit at a wicker table with an air plant as a centerpiece. I notice our coffees smell a bit like mint and fireplaces, and I inhale deeply before I realize the scent is coming from Gabe. My stomach clenches uncomfortably.

Sam steers the conversation to the upcoming Olympic track trials, and I realize he's deliberately picking a topic he knows will cheer me up. Smiling, I take a sip of my vanilla latté and try to shake off the weirdness of the morning.

# CHAPTER
## 21

Thirty minutes later, I hesitantly walk into the schoolyard. Like everything else in town, the architecture of Edgartown High is self-contradictory, seemingly warring between two identities. The front of the school is classic. Red, pristine bricks stand proudly under ivy and a steady stone path leads to the entrance. A brightly lit, all-glass bridge connects the original brick building with a Frank Lloyd Wright-inspired wood-paneled addition that shoots off the back. The bridge is too severe for the traditional look of the old, but too sleek to fit in with the organic aesthetic of the new. Nothing fits together, and yet, somehow, the school seems better for it. There's something to discover with every new angle.

I look at the large oak tree on the left quad. On days we don't commute to school together, Del, Mason, and I meet under the oak and walk into the building together. Part of me hopes they'll be waiting there for me today, ready to make up. But they aren't.

I look at the long stone path in front of me and realize I have to go in alone, something I haven't done since Del and Mason both got the flu at the same time last year. I take a deep breath and re-pin my curls into the bun on top of my head.

On the right side of the quad, Gabe and Sam lounge on the grass with their usual friend group. The horrible Scottie Peters holds center court with a mean-spirited grin on his thin face. With no subtlety or shame, he points at a shy freshman making his way across the lawn and laughs. When I see Gabe and Sam waving and inviting me to join them, I have a burning desire to march over and chew Scottie out.

But I can't do it. I can't go stand with the Scottie crew no matter how much I've come to like Gabe and Sam. So I just nod, wave, and continue inside.

I follow the large swath of shiny wood flooring toward my locker, light spilling in from the half-crescent windows.

When the bell rings, I duck into first period, relieved to escape the uncomfortable feeling of roaming the halls without my friends by my side. Though no one looks at me, I can't help but wonder if they know I'm all alone, friendless and awkward.

By third period, I'm absolutely miserable. In English, Mason nods curtly in my direction and grabs a seat two rows away. We've sat next to each other in every class we've shared since kindergarten.

Mason was my first-ever best friend; we have the pictures in diapers to prove it. When Del moved to Edgartown from Brooklyn in 9th grade, our duo became a trio, but Mason and I always had a special bond. Sure, Del and I bonded over "girl stuff," like a shared crush on Tom Holland, but Mason and I had memories and history that could never be duplicated. Our friendship was unbreakable. It even held strong when Mason started dating Zoe last year. Zoe wasn't a fan of mine from day one, but Mason always protected our friendship. Until now.

I leave third period, getting another chilly nod from Mason as he moves into the hallway before I do. A strong impulse comes over me. I want to run up to him, grab his arm, and shake him until he talks to me. My heart quickens at the image. I need to make this right. I scoot around some dawdling Northsiders with monogrammed backpacks and shiny headbands. They glare at me when I accidentally bump into them. Muttering an apology, I scurry past two hipster Eastsiders who not-so-subtly are exchanging a bag of what appears to be weed.

"Mason!" My voice borders on desperation.

He turns around, but I'm already too late. Zoe is next to him, her arm snaked possessively around his waist.

She nods at me with a coolness that echoes Mason's. "Hi, Annabelle."

I nod back, matching her polite indifference. "Zoe." I don't bother with a proper greeting.

I turn to Mason and try to catch his eye. "Can we talk?"

Zoe nudges his arm. "We're meeting Barry, Lizzy, and the rest of the executive committee in five minutes," she reminds him. Her arm tightens around his waist.

Mason nods. "Yeah, sorry, Anna. Maybe later." He nods again, which might as well be a punch in the gut. They turn, and I watch as they walk away together.

I let out a frustrated sigh. This really sucks.

\* \* \* \*

I dread lunch for the first time since Del moved here. Speaking of Del: Where is she? I haven't seen her since this morning. I glance at my cell, but the only text is from Mimi saying she loves me and that she slipped an extra sweater into my backpack because she saw the weather forecasting a late-afternoon dip in temperature.

I sigh, feeling sad and lost. With nothing better to do, I stare at the picnic area in the upper-class garden. (The Garden Club grows and maintains the space, providing fruits, vegetables, and herbs to the cafeteria. It's also used as an outside seating area for juniors and seniors only.) I spot some Liberal Liaisons sharing a blanket on the ground near the cucumbers. Mason and Zoe are talking to Lizzy, their arms around each other once again. Barry, who's turned slightly away from the circle, glares at Mason, resentment oozing from every pore on his round face. Zoe inspires big feelings in people. I can't help but wonder what it would be like to have that kind of influence.

I see Sam and Gabe sitting with their lacrosse gang at a picnic table near a tomato vine.

My phone dings. It's Gabe: "if you need somewhere to eat, we can come sit with you in neutral territory." Another ding. "You look kind of lost … and depressed."

I look over at him, and he waves his phone in acknowledgment. My stomach dips again, but this time it's because of his smile. It's one of his special smiles, one of those unguarded, full-wattage, almost silly smiles. It somehow makes him even sexier, and I can't help but smile back.

But sitting with Gabe and Sam seems like too much of a statement, one that takes me too far away from Del and Mason and what I know about myself. I turn back to my phone texts.

Me: Thanks, Gabe :) Really nice of you and really appreciated. But I think I need to try and make things right with Del and Mason.

Gabe: And sitting with me and Sam won't help that?

Me: Yeah. I'm sorry, I feel like an ass typing that.

Gabe: No, it makes total sense. Best to smooth it over before you tell them I'm your new best friend.

Me: Hardy har har. You're soooo funny.

Gabe: I think I am.

Me: I'm sure you do.

As our eyes meet, I roll my eyes at him, but then I grin. His nonchalance is contagious. Plus, he's momentarily taken my mind off my bad day.

I make sure he sees that I'm smiling at him. He smiles back with some irony. The sun bounces off his hair. I force myself to look elsewhere.

Rolling my shoulders back, I prepare to eat alone. I scan the seating area trying to figure out where I would look the least pathetic. I spot an empty picnic table tucked in the corner near the herbs.

I sit down and take out my lunch, so hyperaware of everything I'm doing that I feel like I'm an actor in a play. Crumbling up my biodegradable lunch bag, I take in the characteristically elaborate meal Mimi put together. Today, it's avocado toast with pickled onions and pea shoots, with a side of fresh berries and dark chocolate. She also packed a seltzer and a bag of homemade chips sprinkled with kosher salt. On a normal day, Mason would be picking at my meal like a vulture, helping himself to whatever looked good. I get some satisfaction knowing that he's missing out.

I uncap the seltzer, feeling loneliness creep back over me. There's no way to enjoy solitude in situations where you're surrounded by people who aren't alone.

"Hey, lady. Is this seat taken?"

My head pops up. "Del! No, of course not." To my (and Del's) surprise, tears well in my eyes.

"Whoa, Anna, it's okay." Del sits beside me and looks concerned.

"I'm just glad you're here and not mad at me."

Del shakes her head a little. "I'm sorry I was MIA after this morning. Just the whole thing with Mason storming off... I don't know... It was confusing. I wanted to stay neutral."

I nod, mostly understanding, but also resentful that she hadn't taken my side.

"I'm sorry my mess is becoming your mess too."

Del sighs and takes out her lunch. "Yeah, it's annoying."

"Thanks a lot."

"Well, it is, but I wouldn't have it any other way." She smiles at me. "Having each other's back is pretty much the main component of best friendship."

I smile. "True."

She squeezes my hand. "I love you, Anna."

"I love you, too, Del."

I find myself glancing at Mason. Zoe's arm seems to be permanently glued to his midsection.

"He loves you too, you know," Del says, watching my gaze.

My shoulders slump. "He was so cold today."

Del nods. "I talked to him a bit."

"You did?" I look at her expectantly.

"I think the whole thing this morning was just his way of saying he repeatedly feels rejected by you."

Her words catch me off guard. "What do you mean?"

"I mean, I feel kind of rejected, too." She plays with her silver bracelet.

"What?" My shock doubles, and I push my lunch aside.

Del takes a moment to consider her words. "You have this whole thing with Sam and Gabe—this whole vibe. It's a little weird for us, your original besties."

"My only besties."

Del smiles. "I know." She offers me a grape, and I shake my head. I couldn't eat now if I tried. "I also know it isn't easy for you to see Zoe's constant Instagram posts about the executive meetings."

"Ugh. It sucks." I steal another look in Zoe's direction. "It's like she's turned executive meetings into a 'let's exclude Anna' club, right? Or is that paranoid?"

Del pushes back her long, luscious hair over her white cable-knit sweater. "No, it's not paranoid. I think you're right." Bored of her grapes, she snags a raspberry from my Tupperware.

"That sucks. What did I ever do to her?"

Del snorts. "Be too close with her boyfriend?"

"But so are you."

A pensive expression falls over Del's face.

"What?"

"I don't know. She's always making digs that Mason and you are too this, too that."

"Too touchy-feely?"

Del nods.

"Right. I've heard that. It's ridiculous."

Del doesn't look convinced. She chews on her bottom lip. "Do you think she knows something we don't?"

"Like what?" I don't like the tone in Del's voice.

"Like that he has some sort of crush on you?" Her eyes fall to her grapes as if she's suddenly very interested in their composition.

I grab Del's hand. "That's ridiculous." I force her to look at me. "Don't you think one of us would know if that was true?"

Her face relaxes, and she exhales. "Yeah, good point."

"We don't talk about it much but, after everything, I know it can't be easy to watch him and Zoe."

Del grimaces, clearly not happy to be reminded of the time she confessed her feelings—of the non-friendship variety—to Mason, only to be met with silence.

Hurt flickers across her face for a second before she regains composure. "It's not, but I'm used to it. It feels less bad than it used to."

I squeeze her hand. "I'm glad that despite that whole thing, we all still have each other."

"Me too. I'd do anything for our little trio."

Her smile and the specialness of our friendship help heal the wounds of the day, and I affirm that I will make things right with Mason.

* * * *

I wait for Mason outside of his fifth period class. He shoves his hands in his pockets, evidently not thrilled to see me. "Hey, Anna." He looks over his shoulder. I can't tell if he's looking for Zoe or looking for any excuse not to talk to me.

My frustration at his behavior towards me and Del boils over. I punch him in the shoulder and yell, "What are you doing, Mase!?"

"Ow!" He runs a hand over his shoulder. "What was that for?"

"We've been best friends for sixteen years, and you're not talking to me because I messed up this morning? Come on."

A flicker of guilt passes over Mason's face. "I know I've been hard on you today."

"Hard on me? You made me feel totally alone. I've never, ever done that to you. In fact, I've always done the opposite when you needed me the most! Does the name Lincoln ring any bells?"

"We were in fifth grade. That's a little different."

I cross my arms, irritated he's not giving me credit for my bravery as an elementary school warrior.

Mason rolls his eyes, but his expression softens. "Fine, you were there for me in a kickass way. But I don't know, Anna. This morning really threw me. You've been acting so off lately. It doesn't feel like you."

"Are those your thoughts or Zoe's?" I ask, fighting the urge to punch him again.

Mason glares at me. "Don't start this again. She doesn't control me."

"I'm not convinced."

"Trust me. If she did, I wouldn't have gone on your Sunday luncheon with Gabe and gang."

"I knew she was against it!" I point my finger at his chest.

"Of course she was, Anna. It's against everything she stands for. Gabe's dad is super conservative, and several of the Brenson Oakes partners are huge donors of his! Plus, Sam's dad just got that big gas company out of trouble for the oil spill."

"I'm not sure we should be holding people's parents against them."

Mason's features sharpen. "Sure, but in this case, the apple doesn't fall far from the tree. I should know—I was friends with Gabe at one point!"

"That's ridiculous! You don't think it's possible he's changed since middle school?"

"No, I really don't."

We scowl at each other. In the cryptic notes of Beethoven's Ninth, the bell dings again. How fitting, I think.

"Good talk." I turn on my heels to storm away, but Mason stops me. "Wait." He lets out a breath. "That's not how I meant for this to go."

I don't say anything, still too angry to respond.

"I'm sorry." His sincere tone feels like ice water on my fiery temper. "I hate when we fight. Can we talk later? I want to work this out."

I look deep into his moss-green eyes and see that the Mason I know has returned. "Okay," I exhale. "I hate it too. Want to grab dessert tonight?"

Mason throws me a tentative smile. "That sounds good." Then he winces. "Wait. I forgot. I told Zoe I'd study with her to-night."

"Oh, okay. Well, maybe later this week."

Unease spreads between us, and I shift my weight from one foot to the other. The silence spins out for a few more beats. Final-ly, Mason breaks it.

"You know what? I'll make it work. Count me in. 7:30?"

I nod, glad to have my friend back on my side.

# CHAPTER

## 22

When I leave school, I look around for Del because we usually walk home together. My phone dings. "Sorry, something came up with *The Red and Blue*. Gonna be late."

I shrug and re-pocket my phone. As editor-in-chief of *The Red and Blue*, Del often deals with last-minute emergencies.

My phone dings again. I'm surprised to see Del's name reappear. Usually it's impossible to reach her when she's in newspaper crisis mode. "Uh, have you seen Instagram? This isn't going to help your case with the Liaisons…"

My heart skips a beat, but I have no idea what she's talking about. I furiously type back, "No! Checking now!"

My phone chirps again. It's Mason. "Who posted that pic? It looks romantic, Anna."

My pulse is pounding in my ears. I unlock my phone when more texts flood my screen, this time from the girls on my cross country team. "Go for it, Morningstar. Gabe is a HOTTIE!" And "Are you tapping that Anna??" Another teammate, Mary Sue, who is both a Northsider and a particularly judgmental one, texts: "Anna, quite the photo! Have you been reconsidering your cringey Eastside stances? I'm proud of you, hon."

I swipe away their texts, but just as I'm about to tap my Instagram icon, I hear a strained voice call my name. "Anna!" Gabe takes me by the arm and pulls me toward a shaded area near the school's back exit. "Have you seen it?"

"Seen what?" I let out a frustrated breath.

"I think Bethany Cully posted it originally," says Sam, who is leaning against a tree next to where Gabe stationed us. He hands me his phone to show an Instagram post.

"Who is Bethany Cully?" I take his phone, shielding the screen and my eyes from the harsh glare of the sun.

"One of Caroline's henchmen. A sophomore," Sam explains.

"*Henchman* is a bit extreme," Gabe grimaces. "But yeah, seems like it was her. She must have been at the Tavern Inn when we were."

I hardly hear what they're saying as I look at the photo. In it, Gabe is sitting next to me, with his arm around me as I turn to hear what he's saying. I can see our legs brushing under the booth. It looks like we're alone, sitting as close to each other as possible. You wouldn't know from the photo what was actually happening—that I was scooting over so Del could get out to use the bathroom and Gabe was teasing me that I was looking for an excuse to practically sit on his lap. Everyone but Mason laughed.

I stare at the picture on Sam's phone and shift uncomfortably. It looks intimate, sexy. To my horror, I feel strangely aroused.

"The bigger issue is that the *Edgartown Eagle* reposted it." Sam takes out his phone and shows me our local newspaper's account, which paired Bethany's photo of me and Gabe and with the caption, "Red vibe-ing with Blue!"

It has over two thousand likes! And 300 comments! Already!

I give them both a dirty look, though I can tell Gabe feels as awful about all this as I do. "Why did Bethany post this? It's so misleading!"

"Is Caroline pissed at you or something?" Sam raises an eyebrow at Gabe. "After last Friday, shouldn't it be the other way around?"

"What happened last Friday?" I demand after hearing no explanation from Gabe.

His face darkens a little. "She asked me if it would be okay if she hooked up with Scottie."

I bite down on my lip, indignant that Caroline would take such an obvious jab to hurt Gabe, and bothered by the possibility that it worked. Does he still care about her? I know it's not my business, but I feel on edge either way. "It's a major downgrade on her part," I say, trying to sound consoling. I'm actually feeling a whole mess of other emotions. "He's a horrible person. When Del was new here at school and he used to pass her in the hall, Scottie used to say, 'Something smells like curry.' I don't get how you can still be friends with him."

"Trust me, I don't feel very friendly right now." Gabe, staring again at the photo, looks absolutely miserable. Even though I wish the photo hadn't been posted, I can't help but feel hurt by his reaction.

I pull up the photo on my own phone. Gabe and I look happy, the complete opposite of how we both feel now.

"Hmm, that was fast," Sam mutters.

We both turn to Sam, as if forgetting he was still there.

He has a sheepish look on his face. "Guys, don't kill me. I was honestly trying to help. I think maybe I did."

Gabe's eyes narrow. "Sam, what did you do?"

He passes us his phone, this time with his own account open.

My jaw drops as I see he's posted a second photo of me and Gabe at Floppies, a picture I don't remember him taking. In it, Gabe and I have what looks like a week's worth of pancakes between us, and we're smiling. This caption reads, "Edit: Just good buddies. No romance here."

He smiles gamely, as if we should thank him for a job well done. Then suddenly all three of our phones chime.

I really want to smack Sam when I see another notification from the *Edgartown Eagle*. Once again, they've reposted our photo with the caption: "Buddies from across the aisle."

Just then Gabe's phone buzzes with an incoming call. He looks ashen. "It's my dad's press secretary." He steps aside to answer, and I notice how his voice lowers as he goes into dutiful-son mode.

Sam glances at the photo again. "Good news is you both look great."

"Gee, thanks." My stomach clenches as I realize Zoe and the other Liaisons have already seen the post and, in all likelihood, are furiously exchanging messages about my journey to the dark side. "I'm glad you think this is such a hoot. My friends definitely won't agree."

"Just trying to find the silver lining." He looks down at the ground, regret evident on his face. "I really hope I didn't make things worse for you both."

I don't know if Sam has helped or hurt, but before I can even ponder the question, Gabe returns with a relaxed smile on his face. "My dad's team is thrilled. They think it's good for my dad's more moderate constituents to see me hanging with Lilly Morningstar's daughter."

As Gabe's grin grows, so does my anxiety. What's good for Senator Delgado surely can't be good news for my mom. When Gabe exhales like the entire problem has disappeared into thin air, I snap. "Aren't you capable of having your own opinion? You were pissed a moment ago about the invasion of our privacy and how deliberately misleading the photo was."

Gabe winces.

I feel my own phone buzzing, and I know I won't get off as easily as Gabe did. The caller ID confirms my suspicions. I quickly hit ignore and brace myself for the incoming flood of texts. "It's Hen, my mom's PR person," I mutter as I read. "She definitely doesn't sound as happy as your dad's team."

"Are you okay?" Gabe looks concerned.

"Sorry, Anna," Sam says, turning red. "I don't get it. Isn't this what everyone should want? For liberals and conservatives to just get along? Aren't people desperate for harmony and civility?"

Not if civility is just complicity wrapped in a warm, fuzzy blanket.

Before I can respond, Caroline Loran saunters over. Her pink, ruffled blouse is tucked into the waistline of her cuffed jeans in an effortlessly chic way, almost as if she's strolled right off the Champs-Élysées. Caroline is tall, but not in a glamorous way, and attractive, but not in a beautiful way, and I'm jealous, but not in an irrational way. Frankly, I don't get why Gabe even cares if she hooks up with Scottie. They deserve each other.

"Gabe." Caroline steps between us, not acknowledging my presence. She gives him a noisy kiss on the cheek, pressing her whole body into his. I try not to spiral into blackness as I try determining whether his reciprocating grin was one of embarrassment or enjoyment.

"Shouldn't we get going? I thought we could go to the Yogurt House."

I look at Gabe, startled. "You two have plans?"

Sam is also looking at Gabe as if he's lost his mind.

Gabe shifts his weight awkwardly. "Caroline, you know Anna, right?"

Now we all stare at Gabe as if he's definitely lost his mind.

"Of course. We've been in school together since we were five. So funny how we don't really talk, like, at all anymore." Caroline draws out each of her words like she's paid by the syllable.

"Yeah, it's a real comedy," I respond, annoyed that my old grade-school friend can still make me feel so small. I suddenly wonder why I'm still standing here with three Northsiders when my morality is probably being unflatteringly dissected in various Liaisons' group chats. "Catch you all later," I say abruptly.

"Anna, wait!" Gabe untangles himself from Caroline and chases after me. His golden eyes flick between mine and something else. "You seem mad."

"I am mad," I admit, "but I don't know how mad or even totally why yet."

Gabe lets out a small laugh. "I admire your honesty."

"Why are you getting frozen yogurt with her, Gabe? I thought you two were over."

"We are, but I'd like to at least be civil." He runs a slightly nervous hand through his hair. "Between the Scottie thing and the Tavern photo ... I just want to clear the air."

"But her friend leaked it!" I object. "She probably had something to do with it, too."

"Yeah, that's part of what I want to talk to her about. I think she somehow thought the post would stop us."

My heart rate ticks up. "Stop us from what?"

"From being friends."

"Oh." I stare over his shoulder to see Caroline crossing her arms and scowling in our direction. "Well, that's dumb and awful."

"Yeah, it is." He follows my line of vision. "But it's what she does. Caroline lashes out when she feels rejected. She hasn't had it so easy."

I roll my eyes. "She's a Loran. She's probably one of the richest people in the state." Caroline's grandfather was one of the biggest real estate developers in the South, and she never lets anyone forget it.

"Look, I really hurt her when I ended things between us. Caroline has trust issues."

I shake my head. "Look, that sucks and all, but she's still a bully. I don't get you, Gabe. Why do you keep people like her and Scottie in your life?"

"Gabe, are you coming or what?" Caroline whines, irritation lacing her tone like acid.

He asks her to give him a minute and turns back to me. "Look, Anna, Scottie and Caroline have been in my life since we were kids. Their parents are super close to mine."

"And major donors to your dad's campaigns," I spit out.

"Yes, they are." He straightens his posture defensively.

"So you're just going to roll over because of that, and let them treat you terribly?"

"You mean kind of like how you've been lying to your mom and best friends about not buying books at Bookcourt, even though you have been? How you don't even feel comfortable having a differing opinion than the Liberal Liaisons?" Gabe's eyes flash in anger. "That kind of rolling over?"

I can barely sputter out a response.

"Listen," he continues, "it's complicated for me. I hurt Caroline, and that makes me uncomfortable."

I gather my wits and finally strike back. "You just don't like having tension with anyone. You'd rather be fake than upset people."

Gabe flinches. "I wouldn't exactly call you the paragon of honesty, Anna. And besides, we can't all go around talking about our feelings as loudly as you do all the time."

I glare at him. "Real nice, Gabe." I want to spit back a clever retort, but suddenly find myself subdued, half because I'm overwhelmed and half because I realize just how apt his insult was. I feel my psyche spiral downward a little further. "Maybe you have a point."

Gabe shakes his head, his eyes softening with regret. "I don't want to fight with you." His voice quiets. "Honestly, I'm not even sure what we're fighting about."

"It's been a weird day," I manage to choke out. An awkward silence sits between us, and I realize I'm taking things out on him because it bothers me that he's spending time with Caroline and scared that I even care. "It's been an off few weeks. I'm not handling anything that well these days."

Gabe raises an eyebrow but he doesn't push.

"I'm not in a great place with most of the Liaisons," I clarify. "My friends are all mad at me or think I've lost my moral center."

"You still have Del and Mason," Gabe offers.

"I have Del. But Mason…" To my surprise, my voice cracks, and I can't get out any more words.

"Hey, there." Gabe steps closer to me, his arms encircling me, and I find it difficult not to melt into him.

Caroline stomps over to us. "Gabe, can we please go?"

Gabe doesn't release me. Instead, he looks over his shoulder at her. "Hey, Caroline. I'm sorry to do this, but I have to reschedule."

"Why?" Her face falls instantly, and I almost feel sorry for her.

"Anna and I have had a crappy day. I think we need to decompress together."

I turn in Gabe's embrace, shocked and touched. I really *do* need friend time to decompress! But then I see Caroline's shattered expression.

I put a hand on Gabe's arm and wiggle out of his hold. "No, no. It's okay. You two have plans. You should keep them."

Gabe starts to object, but I nudge him in Caroline's direction. He follows my gaze, and a knowing expression settles on his face. He looks back at me and slowly nods. He whispers, "I guess I should go."

"I guess you should," I respond quietly.

Caroline is furiously brushing back tears and trying to compose herself. "So Gabe, are we going now that Anna the Great has given you permission?"

"Yeah." He pauses. "And she is great, so watch the tone."

Caroline's face pales. "I'll meet you at the car." She storms toward the student parking lot.

Sam claps a hand on Gabe's back. "Good luck, buddy."

Gabe nods. "I'll need it."

"What exactly is the deal with Caroline?" I ask Sam once Gabe is out of earshot. "That was intense."

"Caroline's an intense person. But she's always really wanted Gabe, and not just for the obvious reasons either. He's different for her."

"How so?" I cross my arms, then uncross them trying to conceal my desperation  for any details about Gabe and Caroline's relationship.

"Look, her parents kind of suck. Her dad's been married three times, and her mom? Well, she isn't so interested in being a mother. But Caroline always thought her relationship with Gabe was genuine. Real. He was the only constant in her life. So when he started losing interest, she got desperate."

I want to argue that Caroline's family drama doesn't excuse her awful behavior, but I try to imagine a world without Mom and Mimi's endless support and love, and I can't.

Sam senses my softening stance and continues, "And Gabe cares about her. That's why he wanted to hang with her today. I think he probably wants to warn her to be careful with Scottie."

"I don't get it. If Scottie is such a close friend of Gabe's, why would he want to hook up with his ex anyway?"

"Scottie is insanely jealous of Gabe. He's had a thing for Caroline forever, but Gabe got her first. Scottie also wanted to be lacrosse captain, but Gabe got that too. You get the picture. But, on the other hand, they go way back. When Gabe and Mateo were little, before Bea was born, they'd stay with the Peters family while the Delgados were campaigning."

I tilt my head to the side. "So they're basically frenemies."

"Pretty much."

"No offense, but it kind of makes me lose respect for both you and Gabe knowing you're friends with Scottie."

Sam laughs and throws an arm around my shoulder. "I appreciate the feedback, Morningstar. Does that mean you won't be coming to Gabe's party this Friday?"

"I can't. I have plans with Del and Mason." I've missed the last two parties that Gabe has thrown, and I can tell the boys are miffed that I keep turning down invites.

"You're sure it's not because you don't respect us, like you were just saying?"

"I'm eighty percent sure," I respond with a laugh, and let my head rest on Sam's comforting shoulder for a moment.

# CHAPTER 23

From afar, I spot Mason waiting for me at a wrought-iron table at Buttermilks, a dessert and wine shop in town. I love how the outdoor space, with its twinkle lights, flowers, and a tall wood fence enclosing the space, feels like a private backyard. Mason is early, as always; it's one of his most reliable characteristics. His eyes dart between his phone and the tables around us. His blond curls stick out from underneath a black beanie, and his red scarf hangs loosely around his neck. A pair of sophomore girls whisper about him from a table in the corner, but Mason is oblivious to their attention. He doesn't appreciate his own appeal, which makes him even more appealing.

He spots me and straightens his shoulders. His familiar smile is a little strained.

A wave of uneasiness rolls over me.

"Hey." I sit down, wanting to erase the tension between us as soon as possible.

Two chocolate boxes arrive at the table. I smile. It's what we used to order in middle school after saving all our allowances to splurge on Buttermilks' famously decadent dessert, which consists of a dark chocolate base, a milk chocolate center, and a white chocolate-shaped bow on top. I take this as the best type of peace offering: a delicious serving of nostalgia.

"Well, you clearly know the way to my heart."

Mason's eyes round, and he gives me a strange look. "Do I?"

I gesture at the dessert. "Does this mean you're not mad?"

Mason puts his elbow on the table and looks down. "I don't know what I am." He examines his hands rather than meeting my eyes. "Except a little embarrassed. I know I overreacted."

I exhale a long breath. "And I wish I hadn't invited Gabe and Sam to Coffee Wednesday. I wasn't thinking."

We both take bites of our chocolate boxes. I start with the bow, but soon the entire structure crumbles into a pile of broken pieces. I feel deflated as I stare at the chocolate shards on my plate.

"This is still awkward, isn't it?" I say. Unlike with Gabe, whose expressions I need a cipher to decode, I can see every flicker of emotion as it crosses Mason's face.

"Yeah, it is," Mason replies, cycling between frustration and distress.

As I take in his tortured expression, I start to smile.

His face settles on confusion. "Why are you smiling?"

"I just love that you feel things so intensely." I remember Gabe's dig about how loudly I express my feelings. "It makes me feel better about my own emotional state to know it's not just me."

Mason cocks his head to the side. "Is that an insult or compliment?"

"A compliment, of course! No one wants to be in constant emotional crisis alone."

Mason laughs. "That's true." He pauses. "Is that why you like Gabe?" Though I was just thinking about him, I'm still shocked to hear Mason mention his name.

"What do you mean?" I stuff a large sliver of chocolate into my mouth and don't have enough time to chew it before Mason asks me a follow-up question.

"Because he's not emotional?"

I swallow roughly. "I'm not sure I'd call him unemotional … It's more like he's super stable. It's hard to rock him."

"And that's a good thing?"

"It can be steadying. I feel like Del kind of does that for us in a way too, right?"

Mason fidgets with the fringe of his scarf. "Yeah, I guess. And Zoe is that way too. She's steadfast."

"I guess I can see that," I lie, biting my lip to keep from stirring the pot now that he seems more at ease.

"What?" he asks, knowing me too well.

I pause, gathering my thoughts. "It feels like you've been pissed at me since I started conditioning training."

"I don't know if 'pissed' is the right word."

"Then what?"

"Let down, I think."

"Ouch."

"I know that's harsh, but it seems like you don't even care about missing Liaison meetings."

"Of course I care!" I notice he hasn't touched his chocolate since his first bite. "I miss seeing you and Del and being in on everything but, to be honest, it's a relief to get some space from your girlfriend."

"I know Zoe isn't your favorite." He leans back in his chair. "But she's a good person."

"Yeah, well, she's a pain in my ass, but I get it."

Mason gives me a look.

"I do!" I insist. "She's uber-virtuous, but she can also be unrelenting at times. And this whole Bookcourt thing is too much for me."

Mason frowns. "I know it's complicated for you, but can't you see where we're coming from?"

"We?" I fold my arms across my chest. "You agree with Zoe completely? You don't see any nuance here at all? What about all our memories at the Bookery?" I can't count how many coffees and muffins we've eaten together in that café over the years.

Mason's cheeks are conspicuously flushed. He stretches out his fingers as if they are unbearably tense. "If you want my honest opinion, I think you're being too emotional about the situation, and because of that, you can't see any of this clearly."

He reaches for my hand, but I pull away from him.

"Too emotional?" I strip all warmth from my voice. "You

mean because Ms. Adler helped me through one of the most challenging times of my life? You're right, I am emotional about it."

"I wish you'd feel a little more compassion for the workers."

"I do! But I also know how Ms. Adler treats her employees. Like how she helped house Kim and her children when they had nowhere to go, and how she co-signed Shelly's loans. Those things matter!"

"But what happens when Ms. Adler retires, Anna? Then what? It's bigger than one person. What do you think will happen to Kim and Shelly and the rest of them then?"

"Well, if Ms. Adler has to lay off employees because of the boycott, they're not much better off, are they? Lots of bookstores, even without this kind of pressure, are closing across the country. What you're doing is dangerous!"

Mason looks at me as he's never seen me before, as if I'm an absolute disappointment.

"Mase," I soften my tone, "I know this is complicated. I'm just trying to figure this out for myself, and the way you and Zoe are approaching this doesn't make sense to me. It's like your principles make you blind to the specifics."

"And you don't think your relationship with Ms. Adler makes you biased and blind?"

I sink back in my chair. "I'm not sure… Maybe. Probably. All I know is I want Bookcourt to flourish. I love that place."

"We all want it to flourish, but I want to make sure no one is stepped on in the process."

The night air has gotten chilly, and even the heat lamps above us don't warm me up. I look at Mason, sure we've hit an impasse.

"Can we move past this? I don't want to feel all this tension with you."

"I don't want to either. What would I do without my banana?"

I smile at him and allow him to take my hand. His middle school nickname for me melts the ice somewhat. "I don't want anything getting in the way of our friendship. Not Bookcourt or Zoe or the fact she's clearly trying to exclude me from all these executive committee-only lunches …."

Mason winces. "I'm trying to get her to cut those out, but she won't listen. She swears it's not personal. There's just a lot of work to be done right now."

I snort.

Mason arches an eyebrow. "Speaking of snort-worthy things, there's one thing I need to know."

His serious tone takes me by surprise. "What?"

"Are you sure you don't have feelings for Gabe?" He looks at me expectantly.

I blink, taken aback. "Why are you so focused on this?" I think about how Mason lost it on Wednesday. "Is It because he's a Northsider? For what it's worth, Gabe's views really surprise me sometimes. They aren't what you'd think."

Mason steels his jaw. "Gabe is solely on the bad side, Anna. Don't let your little crush delude you."

I blush. "I don't have a crush on him. That's ridiculous."

"Do you promise?"

I feel a little thrown, but promise him that I don't have any romantic feelings toward Gabe.

Mason lets out a breath. "Okay, good. I didn't really think you did." He looks serious again for a second. "Look. I hate it when we fight. I want to have my best friend back. I've really missed the no-awkward-tension version."

I link hands with him, but I'm not sure anything is resolved. Still I say, "I've missed it too."

# CHAPTER
## 24

It's the first Saturday of the month, and as promised, Sam, Gabe, and I are in Bookcourt shelving a mountain of titles in the children's section.

Sam looks rumpled, as if he isn't quite awake yet. His blond hair sticks up every which way, making him look younger and even more boyish than usual. Meanwhile, Gabe, despite stifling a few yawns, looks like he's escaped from a GQ cover shoot with his pressed collar and freshly combed hair.

I smile affectionately at them both as Gabe hands me an Eric Carle book. I try not to react when his finger brushes mine.

Ms. Adler beams at us and pulls me into a warm hug. Her skin is papery soft and, the smell of lavender wafts off of her.

She's thanking us profusely for coming to help when I notice the dark shadows under her eyes. "How are you doing, Ms. Adler?" I ask, feeling weird asking an adult anything personal.

Ms. Adler squeezes my arm. "I've been better, sweetie. But having you and your strapping fellows here makes things a little easier." She winks in Gabe's direction, and he blushes slightly and says, "Yes, ma'am". Sam winks back, but the effect is diminished when he lets out a huge yawn.

Leaving us to our work, Ms. Adler heads to the other side of the store and starts shelving in the poetry section.

Gabe offers the side of his coffee cup for a silent toast, and Sam and I tap our cups against his. My eyes linger on Gabe's. The morning light streaming through the bookstore makes his eyes look even more golden than usual. Soon, we're working side-by-side again. The work is tedious, but Sam makes it fun, regaling us with stories from the previous night. Apparently, he ended up at an Edgartown College frat party with a French major trying to woo Sam with good poetry read in bad Italian.

I shake my head in wonder. "Sounds worldly."

"A weird but memorable night," Gabe adds. "What did you do?"

I fill them in on movie night with Del and Mason and our attempts to make cocktails from a mixture of alcoholic beverages purloined from each of our homes. They were gross and nearly undrinkable, but that didn't stop us from consuming them anyway and laughing most of the night away.

As we work our way through the carts, I wave to Kim in the fiction aisle and to Shelly in her beloved sci-fi section. When no other employees materialize, I realize they must be the only ones still showing up for work.

"Alfred," I hear Ms. Adler call from her spot in poetry. "Are you leaving? We could really use some help with stocking."

Curious, I peek around the shelves to spot Alfred, Ms. Adler's elusive son, whom I hadn't realized was in the store. I'm surprised by how much he resembles Ms. Adler, but with a fuller face and smaller eyes. He pauses and turns at the sound of his name, a large leather folder gripped in his right hand.

Ms. Adler moves closer to her son, so I can't hear what they're saying, but their furrowed brows and stiff posture make it clear it's a tense conversation.

In fiction, Kim is watching the Adlers with narrowed eyes.

"I'll be right back," I whisper to the boys and scoot away before they have a chance to protest being left with the brunt of the remaining work.

"Hi, Kim," I say, pretending to read the titles of her newly stocked shelf. It's strange seeing Kim on the floor. Her usual spot is behind the counter at the Bookery, kneading dough. Since the boycott started, the Bookery has shuttered. With barely any foot traffic, the pastries and sandwiches were mostly going unsold and uneaten each day.

"Hi, Anna." She throws me a tired but friendly smile. "How are Del and Mason? I miss them. Their coffee orders were always a lot simpler than yours."

"They're both doing pretty okay," I answer. There are so many questions I want to ask Kim that I have to bite my tongue to keep them from spilling out.

"It's awfully nice of you and your friends to come help out." Kim's faint Southern drawl is sweet and comforting. "I know it means a lot to Ms. Adler."

I manage a smile. "Um, Kim, can I ask you something?"

"Of course."

"No pressure if you don't want to answer, but what's going on with Ms. Adler and Alfred? Is everything okay?"

Kim presses her lips tightly together, her eyes narrowing. "I don't know, but the last time Alfred left with that leather folder, Brenson Oakes was hired."

"Yikes."

"Yikes indeed."

A pit forms in my stomach. I'm about to walk back to my station, but then I abruptly turn to face Kim again. "Did Terry really eat an edible in the children's section?"

Kim grimaces. "Unfortunately, yes, though it was near closing, and no kids were around. But still…yes."

I sigh. "Terry loved that section so much."

"Yeah." Kim looks hesitant. She glances over her shoulder to ensure that Ms. Adler is occupied in the poetry section. "Between you and me, let's just say Terry wasn't the only one letting loose that day."

"What do you mean?"

"It's always a little messy when Alfred is around." She scans the store again. "Where do you think Terry got the edible from?" Her mouth twists distastefully. "But only one person got fired."

My jaw is officially on the floor. How could Ms. Adler fire Terry but let her own son off the hook for the same offense? I look over to find Ms. Adler restocking copies of Sally Rooney's latest novel. None of this sounds like the woman I've known for over a decade.

Kim folds her sweater-clad arms over her chest and sighs. "This place usually feels so special, but now with the boycott and Terry gone, it all feels so up in the air. I worry for Ms. Adler. But, then again, it's not like her money troubles started with the boycott."

*Money troubles?* Before I can follow up, Shelly yells across the store for Kim's help. Kim pats my shoulder, then heads to the stockroom to help Shelly move boxes.

Stunned, I return to Gabe and Sam.

"You okay?" Gabe asks. "You look like someone gave you a plastic straw."

"I think so." I pull out my phone and text Del to meet me in thirty minutes. Then I turn my attention back to the books, kneeling on the polished wood floor and wondering whether I've been wrong all along.

\* \* \* \*

By the time we're done, the sun is bearing down on us and I'm sweating under my mom-approved fleece.

"So now you want Del to investigate Bookcourt?" Gabe asks as we walk out of the store toward the coffee shop. "I thought we were trying to help save them?"

"Shhh. Keep your voice down," I say. Between the protesters outside and Ms. Adler inside, I don't want anyone to overhear him.

Sam tilts his head. "Were we supposed to wait for some secret code to speak of these highly confidential matters?"

"Ha ha, very funny. I'm just feeling a little thrown by what Kim said …" I trail off, furrowing my brow.

"Yeah, we can tell," Gabe says. "Are you going to fill us in?"

"Yes," I reply far more quietly than I need to. "Just not yet."

Del bikes up, her brakes screeching on the pavement as she stops short. Slowly taking off her helmet, Del looks at me pointedly, and I can tell she's uneasy about what she's getting herself into.

"What were you three doing exactly?" Her voice is clipped.

I hesitate, and Sam beats me to the punch. "We were shelving books at Bookcourt."

I wince, waiting for Del's anger or disappointment.

Instead, she nods.

"You're not angry?" I ask.

Del walks her bike over to the rack and clicks her lock into place. "If I were you, I wouldn't brag about it to the other Liaisons, but I'm sure you had your reasons."

In that moment, it strikes me just how different Del and Mason are.

"So, what's up?" She nods at Gabe and Sam, rolling her eyes when Sam throws her a flirty wink.

Making sure no one else is within earshot, I dive into my conversation with Kim and describe what I learned about Bookcourt.

"Okay, so it sounds like we need to figure out if what Kim is saying is true. What did she mean when she said there were already money problems?"

I shrug my shoulders. "No clue. Until now, I've never heard of any such issues."

Del purses her lips and squints her eyes like she always does when she's thinking deeply. Finally she says, "Okay, I have a plan, but I'll need Sam to execute it."

"Me?" Sam oscillates between utter confusion and delight.

"They all know Anna too well, and Gabe's father is too public a figure to use," she explains, and then turns toward Sam. "Are you going to help me or what?"

Sam smiles readily. "Anything for a queen such as yourself, Del."

Gabe and I laugh. Del rolls her eyes again.

Del pulls Sam behind her, off to chase whatever angle she's come up with, abruptly leaving Gabe and me alone.

"I'm going to grab a bagel. Want to come?" he asks.

"Sure." My pulse ticks up a beat as I fall in step with him and breathe in his clean-showered scent.

We join the other ten people in line for Baked Dough, the bakery with the best carbs in town. Just the thought of their fresh-out-of-the-oven Montreal-style bagels makes me drool.

As we stand in line, I notice a group of Edgartown College girls blatantly giving Gabe a once-over, and I shift uncomfortably.

"Those girls are totally staring at you," I say, affecting an air of nonchalance. "Is it always like this for you?"

Gabe's cheeks turn slightly pink. "I don't know. Sometimes."

"Wow. To be so beautiful…" I nudge him with my shoulder. "Must be nice."

Gabe pointedly ignores me. "It sounds like Ms. Adler is in a bad spot with her son. Has anyone spoken to her about it?"

"I doubt the employees feel they can." I blow some errant curls out of my eyes. "And it sounds like maybe Ms. Adler isn't so innocent in all this after all. Maybe I really was blinded by loyalty this whole time." My face flushes with shame.

Gabe places a gentle hand on my right shoulder. 'Hey, there. Let's not beat ourselves up. You're doing your best to see all sides."

"It didn't take Zoe or the rest of them long to figure everything out. They knew right away something was fishy."

"They made up their minds right away. It doesn't mean they're right." Gabe puts his other hand on my left shoulder and turns me until my eyes meet his. "Give yourself some time to make sense of the situation. Sometimes it's okay not to rush."

"I guess that's not a bad suggestion," I say with little conviction.

"But…?" Gabe raises a playful but challenging brow.

"It just seems very non-radical."

The corner of Gabe's eyes crinkle in laughter. "Is that a requirement for a good idea?"

"Maybe it should be," I huff.

"All I'm saying is if you think there's more to the story, then there probably is. I trust your instincts, Morningstar. You should too."

We've made it to the front of the line. Gabe turns to the cashier and orders an everything bagel with cream cheese and "whatever she's having."

His boyish grin sends my heart racing, a fact I note and then quickly push to the far recesses of my mind.

# CHAPTER

## 25

The next few weeks feel almost normal. With Mason and me having made up, and the Bookcourt stuff somewhat on the back burner with Del doing her journalistic sleuthing, Mason, Del, and I spend a ton of awesome, tension-free time together. Coffee Wednesday is re-established. Taco Tuesday is in full swing. We even take long meandering Sunday walks and delve into what is bothering us most at school. (Me: not being on the Liberal Liaisons executive team and some lackluster sprint times at practice. Mason: the lack of socioeconomic diversity at our school. Del: how badly dressed and uninspired everyone always is.)

It's the first time in months that my friendship with Mason feels steady, and what a wonderful feeling that is. It's as if a tear in my favorite sweater has been mended.

By Wednesday morning, I'm feeling so great that even Mom's request that I change my clothes can't undo my good mood—not that she said anything aloud about my outfit. She always claims she'd never interfere with something as superficial as a wardrobe. However, sometimes her eyes clearly say, "Eh, you can do better than those mid-rise, pre-distressed jeans, honey."

Today, Mom and I are enjoying a pastry breakfast that would horrify Mimi, who left early for work. Sometimes it irks me that Mom can eat whatever she wants and stay thin, but during pastry mornings or cake dinners (the latter occurs when Mimi is on-call overnight), I'm thankful for her sweet tooth.

As I head out, my outfit much-improved thanks to Mom's advice, I smile. It's a crisp fall day: The sky is clear, the air smells smoky, and it's cool but not yet cold. I hop on my bike and ride to Reveiller for Coffee Wednesday. All feels right with the world.

Del and Mason are there when I arrive. As I walk up, I smilingly study them. Del looks Brooklyn-hip, as always, in fur-lined clogs, black skinny jeans, and an oversized sweater. Her hair is loose, framing her heart-shaped face, but then I notice she's frowning and pointing her finger, seemingly in mid-debate with Mason.

As he retorts, Mason nervously taps his hand on his knee.

"Hey, hey!" I call out sunnily, happy to be with the people who know me best for a precious forty-five minutes before school starts. They jolt at my greeting, and my heart sinks when I see their guilty expressions.

"Uh oh," I say, hoping to lighten the mood. "Am I in trouble again?"

Del looks sheepishly at Mason. My heart flutters in my chest.

"What?" My voice cracks with anxiety.

Mason shoves his hands in his pockets. Del straightens her shoulders.

"What?" I repeat.

"Look, Anna, something crappy happened," Mason begins, "and we don't know how to handle it. Zoe's dad is hosting a fundraiser, and it's kind of a big deal because Amanda Gorman will be there."

I clap my hands together in delight. Amanda Gorman is my all-time favorite poet.

"But Zoe's only inviting the executive team." Mason winces. "She's saying her dad doesn't want too many kids there."

"Okay, sounds cool. What's the dress code? Do you think she'll still invite me anyway? Like make an exception?"

Mason turns red. "I'm sorry, Anna. She's not inviting you. I talked to her about it. Actually, I begged her, but she won't budge."

I nod, unsure what else to do. "And you two got invites?"

I ask, even though the answer is obvious. So much for my joyful morning coffee with my best friends.

Del and Mason nod uneasily.

"And you want to go?"

They nod guiltily.

I sigh. "Okay." I sigh again. "It does suck that I'm not invited, and it sounds super cool, but I wouldn't want you guys to miss it."

Del and Mason exchange looks of relief.

"I'm sorry, Anna. This really sucks, but you know I'm obsessed with Amanda Gorman," Del says, staring at her clogged feet.

"I get it. I do."

Del links arms with me on one side, and Mason follows suit and takes my other arm.

"When is this fabulous soiree?" I try not to sound bitter even though I feel terribly left out.

"Friday." Mason grimaces, knowing we were supposed to do our monthly dinner at Bourdin's.

"Of course it is."

Del looks ashamed. "This really sucks. We don't have to go."

Mason looks down, a pained expression on his face.

"No, we can't all miss it. Sounds like it'll be the event of the year."

"Ugh, Anna, this whole thing feels out of hand."

I nod numbly, trying to smile and not show them just how deflated I feel. It isn't until we start walking toward school, my smile frozen in place, that I realize I never even ordered my morning coffee, which isn't helping my plummeting energy level.

"Thanks for being so cool about it, Anna Banana," Mason says.

I really, really don't like Zoe Dart. I want to let out a loud grumble, but decide against it. Weakly, I smile at my two best friends as we walk down the street, feeling that awful, strange distance once again.

# CHAPTER
## 26

$\text{B}$y Friday, I'm totally bummed. My Instagram feed is taunting me with pictures of the executive committee prepping for Zoe's party. I sit on the couch, in sweats, without any plans. I tap another Liaison's story. Looks like Zoe snuck some champagne out of her parents' collection as Lizzy, Zoe, Del, and Mason toast the night in a Boomerang video that I can't stop watching.

In the kitchen, Mimi and Mom are preparing fall-inspired cocktails and a Pinterest-worthy crudité platter for a dinner party they're hosting at our place tonight.

Everyone has a fun Friday night planned except me.

Another picture of Zoe's party pops up on my Instagram.

"Ugh!" I yell and toss the book that I've been trying to read for the last hour across the living room.

Mimi hands me a virgin cocktail with a festive cucumber garnish. "Looks like you could use this."

She sits down opposite me on the couch.

"Are you okay, honey?"

I shrug, but tears are already welling in my eyes. "Like, compared to most world issues, yes I'm okay, but also no, not internally."

Mom walks in with a glass of wine. She sits next to Mimi and tilts her head in concern. Her concern is less warm and more analytical than Mimi's, and therefore a lot less comforting. "I heard Mr. Dart is having quite the party."

"Yeah," I say miserably. "Amanda Gorman is going to be there."

"And why aren't you going?"

"I wasn't invited."

"Mr. Dart is keeping it adults-only?"

"No, Del and Mason are there. Some others, too. Just not me." I sip my virgin cocktail and although it's refreshing, it doesn't really do much for me.

"This is still about the Bookcourt protest you wouldn't join?" Mom leans forward, genuinely worried about my sinking popularity.

"Not exactly. It's more because of my Monday athletic training thing."

"Ugh," says Mom, echoing my earlier sentiment. "Either way, you can't just sit here and mope. Make your own fun."

"But of course, if you want to just have a cozy night in, that's fine too," Mimi adds supportively.

I bite my lip. "But all my friends are at the event."

"All of them?" Mom pushes. "No one from the track team is around?"

Suddenly, I remember Gabe's party invitation. His parents are in D.C. again. Would it make me the ultimate sellout to go to a Northsider party while my friends are literally at an event to better the world? But on the other hand, I would love to be where my friends are, and I was excluded.

So why should I do nothing tonight? And, to be totally honest, I've always been curious about Northside parties. I can't even picture what a party looks like without someone standing up and breaking into spontaneous slam poetry.

I bounce off the couch. "I was actually invited somewhere tonight."

Mimi claps happily. "That's great."

"Where?"

I freeze. Mom will have a fit if I tell her I'm going to a party at Gabe Delgado's.

"Eh, just the home of one of the new kids from the team."

"Do you want me to drive you?"

146

"No. If it's okay, I'll drive myself. Or I can bike?"

Mom nods. "You can take the car, but if you drink, you take a Lyft or call us. Promise?"

"Promise."

"Of course, we prefer you don't drink at all, honey, but if you do, yes, please call. I'll have my phone with me," Mimi says anxiously.

I hurry up the stairs to my bedroom. What the hell am I supposed to wear to a Northsider party?

# CHAPTER

## 27

I walk into Gabe's house with great apprehension. The house, replete with white Tuscan columns and furniture so pristine it appears to be for display only, screams luxury. I look around, hoping to spot a friendly face. But all I see is a sea of Northsiders dressed in too many pastels. What was I thinking coming here?

I look back towards the door, ready to make my escape, when I hear a voice from across the room yell, "Anna, you came!"

My heart flips a little as I spot Gabe. He looks ridiculously handsome in Levis and a white polo shirt.

He motions for me to come over to where he's standing with Sam and, to my chagrin, Scottie.

Without a choice, I make my way over. Sam hugs me and hands me a beer. I smile, then frown. "This hasn't been roofied or anything weird, has it?"

Sam looks horrified. Gabe laughs.

I glare at him. "You know that happens, and it's serious."

"I know, Anna." Gabe can't control his grin. "But that's an unopened can of Bud Light."

My cheeks flame. "Oh, right."

"But, hey, you can never be too safe." He winks at me and laughs again.

"Shut up." I shove him with my hip.

Scottie looks at me, Sam, and Gabe. "Well, isn't this chummy?"

Scottie isn't as broad or as handsome as Gabe or Sam. His hair is thick and shiny, but his face is thin and long. Truthfully, he always reminds me of a ferret.

"What can I say, Scottie?" Sam swings a friendly arm around me. "Those who train together, hang together."

I beam at Sam, appreciating how easily he can alter the mood.

Gabe looks at Sam's arm around me and frowns. I can't tell if he disapproves of Sam's boldness or his lack thereof.

"Oh, Gabriel, Caroline just walked in." Scottie whistles. "She's looking mighty *caliente*." He butchers the Spanish pronunciation and leers at Caroline, who instead locks eyes with Gabe and gives him what can only be classified as a come-hither look.

Gabe shoves his hands into his pockets. "If she'll have you, she's all yours now, friend. We cleared the air last week."

Scottie gives Gabe a sour look. "I don't need your rejects, *amigo*. But thanks."

I'm relieved when Scottie leaves us to go harass some other unlucky guest.

"What an asshole," I say, popping open my beer.

"Yup, that's Scottie," Sam agrees.

I look at Gabe. "What's with those Spanish words? That felt micro-aggression-y to me."

Gabe shrugs. "Yeah, it probably was." He takes a sip of his beer as if he doesn't have a care in the world.

"You know that's a bad thing, right?"

"Yeah, Anna. Duh. But he's my friend, sort of, and it's my party."

My mouth falls open. "It's really messed up. Micro-aggressions are, well... aggressive."

Gabe laughs and takes another sip of beer. "You really have a way with words, Morningstar."

When I continue to stare at him, he elaborates, "He's just trying to cut me down. It's always bothered him that Caroline chose me over him initially. But I'm choosing to ignore it. I said what I needed to say to her about it, so now I'm done."

My eye starts twitching. "But it's kind of disrespectful, isn't it?"

"Sure, but I'm not going to let it get to me," Gabe insists. "I don't see how getting into it with Scottie at my own party is going to help."

"So, you're just going to ignore it?" I ask, incredulous. "Do nothing?"

"That's exactly what I'm going to do. I don't owe anyone a reaction or a response, not even you, Miss Liberal Liaison."

He has a point, and I feel my cheeks, already flushed from my few sips of beer, redden further.

"So, I'm going to have a pretty fun night at my own awesome party, and that's that." Gabe smiles at me, lightening the mood. "Anna, please remember you're at a party. Try to have fun and not take on the world's woes on a Friday night."

"I'll take that under advisement," I mumble into my beer.

\* \* \* \*

Going to a party where you feel out of place is merely uncomfortable. Going to a party while doom-scrolling through a nonstop social media feed of your supposed "real" friends at a once-in-a-lifetime event is outright depressing. It's so depressing, in fact, that I cope with my feelings in a very un-Anna-like way: by binge drinking.

My arm hurts as I pump the handle of the keg, unsuccessfully trying to fill my third cup of beer. "Why is there so much foam?" I ask no one in particular. I'm enjoying how my brain is drifting into a calm haze. "I should really drink more. This is awesome."

"Well, darling," Gabe interjects in his usual Southern drawl mixed with political polish. "You need to tilt the cup at an angle." He leans against the wall, well-defined arms folded casually across his chest and an amused smirk on his face.

I roll my eyes at "darling," but tilt the cup as instructed and am pleased to achieve the proper beer-to-foam ratio. "You know it's sexist to call me 'darling,' and it's just plain weird for a high schooler to say it at all."

Gabe rolls his brown eyes back at me. "Well, *you* know it's weird to be the last guest at a party you didn't even RSVP to."

I look around his living room, surprised to find that, despite the pounding music, we are alone. "Whoops."

Gabe laughs at me, and his eyes light up. It seems unfair how handsome he is, how his stupid perfect cheekbones give him a lovely, romantic air. I have an awful impulse to run my hand along his jawline.

I lean forward and trip. Gabe catches my shoulders. His eyes round, but I think I see a glint of something else in them. Could it be desire? I blink and stand on my toes to examine him more closely.

"Anna, you're drunk." Gabe lets out a small breath. Now I'm standing so close to Gabe that I feel his breath kiss my skin, and I shiver. I wonder what it would feel like to be crushed in his arms. I lick my lips unconsciously.

Gabe watches my tongue trace my lips with what looks like wonder. He shakes his head and abruptly removes his hands from my shoulders.

I make a small sound of protest. His face is flushed, and his eyes suggest he's confused. "Oh my god," I say with delight, "you want to kiss me!"

Gabe laughs. "Maybe I do, but—"

I launch myself into his arms. Gabe stumbles into the wall behind him but manages not to drop me. My legs wrap around his waist, and I can feel the hard, flat surface of his abs. I'm so flustered and hot that I wonder if I'll faint. Tilting my head towards his, my heart beats erratically as my eyes flutter closed. My hazy brain tries to take in this momentous occasion when—

*Boom.* My butt hits the ground. "Ouch."

"Sorry!" Gabe rushes to help me up, looking guilty for dropping me. However, after hauling me up, he takes a gigantic step back. "Stay," he commands when I step toward him.

"Why?" I slur, pouting as he takes another step back.

"You're too drunk, Morningstar."

I blink, eyes glazed over. "I can't decide what to do first," I say.

"Finish my beer or call you an asshole."

"How exactly am I being an asshole?"

"Because now I like you even more! And you're supposed to be the type who takes advantage of the situation!" Unfortunately, I'm so drunk that I spill half of my remaining beer directly onto my shoes.

Gabe rolls his eyes. "That is beyond insulting, but I'll tell you what…" He pauses to refill his beer cup with an admirably foamless pour. "Let's go to the kitchen and get you some water. Then you can help me clean up, and maybe afterward, you can yell at me. Deal?"

I'm too drunk to resist his proposal. I tap my cup to his. "Deal."

"Hold on. Let me take that." Gabe tries to grab the beer out of my hand, but I dance past him and down it with glee.

Gabe lets out an exasperated but amused groan.

\* \* \* \*

Fifteen minutes later, we're eating cookie dough and finishing our drinks—beer for Gabe and a tall glass of water for me—in the Delgados' white and copper kitchen. My head is full-on swirling.

I lean forward with a mouth full of cookie dough. "That's the most beer I've ever had." I smile as if we're co-conspirators.

"Thanks for the lovely display of cookie dough and the fun fact." Gabe grins.

I crack up, laughing so hard in my inebriated state that I fall off the barstool.

He shakes his head but smiles as he pulls me back up. "What's so funny, drunky?"

"I am a drunky-monkey!" I giggle far louder than is appropriate. "It's just—you're so preppy. I mean, you're wearing a white polo shirt with a popped collar! I bet you've never even heard a woman burp before you met me."

Gabe looks at me and shakes his head. "My mama taught me only men do those things."

My jaw drops with rage, but his self-satisfied smirk throws

me. Is he teasing? The alcohol weakens makes my ability to detect sarcasm. "Sexist! Sexist boy," I accuse him.

Gabe breaks off another piece of cookie dough and raises his hands in surrender. "I was joking. My little sister burps all the time."

"I'm sure she'd be happy to hear you say so. Such a gentleman."

"Just like my daddy."

I wrinkle my nose, remembering whose kitchen I'm in. "No comment."

Gabe eyes me. "Luckily you can't vote yet, so I'll ignore the fact that I'm entertaining a member of the opposition in my kitchen."

I tilt my head and really look at him. Who would have thought Senator Delgado's son and Lilly Morningstar's daughter could continue to find common ground, even if it was over raw cookie dough and stale beer?

"You're staring at me," he points out. "I know my good looks can be blinding, especially since you basically attacked me in my living room, but stop it."

I blush. "Yeah, okay. You're hot in a preppy way, but that's not why I'm staring."

Gabe bursts out laughing. "I have to say, Annabelle, I'm pretty charmed by your honesty."

"You are?" I blush harder, as the thought of charming Gabe sends goosebumps down my arms. "It's really more of a shtick—like I know it makes me funny, but there's plenty I'm not honest about."

"Like what?"

"I'm not telling my deepest secrets to someone wearing a popped collar."

"Okay then." Gabe pulls off his shirt.

I gasp, immediately turning bright red, and try not to stare at his perfectly toned chest and abs. I've seen him shirtless a few times before at practice, but there's something about this moment—the privacy and intimacy of it all—that makes it feel different. I sit on my hands so I don't try to touch him. A weird itch develops between my shoulder blades.

Just when I thought things couldn't get any more awkward, Gabe's older brother, Mateo, walks in. He's a freshman at Duke, and, like Gabe, is one of the most beautiful men I've seen IRL. The Delgado family may have questionable politics, but damn, are they good-looking! Back when Mateo attended Edgartown High, he was a legendary ladies' man, and I can certainly see why.

Mateo looks first at me, then at his bare-chested brother, and breaks out into a perplexed grin. "Oh, sorry to be interrupting."

I want to die. "Oh, hi, Mateo." He was on the men's cross-country team, so I know him a little from school. "This isn't what it looks like!"

Gabe watches my reaction with joy. "Yeah, bro, I mean my being half-naked at the request of Annabelle is totally innocent."

"Shut up, Gabe," I snap.

"What?" Gabe lifts his hands. "What I said was true." He turns back to Mateo and sniffs his brother affectionately. "Still using natural deodorant, I see."

Mateo sticks his armpit in Gabe's face and winks at me. "I'd rather stink than get cancer." He laughs as Gabe pushes him off. "Have fun you two." He salutes us as he heads out of the room.

"Mateo Delgado wears natural deodorant?"

"Yeah, a college thing, I guess." Gabe shrugs, before offering me the tube of cookie dough. "But, whenever I have parties, he's always cool about looking the other way."

"What's he home for?"

"My parents wanted him to supervise us while they're in Washington for some dinner thing. They're coming back at 6 am, so I gotta get this place spotless before then."

"The senator doesn't approve of underage drinking?"

"Yeah, no, he doesn't. Speaking of which, I better start cleaning up. And since you ate more than your fair share of cookie dough, I think you should help."

"Totally!" I agree and immediately fall flat on my face trying to hop off the stool.

# CHAPTER

## 28

Sunlight streams across my face. A loud and powerful jack-hammer is smashing away in my head. I turn my face into my pillow and notice a strange smell—piney aftershave combined with body odor. My eyes fly open.

I'm in a room that's not my own. A boy's room. A fancy boy's room with wood-paneled walls, ornate light fixtures, green plaid bedding, and posters of soccer players tacked haphazardly onto the walls.

I sit up frantically and jump out from underneath the covers. Phew! I'm still wearing the same clothes from last night. I smell my shirt and gag as the stench of stale beer overwhelms me. My curls are sticking up all over my head, and my attempts to pat them down only make it worse.

The door swings open, and I yelp as Gabe walks in with his hands over his eyes.

"Decent?"

I desperately try one last time to put my hair into place. "Yes." I smile as if this moment isn't unbearably humiliating.

"How's my favorite monkey doing?" he teases.

"That's Ms. Drunky Monkey to you," I manage to joke back as memories of the preceding night slowly start to come back to me.

Gabe looks at me and winces. "You look a little rough. Since you don't have my natural charm, you can't really get away with the morning-after look."

I grip the edge of his duvet until my knuckles pale. "Morning after? Did we… did you—" I can't quite find the words.

Now Gabe's cheeks flush. "No, no, you just passed out, and Mateo and I carried you upstairs. Since you were snoring so loudly, I bunked with him." He smiles sweetly to let me know he's joking.

The thought of the Delgado boys carrying me up the stairs generates conflicting emotions—a strong desire to die of embarrassment, while at the same time feeling more alive than ever.

"Why don't you come down for breakfast? My parents saw your car and know we still have company."

Parents. *My* parents. Oh god. "My parents have no idea where I am!" Frantic again, I search for my phone.

Gabe hands it to me from his pocket. "I think it's taken care of." He pauses. "I read your texts."

"You what?"

"I didn't want your parents sending out a search party for you, so I got Del's number from Mary Sue." He gives me a sheepish smile. "You're welcome?"

I look over my texts:

Del at 12:34 pm: Where are you??? Your mom is freaking out!

Del at 12:48 pm: Gabe Delgado just texted me. He says you're with him. What are you doing with Gabe at this hour?! I need one hundred details IMMEDIATELY! Lucky for you I saved your butt! When your mom texted me, I said you were at Mary Sue's house. Did I mention I need DETAILS like now!

Del at 12:55 am: Now I'm freaking out. I think your parents would actually disown you if you lost your V to a Northsider!

I glare at my phone, embarrassed.

"For someone whose friends just covered for her, you don't look too happy. Is it because you're a virgin? I hear that sucks."

158

He pauses mockingly. "Or is it because you slept in a Northsider's bedroom?"

I throw a pillow at him.

"It's just… how did Del know I was okay? Shouldn't she have been more worried about me? What if you were taking advantage of me?"

"I think she probably assumed we were good enough friends for me not to harm you."

"She doesn't know you well enough to know that. I do, of course, but she doesn't."

Gabe smiles while simultaneously looking horrified. "You're funny. Your logic is faulty, but you sure are amusing."

"Anyway, my point is that Del should have been more worried about me, don't you think?"

Gabe looks at me like I've lost my mind. "Well, luckily, I didn't take advantage of you, and you weren't busted by your parents. So, it seems like you should be thanking her. But you're Annabelle Morningstar, so I'm sure you'll make it wildly more complicated than it needs to be."

A grandfather clock dings nine times. "We're late. Here, you can borrow this shirt. Oh, and feel free to use the shower. See you downstairs in a few."

I catch the white button-down he tosses me. It smells just like his pillow—piney and musky and exactly like Gabe. He closes the door behind him, and I head into his bathroom. Plush blue towels hang on the door alongside an even plusher robe. I wonder where the Delgados buy their towels. Why aren't our towels this plush and soft? I commit the label to memory before stepping out of my clothes and placing my aching head under the wonderfully warm, rushing water.

\* \* \* \*

I make my way down a long hallway until I reach the top of a spiral staircase. Descending slowly, I call on my inner Beanie Feldstein to make the most of this entrance.

Mateo appears at the bottom of the staircase. "They were

159

about to send a search party for you." He throws me a kind smile. He's wearing a faded green t-shirt that sets him apart from his otherwise formal family.

"Easy to get lost here," I tell him. "This place is huge. Like movie-star-house huge."

Mateo grimaces. "It's embarrassing. Like, why would anyone need this much space?" He shrugs. "Not my style."

I look at him curiously as he leads me into the large kitchen. "Natural deodorant? Worrying about taking up too much space? Are you sure you're one of them?"

My question leaves my lips just as Mateo swings open the salon-style doors leading to the peach-colored dining room.

Senator Delgado, Mrs. Delgado, Gabe, and Beatriz, Gabe's twelve-year-old sister, all stare at me. Gabe glares, Mateo coughs in his hand, and Beatriz looks back and forth between me and her dad as if she can't wait to see what happens next.

"'One of them?'" Senator Delgado lets out an appealing laugh, deep and throaty like Gabe's, only louder and more startling.

I flush red. "Uh, I just meant, sir, I mean, Senator, I read that you aren't a huge supporter of the environment."

Senator Delgado holds my gaze. He pauses, perhaps relishing the intimidating silence. "Is that so?" The question lingers in the air.

"Though I, for one, never believe what I read." I lie, as I live for gossip and believe almost everything I hear.

The senator continues to stare at me, and I step back. Something sharp digs into my shoulder, and I turn to find two protruding antlers atop a taxidermied deer head mounted on the wall. Its black eyes stare blankly at me, and I yelp, startled, knocking into it once more. The deer rattles but doesn't fall.

Mateo and Gabe both exhale deeply.

I turn to face the firing squad, faking my best smile. "At least he's already dead." I turn back to the Senator. "Sorry for bumping your..." I search for a word. "Trophy?"

Mrs. Delgado, who is chic in a Kate Spade sort of way, lets out a gentle laugh, which seems mismatched with what she says next.

"Just to be clear, the reason that deer is dead is because I'm the best shot in the Southeast."

"Ugh, don't remind me," Bea protests. She looks forlornly at the deer. "Bambi…"

"Oh honey, don't be so dramatic."

"She can't help it. I don't know what they're teaching her at school, but she's so riled up all the time." Senator Delgado shakes his head, then tousles his daughter's hair.

"Like you should talk, Dad! You literally barfed when mom shot that deer."

Mateo and Gabe burst out laughing.

"It was disgusting," Gabe says to me.

"The shooting or the barfing?"

"Both."

Senator Delgado breaks out in a warm smile. "I've never been good with blood."

Mrs. Delgado nods. "He nearly fainted anytime one of the kids scraped their knees. He's absolutely useless on a hunt."

"Yeah, Dad is a total softie," Bea confirms.

A *softie?* It's hard to think that way of a man passing some of the country's most conservative legislation, but in this moment, seeing him surrounded by his wife and teasing kids … it's, well, confusing.

"I may be a softie, but I'm not a dummy." He turns to me. "So, Miss, please tell us why you found the need to keep Gabe company all night?" He gives me and Gabe a stern look.

"Well, I'm embarrassed to say, but following some less-than-fortunate, life-derailing events, I let myself get in a rare state that made it so I couldn't drive home."

Mateo's lips quirk in a smile. "*Life-derailing?* Sounds serious."

"You were drunk!" Bea's eyes light up. "What's that like? I'm so curious about being drunk. Gabe let me take a sip of his beer once, and I thought it was so disgusting." She lets out a pained sigh. "Tragically, I don't think I'll ever be able to get drunk."

Now it's Mrs. Delgado's turn to glare at Gabe. "You gave her alcohol?"

Gabe puts his hands in front of his face. "I let her dip her tongue in a beer I was drinking … just once."

Senator Delgado gives his son a hard look. "And why were you drinking, son? Last time I checked, you're still in high school and well under twenty-one. Despite what certain lobbyists may say, the drinking age in this country, for better or worse, is—"

Mrs. Delgado swiftly cuts him off. "You all know the house rules: No politics or pageantry before noon."

All the males at the table immediately fall silent.

I'm taking all this in when Bea whispers loudly in my ear, "My mom is a badass."

I laugh. "Did Gabe teach you that word?"

"You catch on quickly," Mateo, sitting directly to my right, says.

Gabe smiles, all innocence. "I'm starving! Mom, can we eat?"

"Grace first."

Mateo and Bea each take one of my hands. This is weird, I think, but I follow along as the senator leads us in thanks for the meal.

When I open my eyes, a maid appears with platters of food and sets them on the oak buffet against the wall. She uncovers the trays—eggs, pancakes, and a fruit salad. Moments later, she reappears to fill our water glasses and place pastry baskets and pitchers of orange juice on the table.

"Marla, how's Michael's semester going?" the senator asks the maid.

Her face lights up. "He's loving school and working hard, Senator. We're so proud of him."

"He's such a wonderful young man," Mrs. Delgado replies. "We're just sad he's missing Thanksgiving this year."

"Hey, if I had the chance to go to Peru on an archeological dig, I'd skip Thanksgiving too," Gabe says. "When I talked to Michael last week, he sounded pumped about the trip."

I watch this exchange with interest, surprised to find the Delgados are close to Marla and her son. I assumed they'd be the type to treat their staff with cool indifference.

162

Soon after, Marla leaves the room with the empty serving trays, and the family is eating in earnest.

"Mom, can you do that special salt and ketchup combo to my eggs again?" Gabe asks between huge forkfuls of food.

"Sure, hon, but it's not really that complicated."

I start chuckling.

"What?" Gabe looks at me across the table, head tilted in confusion.

"Nothing. Just it's funny that you need your mom to prepare your eggs."

"Why?"

I laugh harder. "It's a little baby girl-ish."

"Hey!" Beatriz glares at me. "Why did you say baby girl instead of baby boy?"

Gabe almost spits out his coffee because he's laughing so hard. "Well, look who's anti-feminist now."

\* \* \* \*

An hour later, Gabe and I head out his front door.

"May I walk you home?" His tone is sweet and unassuming, and I feel strangely cared for, even though I'm sure the offer is just the result of good manners.

"I drove, remember? The whole sleeping-over thing that led to me crashing your family breakfast," I joke.

"Oh, right," Gabe replies sheepishly. "I'll walk you to your car then."

"Okay, thanks." We start down the pebbled path. I wish so badly that Gabe's offer to walk me home more than just his innate politeness and he really was just looking to spend extra time with me. A flush creeps up my neck as I remember how I practically threw myself at him last night. I suddenly feel like hiding.

We're halfway down his driveway, shaded by large trees that line the gravel road. I stop walking somewhat abruptly and turn to him, he mirrors my stance so we are facing each other. "Thanks for taking care of me last night. You were a true gentleman."

Gabe nods. He tucks his fingers in the belt loops of his jeans and rocks back on his heels. "I have a question."

I lift my eyes to his and feel a pang in my stomach as I stare into his searching gaze. Suddenly, I dread the near future when I have to be apart from him. "Yes?"

"Are you sober now?" He takes a step closer to me. The smell of spearmint floats across my nose. An unfamiliar look settles on his face that sends my pulse scrambling.

I nod, the large frog in my throat preventing me from forming words.

"Good." He takes me into his arms and gently presses his lips on mine. A gentle brush that ignites my insides. I respond immediately, pressing urgently against him. I feel his body grumble with a low, teasing sound as he changes the angle and deepens the kiss.

A soft moan escapes me as I run my hands though his silky hair. I pull his head closer to mine. His mouth is warm and soft, his skin heats under my touch. I want every inch of him. I move my lips to his neck, gently trailing kisses down the column, his sharp intake of breath emboldens me. A million tiny diamonds burst inside my mind as heat envelops me. I want this moment to last forever. He guides my mouth back to his and gently sucks on my bottom lip, which sends a fresh wave of frenzied need through my system. I stick my tongue into his mouth.

Bliss surrounds us.

# CHAPTER
## 29

For the rest of the weekend, I avoid Mason and Del. I can't bring myself to respond to their texts or calls when this huge, earth-shattering thing has just happened that I'm not ready to share. Instead, I hide under my covers reading romance novels for the rest of Saturday and hike at the Greenway with my moms on Sunday.

Getting ready to go back to school on Monday feels weird. I can't believe I made out with Gabe Delgado...even that I'm the sort of person Gabe Delgado would make out with. Even more unbelievable, I can't believe it was so amazing. All I want is to do it again... and again. And again. Thoughts of his golden eyes and soft lips pop into my mind when I least expect them to and linger.

Gabe and I agreed to take the weekend to gather our thoughts. I groan and open my bathroom mirror—is it at all possible he feels anywhere near as affected by all of this as I do? Probably not. He's had a serious relationship before. I'm sure our kiss barely registered with him. I groan again.

Just as I'm applying a dollop of toothpaste, I get a MAD summons from Del. (MAD is code for a Mason, Anna, and Del emergency hang. When one of us rings the MAD bell, we all show up, no questions asked.)

So, twenty minutes later, I'm sitting in our usual corner booth at Floppies when Del plops down in front of me. "You've been avoiding me." Her arms are crossed over her favorite striped sweater. I'm about to deny it when Mason appears out of nowhere.

"And me."

He shrugs off his wool peacoat, looking more like the Ivy League college boy he'll soon be rather than the high school junior he is.

A waitress stops by and takes our order.

"I haven't been avoiding you," I say as soon as we're alone. "It was just a busy weekend."

Anger flashes in Mason's eyes. "So, you're going to Northsider parties now?"

"Mase, we talked about this." Del puts a reassuring hand on his forearm. "Calm down."

"You talked about it?" Suddenly, I sharply feel the distance between us again. How do they always manage to end up on the same side while I'm left alone on the other?

"Yeah, of course we did." Del sounds tired. "You slept over at Gabe Delgado's house after attending the RNC equivalent of a high school who's who."

"What she said," Mason says bitingly.

Del eyes Mason, then shakes her head as if deciding not to deal with him. "So, what happened?"

"What happened?" I repeat, sipping my water. "I had nothing to do Friday night while you two were at the coolest event ever." I pause for dramatic effect. "Remember? Mason's girlfriend canceled me for not boycotting an independent bookstore?"

"Don't be ridiculous, Anna," Mason says. "You weren't 'canceled.'"

"Yeah? Well, that's what it felt like."

Mason turns to Del and continues speaking as if I'm no longer there. "She hangs out with Northsiders for one weekend, and now she sounds like Fox News railing against cancel culture."

"Guys, can we cool it?" Del slaps her palms down on the table, rattling the silverware. "This doesn't feel productive. We all know Zoe is being super-punitive, and that she takes self-righteousness to a new, higher level. We also know Anna is potentially going off to the dark side."

"Hey!" Mason and I exclaim in unison.

Del narrows her eyes. "Zip it. I don't want to hear anything else on the subject. New topic please."

No one says anything, so Del presses her lips together and continues, "Anna, it sucks you couldn't come Friday."

Finally, Mason unclenches his jaw. "Yeah. Del and I felt bad about it all night."

"Mason even told off Queen Z over it." Del nudges Mason encouragingly.

My eyes round. "You did?"

He shrugs. "It wasn't a big deal."

Del nods to let me know it was a very big deal, and I feel a weight lift off me. For the first time since I found out about the party, I feel like maybe this will all be okay, like my team just might be back in place again.

"So spill," Del tries again. "What happened at Gabe's?"

I take a deep breath and start to tell them everything, from feeling crummy for being left out, to getting too drunk and sleeping there, to my awkward, next-morning breakfast encounter with the full Delgado clan, to accidentally being the last party guest to leave Gabe's.

Mason's face is eerily still, but Del studies me curiously.

I'm about to share what happened next, but something stops me. For some reason, I can't go there yet. I don't want to risk any more upset.

"Sounds like you like them," Del says softly. Mason crosses his arms at his chest and huffs. "The Delgados?"

"I do, mostly."

"How can you like someone who supports so many horrible things?" Mason presses.

I don't know how to answer that. I think of all the human and environmental atrocities on Senator Delgado's voting record over the past decade. "You're right. I shouldn't."

"But you do anyway?"

"I guess it's confusing. I mean, Gabe isn't his father."

Mason doesn't seem satisfied, but Del jumps in before he can say anything further. "Does it really matter? When someone's just a teammate, who cares how their parents act or don't act?"

"Exactly," I say, eager to ease the table's suffocating tension. Of course, I don't mention that "teammates" usually don't stick their tongues down each other's throats.

**** 

I should have known that my acting abilities would be no match for Del's investigative talents. Later, when Del grabs me between second and third period and pulls me outside into a corner of the archway that connects the two sections of the building, I know I'm caught.

"What was that this morning?"

"What do you mean?" I try to remember what the telltale signs of lying are. Shifting pupils and excessive blinking perhaps?

"Mason was so intense. You should have seen him at the party. He went off on Zoe."

I'm relieved and perplexed by the direction of our conversation. Didn't I have "I made out with Gabe Delgado" tattooed across my forehead? "Well, we've been friends our whole lives. Maybe Mason finally remembered to have my back?"

Del shakes her head. "I don't know. It's weird."

"Weird how? He's still pissed at me because of missing Liaisons and the Gabe and Sam stuff."

"I don't think Sam has anything to do with it." Del looks troubled, but I can't press her on it because Gabe and Sam are making their way across the grass in our direction.

It's the first time I've seen Gabe since our six minutes in heaven. His eyes meet mine, and I couldn't break our gaze if I tried. My feet are rooted to the floor as confusion and lust turn my insides inside out.

Sam clears his throat, and I rip my eyes away. Del looks between us, bewildered by the interaction. Gabe snaps out of it.

"Morningstar," Gabe says, shooting a fake finger gun at me. I roll my eyes. Have I been so swept off my feet that I can barely think straight around someone who makes finger guns? This can't be good.

"Hey, Del." Sam waves, with a slightly lovesick expression in his eyes.

Del sends a breezy wave back.

"Don't mimic shooting a gun," I call to Gabe.

"What?" he says back with a shrug.

"I wear orange!" I yell, evoking the gun control color.

Gabe shakes his head with a laugh as he walks toward the end of the archway. "I have no idea what you're talking about, Morningstar, but sure thing." He shoots me double finger guns and disappears into the crowd.

"He's ridiculous."

Del eyes me. "Boy, do you have the hots for him."

My cheeks flame. "Um, well, I don't know."

Del rolls her eyes. "This is worse than I thought. Your mom is going to flip out if she finds out."

I narrow my eyes. "Okay, so what if I find him a little, tiny bit handsome? It's just a superficial thing."

Del bursts out laughing. The bell rings. Del gives me a wave as she heads off toward her next class. "Happy Northsider daydreaming. I love you even if you're dipping your toes into dark, scary waters."

"I love you too, even if you're wrong about where my toes are dipping." Sure, I kissed him, but that was pure lust. It's not like I actually *like*-like him. It's not truly the dark side unless you're also catching feelings.

"We'll see." Del gives me a knowing smile and flounces away.

# CHAPTER 30

From there, my day gets weirder.

My conversation with Del still has me spinning. What would she say if she knew about my kiss with Gabe? Would Mason get even madder? I shake my head, wanting to pause my racing thoughts. Am I going to lose my friends over this?

Some kind of friend survival instinct screams *Don't go there!* from the deep recesses of my psyche. I let my mind curve back to easier thoughts of Gabe pulling me flush against his impossibly toned physique. I remember the sight of him without his shirt on. I draw a sharp breath, feeling warm just thinking about the absolutely cosmic, earth-shattering feeling of being in his arms... indeed, of his lips on mine. A sigh escapes my throat right there in the hall. Maybe I *have* gone to the dark side.

I shake my head for the umpteenth time and am on my way to Chemistry when someone grabs me by the arm and drags me into an empty hallway behind the science lab. To my surprise, it's Caroline Loran, and she doesn't look very happy.

"Is it true that you slept over at Gabe's on Friday night?" Her voice sounds strangely high-pitched.

I fold my arms across my chest and say, "I'm not sure why you think I owe you an answer." I want to say something much meaner but, remembering Gabe's charitable interpretation of Caroline, I bite my tongue.

"Listen to me, you frizzy-haired loser." Then again, there is something to be said about putting an entitled brat in her place.

"I think my curls are really well-defined lately." I touch my head. Del introduced me to the world of curly-haired salon specialists, and it's made a world of difference, or so I thought.

"Gabe and I are not over. Our breakup is temporary." She unconsciously touches a silver bracelet on her wrist, and I wonder if it's simply a relic of their onetime relationship. "Just thought you should know that."

I temper my expression. "You sound delusional."

Caroline's eyes narrow. "I don't even get why he wants to hang out with you. You're not that pretty, and you're awkward. And you almost seem proud of your awkwardness, which makes it even weirder."

It would be too easy to weaponize Caroline's own insecurities and use them against her, but I can't shake Gabe's mediating voice in my head. "Great talk," I say. "Always inspiring."

Still, I'm no angel. I spot Gabe and run across the small courtyard to where he's standing with Sam. I make a big show of kissing them both on the cheek. Sam looks utterly confused, while Gabe turns progressively pinker.

"Sorry, just trying to piss off your girlfriend," I explain. Turning, I see Caroline glaring in my direction, and I throw my shoulders back in victory.

"*Ex*-girlfriend," Gabe reminds me.

Sam shoots me a knowing look.

"It ain't over till it's over," I say, reading Sam's expression out loud.

Gabe shrugs both of us off. "Whatever." He glances back to where Caroline is still fuming.

"Don't know how smart that one was, Anna."

"Whatever. I've handled far worse. Zoe Dart is much scarier than Caroline Loran."

"I wouldn't be so sure of that," Sam says uneasily.

The bell plays. "Fun chat. I didn't know you all are so scared of Mean Girl," I laugh, getting ready to run off to class.

Gabe rolls his eyes as the bell ends. "Go learn something and let us be."

"Gladly!" But we smile at each other, and my stomach flutters.

# CHAPTER
## 31

By day's end, Sam and Gabe's warning proves all too prescient. Caroline posts an Instagram photo of me kissing Gabe on the cheek and captions it: Hmm ... *a sleepover and now some bipartisan kisses in the courtyard. I wonder what @LillyMorningstar would say about such canoodling.* I want to disappear. My only hope is that Hen, who helps manage all Lilly Morningstar social media accounts, sees the tag and not Mom.

Even worse, I know Mason follows Caroline. It's hard to keep insisting that we're just teammates when that photo looks anything but platonic. I feel nauseated.

My phone buzzes.

Gabe: Told you, darling.

I text back: Ugh. At least this one didn't make the news. Pretty sure this is exactly what Hen told me not to do.

Gabe: I'm sorry, Anna. Let me see what I can do.

Scanning the area for Del, I walk down the school's front steps toward the street. Del always knows what to do in a crisis.

The first person I see is Zoe. Her piercing look stops me dead in my tracks. "Can I talk to you for a second?"

"Sure," I reply cautiously. Why does Zoe always look like she knows all the secrets of the universe?

"I just wanted to say that if you ever want to strategize on how to get Gabe to see things in more of a socially conscious way, I'm happy to brainstorm with you."

I am totally taken aback. Why would the girl who has made my last few months a living hell now want to brainstorm with me? Is she a robot or the ultimate do-gooder? "Oh, thanks, Zoe. I'll keep that in mind."

"If you can get to Gabe, maybe Gabe could get through to his father," she presses, smiling at me as if I'm suddenly the teacher's pet.

I nod. "Yeah, that would be something. That's for sure."

"It really would! Well, let me know. I'm sure Mason would help too." Her eyes swim dreamily at the mention of her boyfriend. "He's so good at thinking things through."

"Yeah, I know first-hand how good Mason is at that. We've been best friends our whole lives."

Zoe blinks. "Yes, of course." She shifts her backpack from one shoulder to the other and says, "Well, I have a lot to do to get ready for the Planned Parenthood rally next week." She pauses. "You'll be there?"

"Of course."

"Maybe you can bring Gabe."

"Stranger things have happened."

"Exactly. Okay, bye, Anna." She turns to leave and then turns back. "I hope there aren't too many hard feelings about the times I've had to make meetings executive team only."

I'm too confused to muster an answer, so I just shrug.

"Mason said you might be upset."

"Well, as you said, Mason's a deep thinker."

Zoe blinks at me. "It wasn't personal. I hope you know that."

"Okay, well …" I trail off.

Zoe looks at me, waiting for me to finish my sentence.

"Well, have a good rest of your day," I finally manage.

She nods slowly as if accepting this as the end of our conversation. "You too."

"Bye," I say, awkwardly waving as I scurry down the stairs.

****

On our walk home, I tell Mason and Del about my weird conversation with Zoe.

"Seems a little random," Del suggests, looking at Mason apprehensively.

To our surprise, Mason agrees. "Why would you have any sway over Gabe Delgado just because you train together?"

"We are friends," I remind him, though I internally debate how truthful that really is.

"Don't remind me," Mason mumbles.

My phone dings again. "Ugh. Caroline keeps tagging me to that post even though I've untagged myself, like, ten times. She's in a total rage."

"What do you think Lilly is going to say if she sees the post?" Del asks nervously.

"By the way, what did that post say?" Mason asks. He tries to sound calm, but I can hear the annoyance in his voice. "Why were you kissing him?"

"I also kissed Sam!" I blurt out, though I know it doesn't help. "On the cheek, I mean."

"Will Mimi be home?" Del asks, carefully steering us away from another fight. "Maybe she can talk some sense into your mom."

"I doubt it. She usually works late on Tuesdays."

Mason and Del exchange worried grimaces.

We walk up the gravel pathway that leads to our wraparound patio. I sigh. "Time to face the music."

I push open our light blue door, we all kick our shoes, and stow them under the console table.

Mom pops out from the kitchen and into our minimalist living room. An abstract painting by one of Mimi's favorite artists dominates the space. Mom and I both hate it. "Mason, Del, what a treat." She beams at my friends. I often joke (okay, worry) that she likes my friends better than I do. Just to piss her off, maybe I should show her Caroline's post about me and Gabe, I think, avidly watching her chat up my friends.

177

"Honey, I had the most interesting call from Hen," Mom says with a knowing look. I cringe.

She lays out a platter of hummus and pita chips. "She claims not only did you sleep over at Senator Delgado's house last weekend, but there's another round of incriminating pictures of you and Gabe online. But I told Hen there's no way that happened, as my Annabelle, and her best friend Del, are two upstanding young women who would never trick me."

Del looks horrified.

"It was only one picture," I say, knowing it's a terribly weak defense. "Okay, cut the dramatics, Mom. We know we're busted."

Mom pats Del reassuringly on the shoulder. "It's okay, honey. If you all never snuck around or fibbed, I'd think there was something wrong with you. You're teenagers after all."

Del brightens. Her parents are stricter than mine. "Thanks, Lilly."

"So, honey, what exactly were you doing all night at Gabe Delgado's?"

"You don't seem upset?" I ask, confused.

Lilly laughs. "Anna, I know you too well to think anything actually happened. You'd never be romantically interested in a Delgado."

I nod though my insides are burning with shame.

My mom continues, "Although I need to warn you, Mimi is super upset you lied to us."

Del and Mason give me a look as if to say, "We got that one wrong."

I slump down on top of a barstool. "How upset?"

"She thinks we failed to make you feel safe enough to trust us. So, pretty upset."

I let out a sigh. "Great. I'll prepare myself for the waterworks."

Mom puts her arm around my shoulder. "Honey, though I'm not quite at Mimi's level," she pauses, clearly enjoying getting to be the good cop for once, "I do expect you to be honest with us. It's not okay for us not knowing where you are. Plus, it's unfair to rope your friends into a lie."

"I had no idea, Ms. Morningstar," Mason says in the ultimate suck-up move. I shove him with my left hand and grab a pita chip with my right.

Mom nods. "Okay, enough of this. Later, when we're alone, we'll talk about this with Mimi."

Del and Mason seem relieved this particular discussion is over. The topic quickly shifts to Del's recent stories for *The Red and Blue* and Mason's latest semi-viral YouTube video. For once, I'm relieved not to be exciting enough to be at the center of the conversation.

# CHAPTER

## 32

It's Sunday morning, and I'm lazing under the bed covers when I hear Mimi call upstairs to me. "Um, Annabelle, honey? You have a guest."

I blearily look at the clock on my nightstand. Who the heck is visiting me at 9 am on a Sunday? What self-respecting person is even up at such an hour?

"Like an in-person visitor?" I yell back. I figure it's either my grandmother on FaceTime or Del. Mason never wakes up until noon on weekends.

"An actual, real-life person," Mimi confirms.

"A person I need to change out of my pancake PJs to see?" I'm sporting my absolute favorite pajamas that Del got me as a gag gift last Valentine's Day. They're purple fleece patterned with cartoonish dancing pancakes.

Now I hear three laughs. Two are my parents' and the third is... Gabe's! I throw off my covers and run to my dresser to change.

I get a text from Mom: "Anna, honey, if the sound of feet running means you're trying to quickly get dressed… Gabe is here in athletic gear."

"Thanks, Mom!" I text back and throw on performance leggings and a mesh shirt. I brush my teeth, tie my hair in a high pony, and wash my face. I give myself one last once-over before hustling down the stairs. My heart beats nervously at the idea of Gabe talking to my moms.

I hope they aren't, like, being mean to him or anything!

But as I skid into the kitchen, I see Mimi pouring Gabe a cup of coffee, while Mom hands him an ice water with a lemon wedge, the way she always serves it.

They're asking Gabe about his classes this semester, and not, as I feared, grilling him on his dad's immigration policy.

They all look up when I enter.

Gabe's face lights up, and he stands to greet me. "Hey, Anna." I suddenly realize that, after the Caroline drama took centerstage, Gabe and I never had our talk.

My moms exchange a knowing look.

"Hey," I say, feeling a little glow-y at the sight of Gabe's beautiful face in the kitchen's morning light.

Mimi endearingly studies my face.

"I wanted to see if you were up for an extra training run?" Gabe asks.

"But it's our day off."

"I know, but I usually do a Sunday run anyway."

"You do? Why?"

Gabe looks embarrassed. "Uh, I guess I just want to make sure I'm giving my recruitment chances everything I've got."

"So how long a run are we talking about here?"

"I usually do a five-mile loop. I actually found an amazing trail on the Greenway I think you'd like. But, since we don't have school on Monday, maybe we could do a longer run." It's Teacher Development Day tomorrow, so our training session with Coach Farmer is canceled.

Five miles on a Sunday? I groan at the thought of exercise, but I feel a jolt of energy at the idea of more alone-time with Gabe.

"Okay, fine. I'm in, but can we please stick to the five-miler?" When Gabe nods, I add, "And I get to pick lunch after."

Gabe lifts a brow. "Sounds like you just want an excuse to spend the whole day with me."

"Let's not forget who showed up in whose kitchen at the crack of dawn."

Gabe laughs. "Busted."

Mimi clears her throat to remind us that she and Mom are still here. Gabe and I both jump a little, and I feel sheepish. "Well, kids, have fun." She hands both of us a water bottle from the fridge. "Hydrate."

"Have a good run." Mom leans over to whisper in my ear, "Okay, so maybe I was wrong about you never being interested in a Delgado."

I shush her and follow Gabe to his Jeep, hoping my moms don't notice just how widely I'm smiling.

* * * *

Thirty minutes later, I'm behind Gabe, huffing a bit on a beautiful, low-incline Greenway trail. Red and orange leaves crunch beneath our feet as we run across the dirt trail, dodging rocks and tree roots. Three miles into the run, we switch to the Heron trail, and head out of the forest and up to rock bluffs. For another mile, we tackle a challenging uphill climb. Then we reach a summit that offers a perfect view of the cloudless sky. Gabe asks if I want to sit for a few.

"Sure." I put my hands over my head to catch my breath. Gabe offers me my water bottle, which he'd been carrying in a small backpack.

I look at him. He wipes his forehead and uncaps his bottle.

He catches me staring and smiles. "What?"

"That was really great. What an awesome route."

"Yeah, I love being out here."

"I really admire how dedicated you are to improving your game. Not everyone has that kind of discipline."

He nods thoughtfully. "Thanks. I think discipline also has some pitfalls, though."

"How so?"

"It's like how you always tease me for my L.L. Bean Instagram. I'm stuck in this holding pattern, always doing the same things over and over again. It's like I'm always too careful."

"Hey, to your credit, there have definitely been some non-L.L.

Bean posts of late. And, besides, L.L. Bean has its pluses. They make a high-quality flannel."

I beam when Gabe laughs at my quip.

"But how does that relate to training?"

"Because I'm constantly weighing options in my head." He drops to the ground, leaning his back against a big rock. "I know running this extra day will help me be better, so I do it. But I also wonder if I'd be happier if I stayed in bed or just hung out at home or didn't plan things quite so carefully."

I watch the sun reflect on his mussed hair. "I can see that, but it's hard to find a balance. If you hadn't come and tricked me into this indecently early run, I'd probably have stayed in bed for another two hours today. I can be a bit of a short-term thinker that way."

"Tricked?"

I laugh. "Well, I guess that's the wrong word. It was more of an enticement." I blush at the confession.

Gabe's eyes shine with good humor and his smile adopts a flirtatious tilt as he looks up at me. "*Enticed?* How so?"

My face is now officially on fire.

His smile ticks up another two notches into dazzling territory.

"Don't give me that megawatt smile, Delgado. It's not fair."

Gabe reaches for my hand and pulls me down beside him. "I'm just smiling because I'm picturing you in those pancake PJs. They sound really comfortable. Anyone wearing those would probably want to stay in bed for days."

I laugh, happily settling next to him. Our knees brush gently. "I never would have said that if I knew you were down there and could hear me."

He retakes my hand and tugs me closer. I circle my arms around his neck as a dreamy sigh escapes my throat.

"I'd love to see them sometime. It's not often you get to see pancakes dancing."

I laugh again and tilt my head towards Gabe's, inviting the kiss I've been dreaming of for the last four miles. As his salty lips touch mine, I wonder if anything will ever feel so good or so exciting again.

Gabe drops me off after one more mind-blowing kiss, and I stroll into my house feeling so giddy it feels like the world is shimmering around me.

I dance into the kitchen and see a note from my moms informing me they've gone antiquing in the neighboring town of Hudson Village to find some nightstands for the guest room.

I'm dying to text Mason and Del and tell them everything, but I'm also afraid. As my heart balloons in my chest, I close my eyes and blindly type a group text to Mason and Del asking if we can talk. They remind me that, later that night, we're seeing a play together at Edgartown College. Whoops, forgot about that. I ask if we can meet at the theater a little early, and they agree.

Del: Officially dying of curiosity here…

Mason: Me too. So mysterious!

Three hours later, I'm standing outside the Shed, Edgartown College's art center, which has all-glass walls and a wood slat roof. Thanks to the college's thriving theater program, there's always an amazing play to see. Or mostly amazing. Truthfully, some productions are so far out there that I don't quite get what's going on in them, but based on local reviews and what Del, Mason and my moms say, even the weirdest experimental plays are on-point.

Del arrives first. She looks sophisticated in black faux leather pants and a gray oversized cardigan that she paired with moto boots. "Hey there, mysterious lady!"

She gives me a hug.

I hug her back a little too tightly, nervous to spill my news, but also excited to share my bursting emotions with my bestie. "I don't know if I can wait until Mason gets here!" I bite my lip, scrunch up my face, and decide to just go for it, right here and now. "So, this might be a little shocking and hard to believe, but I'm hoping you can be open-minded…" I take a big breath, but before I can get it out, Del interrupts me.

"You and Gabe made out, and you're totally into him."

"Whoa! How did you know?"

Del laughs. "It was completely obvious." She studies my face. "Fess up. You kissed him at the party."

I blush. "Morning after."

"Morning after *what?*" Mason asks as he approaches. Both of us are startled by his sudden appearance.

Del looks at me nervously. I chew my lip.

"Well, Mase, I don't think you're going to love this, but I've made out with Gabe a few times, and I'm super into him," I say in a rush.

The color drains from Mason's face. "Are you serious?"

I turn to Del. "See? He looks shocked. You said it was obvious."

Del seems a little somber. "It was obvious to anyone who wanted to see it."

"What does that mean?" Mason asks.

"Just what I said." Del's words carry an unusual frostiness.

"Okay. Sorry I missed what was so apparent to you," Mason snaps.

"I know it's surprising, but I feel really happy and excited."

"Then I'm excited for you," Del assures me.

We both look at Mason.

"Honestly, I'm still processing this. I don't want to say anything dumb. I just feel really rocked," he finally manages.

We hear the bell ring in the theater, signaling it's time for audience members to take their seats.

"Good timing," Mason says, trying to smile.

I sigh and link arms with him and Del. "Guys, I just need you to know that I love you both so much and would never want anything about us to change." I give them both a kiss on the cheek, and as we take our seats to watch the show, I almost believe everything will be okay.

# CHAPTER 33

I persuade Del and Mason to come over after the play. Since my big announcement, Mason has barely spoken ten words and I'm hoping some fire pit time will loosen him up a bit.

As we pull up to my house on our bikes, the streets now dark, I make out four figures standing in the driveway.

"What's going on?" No one answers.

Mason jumps off his bike and turns around in a huff. "Anna, what the hell? Is this another Sam and Gabe surprise hang? Thought we've been there, done that."

"What?" I stumble off my bike, confused. "No, of course not." But as I walk closer to the house, sure enough, I see Gabe, Sam, and my moms standing in the driveway, deep in conversation.

"I think something is going on," Del says. We all pick up the pace as we make our way up the driveway.

"Honey." Mimi notices us and hurries over to me before I can even greet Gabe and Sam or ask why they're here. She gives me a huge hug and when I try to end the embrace, she hugs me harder.

Confused, I ask, "Everything okay?" I escape Mimi's hug with all of my ribs intact.

Mom looks me in the eye and speaks softly, but firmly. "Anna, while you were out, someone came to the house and graffitied the driveway." She gives my shoulder a gentle squeeze.

I step around my moms, who seem somewhat unwilling to move aside. There, in red paint, scrawled in large, looping cursive is: "Hippie Slut." And I realize that Instagram post was only the beginning of Caroline's rage.

I look up and meet Gabe's eyes. He moves toward me, concern in his eyes, and places an arm around my shoulder, bringing me in for a hug. "This is awful, Anna. I'm sorry." I breathe in his scent and feel calmer immediately. I want to curl into his chest and cry, but I manage to keep my composure.

Mason watches our interaction with a frozen expression, but once our eyes meet, he gently says, "This is totally out of line."

Sam lightly squeezes my shoulder. "Yeah, I can't believe she did this."

"She?" Del stops hunching over the graffiti and stands up straight. "You know who did it?"

"Gabe and Sam actually came over to find you, Anna. Apparently, they suspected Caroline Loran was really upset," Mom explains, giving the boys an approving nod.

"But we were too late. This was here when we arrived."

"How do you know for sure it was Caroline?" Del asks, always the journalist.

"I recognize her handwriting and, as Ms. Morningstar said, she was really spinning out today about…" Gabe pauses and looks at me. "Us. About us."

Mason's face is rigid with anger. "We have to do something. She defiled your property. What a completely heinous person."

"Or a person in a whole lot of pain." Gabe sounds troubled.

"Of course you'd defend her," Mason snaps.

"I'm not defending this. It's indefensible." He looks at the writing on the pavement and frowns. "I'm saying this seems really unhinged and as someone who does know her, it worries me."

Mimi looks fondly at Gabe. "That's a really empathetic view, Gabe."

Mason looks stung. "I wasn't trying to be unsympathetic. I just feel really protective of Anna."

"Of course, hon. I had the same feeling," Mom reassures Mason. "I think our first step is to call the school and the Lorans."

I nod, but I can't really feel anything. "Yes, okay."

The seven of us stare at the paint a little longer.

"We need to get this fixed up," Mom says.

Mimi tilts her head. "Might be difficult to find somebody on the weekend."

"If you don't mind the intrusion, Sam and I could get the lacrosse team over here first thing in the morning to take care of it. We'd like to help." Gabe takes a step closer to me.

"Ugh, then the whole team would see this," I point out.

"Why don't we take a beat and figure it out?" Del asks, taking my hand and squeezing.

"Great idea, Del. Gabe, what's the latest you'd have to let the guys know if we want them to come remove this?" Mimi asks.

"Anytime is fine. Whatever you need."

"Let me call our old contractor and see if he can get someone on it immediately." Mimi pulls out her phone and starts taking notes on it. "Lilly, sweetheart, let's make sure we document this." She then turns to the rest of us. "Okay, kids, why don't you all hang out back, and I'll bring you some warm beverages?"

"Like your famous hot cocoa?" Gabe's eyes light up.

"Ah, so you've tried it before. Interesting, I wasn't aware." Mimi gives me a pointed look.

Gabe's face falls. "It was just an innocent porch swing chat."

Mimi and Mom both chuckle. "We have no doubt. I was just teasing. Mostly."

"So were there a lot of these porch swing chats?" Mason asks as we head to the backyard to add logs to the fire pit.

"There were a few," I say, feeling some joy returning at the mention of my early days alone with Gabe.

We sit down and, right off the bat, I say, "Okay, can we please not talk about Caroline or her lovely artwork for the next hour? I'm fine. I just don't want to think about it."

"Deal," Sam says. "So, how was the play? Was it one of the good ones or one of the weird ones?"

"Do you see a lot of plays at the Shed?" Del asks, surprised.

"Just a few with my parents. I was only saying that because Anna's told us some hysterical stories about the really out-there ones."

Gabe laughs. "Yeah, like the one where, for twenty minutes, the farmer 'milked' some actor dressed in a cow suit? That sounded ridiculous."

I want to disappear into the stone bench so no one can see me.

"Huh? Anna loved *The Feeder*. We all did." Mason looks at me for confirmation.

"Uh, well, I understood its value once I heard Del's thoughts on it and I read that review you sent me. But to be honest, I didn't totally connect with it at the time."

Mason looks strangely betrayed.

"Do you know what I saw there that was super cool? *Copenhagen*," Gabe recalls.

Del nods. "Yeah, I thought that was so well-done."

"Wow, look at us! Just a couple of theater dweebs vibing," Sam jokes.

Mimi comes out and offers everyone a choice between hot chocolate or apple cider, and for the next forty-five minutes we talk about everything except the red paint in front of the house.

Just before everyone leaves, Del and I excuse ourselves to go to the bathroom. Sam and Gabe tease us for making such a cliché move, and Mason cracks a joke about being left with the "enemy" that sounds like he's only half-kidding. Once we're indoors, I take the opportunity to ask Del what she thinks of Gabe.

"I think he seems really great, Anna. I do. I kind of get it more now, but there's something I need to tell you."

"What?" I ask, thrilled by the first part of her statement and apprehensive about the second.

"I wanted to tell you this before the play, but then you sprang the Gabe thing on us."

I nod and motion for her to go on.

"Well, as you asked me to, I've been looking into the whole Bookcourt drama."

"Okay." I gulp nervously.

"We know Alfred hired Brenson Oakes to fight the employees' unionization attempts, but…"

I bite my lip. It's clear by Del's expression she's nervous to tell me the rest. Suddenly, I don't think the drama is about employee infighting and edibles anymore.

"It looks like Senator Delgado's office called in a favor for Alfred to be able to retain the firm. Remember, Scottie Peters' dad is a partner at Brenson Oakes and a huge donor to the senator's reelection campaign."

"Okay, that sounds shady," I say, feeling a little sick. "But why would Senator Delgado and Mr. Peters even get involved at this level of town stuff?"

"I wondered that too until I started reading some of the senator's recent speeches. I think he's going to base a lot of his re-election campaign on opposing unions. Bookcourt and the Adlers are likely pawns in that game."

I blink, my shoulder slumping.

"Do you think Gabe knew about any of this?" Del asks.

Startled by the thought, I manage to say, "I don't know. If he did, I hope he would have told me. He knows how much tension the Bookcourt stuff has caused."

Del and I look at each other for another moment.

I let out a long breath. "This night is not turning out how I expected."

Del gives me a sympathetic glance. "I know."

# CHAPTER
## 34

This bookstore information Del shared with me? I can't get it out of my head. So the next morning, I invite Gabe over to talk. I can tell by his response that he assumes it's about the Caroline situation, and that assumption is confirmed when he sits next to me on the porch swing and starts apologizing.

"I'm so sorry about yesterday. I can't believe she did that."

"Yeah, it was so shocking ... and so embarrassing... and so funny because it's so far from the truth. But it still stings. It's like she's calling me dirty."

"It's pretty messed up that anyone is still using sex to define a woman's worth. How much, or how little, sex you have is your business."

I look at Gabe, a little taken aback. "That is totally true... and so woke of you."

"God forbid," he responds with a smile.

"As awful as it is, part of me is wondering if this ups my social cachet? Like, if the popular mean girl is targeting me, doesn't that make me the star of this very twisted show?" When he stares at me blankly, I laugh. "Don't mind me. I'm just a total mess at the moment."

"You're sort of a wacko, but a cute one." Gabe runs a hand through his hair. "I feel like this is all my fault." He turns to me. "I promise I won't let her mess with you anymore."

"Thanks," I say. I can't resist smiling back at him, but then I quickly frown. "Ew."

"What's wrong?"

"I was just enjoying feeling protected by you. But I can totally protect myself, and I don't want to crave male protection. That's just not me."

Gabe shakes his head like he has no idea what I'm talking about. "Uh, okay."

"I think it's because you're so handsome and such an awesome kisser. It makes the facts of the situation confusing for me."

His face relaxes. "The kisses have been pretty freaking awesome. Speaking of which…"

Gabe inches closer to me. He places a hand on my cheek and gently traces my cheek bone. Every muscle in my body feels like jelly. He leans in closer, and my heart drums with anticipation. I can't wait to feel his lips on mine again, to be transported. But then I remember why I invited him here.

I lightly put my hands on his chest. "Wait."

Gabe looks at me, surprised. The lust still in his eyes sends shivers down my spine. Part of me wants to ignore my questions and jump into his arms, but I can't. "Look Gabe, the real reason I asked you to come talk is because I need to know something." I quickly repeat what Del told me, barely pausing to take a breath. "So it kind of seems like your dad and Mr. Peters brokered a deal between Alfred and Brenson Oakes. Did you know about any of this?"

Gabe's eyes close for a moment and then open. "I didn't know directly, but I suspected."

"And you didn't tell me?"

"I was already starting to have feelings for you when I overhead my dad saying something to Mr. Peters about the firm, and I knew you'd flip out." Gabe looks down. "I didn't want to get in between my dad's politics and you, so I decided it would be better for me just not to get involved at all."

I look at Gabe, not sure what to feel about his passivity. "I feel so upset. Not just at you, but mostly at myself. I was so wrong."

"Wrong about what?"

"The whole Bookcourt thing. It was all a manipulation to hurt workers, led by your father and his evil minions."

Gabe's expression freezes. "Are you joking? It wasn't a Machiavellian plot. My dad is against organized labor for a lot of the same reasons you were defending Bookcourt. It erodes relationships between employees and management, it's impossible to fire bad employees, and it hurts small businesses. I thought we agreed on that?"

"No! I'm completely for unions, in all situations! I was confused before."

"Anna, listen to yourself. Nothing has changed except that you found out my dad arranged for a law firm to help Ms. Adler. You were so worried about her before."

I shake my head, the truth of his words hitting me. "I was being willfully blind. I refused to let myself think that someone I like could be doing stuff that was wrong. In reality, she's left the employees completely vulnerable. Don't you see that?"

"It's a lot more nuanced than that, and you know it."

"Can't you just answer anything directly? Don't you think it's messed up that your dad got Brenson Oakes involved? It doesn't give the employees a chance. It's created a massive power imbalance."

"Look, my dad helped Alfred make a strong point, and I get it was a little much. But it's no more extreme than your friends refusing to set foot in there, a store that's a local staple and may not survive this boycott."

I shake my head. "I hate this feeling."

"What feeling?"

"Not knowing what to do or how to feel."

Gabe looks at me with a steady gaze. "My grandmother says when you're feeling confused, you're usually seeing things right. And I think that's mostly true."

"Ugh. I hope not!"

"Do you know what's even more confusing?"

"What?"

"How much I want to kiss you right now even though I know it feels like we're kind of mad at each other."

I let out a shaky breath. Our eyes lock, and I swear I can hear his heart pounding. Or maybe it's mine. The sound roars in my ears. Acting on pure impulse, I lean in, anticipating the warm, wonderful feeling of his lips on mine, but then a thought occurs to me. I pull back abruptly.

"What's wrong?" he asks.

"There are some things that aren't confusing at all, you know."

"Meaning?"

Air whooshes out of my lungs. "There's something that's been bothering me since we first talked about it at Mooburger. And I guess seeing how you're responding to your dad's involvement in Bookcourt is reminding me of it."

"What?"

"What are your real views on gay marriage? It kind of sounds like you could take it or leave it?"

Gabe looks a little startled. "I absolutely think people should marry whoever they want. No question."

I let out a huge sigh of relief. I grab his lapels and pull him closer to me. I can barely wait to be in his arms again.

He gives me an amused look, and lets me pull him forward. He leans over, I tilt my head, and—

"Wait!" I slam my hands back on his chest.

Gabe blinks. "Now what, Morningstar?" he says with a cross between a groan and a laugh.

"But what about your dad?"

Gabe takes a breath to compose himself. "He voted against it. Dad thinks a civil union should suffice and that marriage is a religious institution."

"That's bullshit."

Gabe nods. "I agree. It's messed up. But that's how he thinks."

I shake my head. "So what do you do to try to change his mind?"

He blinks. "I don't."

"What do you mean?"

"I don't get involved with my dad about that kind of stuff."

"That's what you say about everything! But it's wrong. What your dad is doing is wrong."

"I give him the benefit of the doubt. He needs to please a lot of people to stay in his job. It's complicated."

"Denying two people in love the right to get married is not complicated," I spit out.

Gabe looks wary. "Look, Anna, I agree with you. But my dad doesn't."

"And you're willing to stay silent about such an important issue? We're talking about my family's right to exist."

"Look, the truth is, until I started hanging out with you, my dad's views on gay marriage weren't at the top of my mind. I think his positions on the economy, on national security, on the budget, on job growth are a million times better than the Democrats who run against him. And I placed those issues first."

"And now that you do know me... know my moms?"

"I've been thinking about it a lot more."

"So you'll talk to your dad about it?"

"I didn't say that. He gets enough liberal flack from Mateo and Bea, I don't want to add to that dynamic."

"That dynamic? It's not a dynamic. It affects basic human rights."

"I understand, but I'm not ready to commit to some big confrontation with him. I'm not like you. I don't think there has to be one right way to do things all the time."

"What does that mean?"

"Like even with your best friends, you decide their opinion about a play is the right one, and you dismiss your own gut instinct. Why? You're so afraid to be unsure of anything and to be on the 'wrong' side. Look at how you just flip-flopped your whole attitude about Bookcourt. Nuance matters. Everything isn't black and white."

"Yeah, well, do you know what *is* black and white? A person's right to marry whoever the fuck they want."

"I'm not disagreeing with you about that!"

"Yeah, you're just refusing to talk to someone who makes actual policy about it! I can't believe I was about to kiss you again."

Gabe looks offended. "Same."

We exchange one more furious look before he turns and leaves. I storm inside hoping he can hear the front door slam.

# CHAPTER 35

I'm determined to start the week with as much space from Gabe and any Northsiders as possible. I recommit myself to pursuing social good every day (except Monday, of course). Thank God it's a four-day week at school, and I have time to collect myself before our next training session.

I am fine, just fine, I remind myself. I don't need Gabe Delgado or his kisses! I need someone who will stand up to the wrongs of the world with me.

When I walk into homeroom on Tuesday, Ms. Carrie hands me a note saying that I need to see the guidance counselor. I trudge off to Ms. Thatcher's office feeling uneasy. I hope Caroline isn't there too. I've already had to deal with a mix of concerned, curious, and nosy text messages from both the Liaisons and my track teammates about the graffiti incident. Between that and the way a few classmates stared at me in the hall this morning, I'm not in the mood to deal with anything else.

"Annabelle, have a seat. I want to talk about the spray paint incident." Ms. Thatcher gives me a sympathetic look. She places a box of tissues on a small table next to my seat. I look at them, remembering how, last time I was in her office, I started crying about college. I doubt I'll cry today, but you never know.

"Hey, Ms. T, I'm really doing okay with the whole Caroline

thing. Honestly, I have so much else on my mind right now that being a 'hippie slut' isn't even in my top-three concerns. Though it's embarrassing, I'm kind of just ignoring it. Actually, I've taken a 'I know this will all pass soon' kind of approach. Does that make sense?"

Ms. Thatcher nods as if she almost understands what I'm saying. "Well, it sounds like you're certainly processing your feelings about the vandalism, but I want to talk to you about the school's response."

"Oh?"

"As you know, Edgartown High has a zero-tolerance policy for bullying. So Caroline is at home until we figure out next steps. While the disciplinary decision is being made, we would like to hear your thoughts about the incident."

"Really? You're going to let me decide what happens to Caroline? I don't know if that's really an ideal policy, Ms. T."

Ms. Thatcher smiles. "Not 'decide,' Annabelle. We find it beneficial to hear the victim's point of view. As part of the disciplinary proceedings, I'll be reading a statement on your behalf. The punishment for her behavior can be anything from mandated counseling to full expulsion."

"Full expulsion? Wow."

"I doubt that will happen given…" Ms. Thatcher breaks off and clears her throat, as if she's already said too much.

It's obvious what she's thinking. Caroline's family is way too rich for the school to kick her out.

"Well, anyway, this isn't something you have to decide now. Just consider it over the next few days, and let me know your thoughts. You can either write out what you'd like me to read or come in again, and we can formulate a statement together."

\* \* \* \*

My conversation with Ms. Thatcher consumes my mind for the next two days. Actually, though, it's a welcome distraction from thinking about how much I miss Gabe. We haven't talked or texted since our fight.

Everyone has an opinion about what I should tell Ms. Thatcher. Mom thinks I should go for the jugular, and Mimi, usually a pacifist, agrees, to my surprise. Mason and Zoe (whose opinion I did not directly seek out) say I should carefully document the whole thing so when the rich kid predictably gets let off, we can rally against the school decision. Sam thinks a short suspension would suffice. Del's vote is for community service and suspension.

But even with all these ideas, I still feel lost on how to respond to Ms. Thatcher. I keep picturing Gabe saying that only someone in a lot of pain would lash out like that. I also keep obsessing over his accusation that I don't understand nuance. I guess it's true that I usually do think that I—or at least the people around me—know exactly what to do and what is right.

I find Gabe in the hall after school and ask if he has a minute. He seems surprised but nods. Even though looking at his lovely face makes my heart hurt, I really want to know what he thinks Caroline deserves.

"The school is taking an interesting approach," he observes after I fill him on my meeting with Ms. Thatcher. "Are you asking what I think?"

"I am." I appreciate that he checks to make sure I want his advice. No one else has done that.

"Okay, well, I think Caroline has a lot of demons. She doesn't feel lovable. And yes, I know, poor little rich girl boo hoo, but it's still sad. And for the sake of everyone in our community, I think she needs to work through her anger issues. That being said, consequences are important."

"So a mixture of therapy and an official reprimand of some sort?"

"Sounds right to me, but she did this to you, Anna. You have to decide what feels fair."

"I doubt the school will listen to me anyway. Mason's right that asking my opinion is probably all for show."

"It might be, but I bet it will feel good to speak your part."

"Yeah. Thanks, Gabe."

He nods. I can't read his expression. "Okay then, I have to get going. I guess I'll see you Monday."

"Yeah, sure, see you Monday."

I walk away quickly, not wanting Gabe to see the emotion in my eyes.

The next day at school, I decide to tell Ms. Thatcher I'd like Caroline to return to school, but to also go to therapy and do community service. That feels right. Ms. Thatcher thanks me for my thoughtful feedback. The next week, when all the school's computers are replaced with new ones, I hear they're a giant gift from Caroline's dad. I never find out exactly what the school decides about Caroline's punishment—the school says that's a completely private matter—but I hope she at least goes to therapy.

# CHAPTER

## 36

Thursday night, I'm sitting at the kitchen island staring blankly at my History assignment. I've spent most of the school week pretending I'm more okay than I feel, clinging to Del and Mason and dreading even catching a glimpse of Gabe.

When Mom and Mimi join me in the kitchen, I glance at the microwave clock, surprised they're both home by 5 pm.

"Hi. You all are home early." To my disappointment, their hands are empty. Sometimes when they sense I'm having a bad day, they come home bearing pastries. I note the serious expressions on their faces and think "Uh-oh. Am I in trouble?"

Mom answers "Yes," at the same time Mimi responds "No."

They look at each other and smile. I sink lower into my stool. They sit in chairs on either side of me.

"Listen, sweetie, we know it's been a rough week, so we wait-ed to talk to you about this," says Mimi. "But you have to pay some price for lying to us about sleeping at Mary Sue's."

"Especially when you slept at your boyfriend's house, a fact I didn't realize when I first spoke to you about this."

"He wasn't my boyfriend then, and he isn't now. Remember? We're done," I say glumly, staring down at my lap. I hate feeling so miserable so often.

"Either way, we've gone out of our way to explain to you that as long as you're honest with us, we won't punish you, but that premise is based on trust." Mom's face is firm.

"Was that not clear to you, Annabelle?" Mimi asks, concerned.

I wince. Between Caroline's spray painting and the Gabe fallout, I almost completely forgot about my fib. "It is," I assure her. "I know if I'm drinking or have any questions about almost anything, I can come to you."

"So why was that night different?" Mimi asks.

"I thought you guys would be really mad I was at Gabe's."

"Because he's a boy?"

"Because he's a Northsider...and a Delgado."

Mimi gives Mom a reproachful look. "Lilly, I'll let you take this one."

Mom genuflects slightly. "Honey, I'm sorry if I ever made you feel like Gabe's family was unacceptable to me." She sighs. "Their politics are very hard for me to swallow, but I'll always make room to accept anyone you value. I can promise you that."

I look at my mom, touched. I give her a big smile. She pats my back gently.

"I'm sorry I lied." I look at Mimi. "I should have known I didn't have to."

"And we really can't have this happen again. I need you to understand that, Annabelle. It's not acceptable to lie to us like that. Understood?"

I nod somberly and meet Mimi's eyes first, then Mom's so both can see I'm serious.

"So you're grounded for a week. Go straight to school and straight back home every day. No coffee with Del or Mason. No porch-side chats with Gabe."

"I'm really missing your initial loose attitude, Mom."

Mimi eyes Mom. "Loose attitude?"

"I didn't realize they were romantically involved at the time!"

"By bringing that up, you're really rubbing salt in my wounds here!"

My moms turn to me and give me a stern look.

"Fine, fine. Grounded for a week." I look at them. "I *am* sorry I lied. I really won't do it again. Even though I think depriving me of coffee borders on child abuse."

"Anna," Mimi warns.

"Joking. Got it. Really."

My moms both relax visibly and get up from their chairs to start making dinner. I let out a breath and turn back to my history book, feeling a little more focused. But just as I start to read about the New Deal, a banging at the double French doors off the kitchen catches my attention.

Mimi gets to the door first. "Hi, Del." She looks at Del's flustered face. "Are you okay?"

"I don't know. I was kind of hoping to get Lilly's opinion on something I think I uncovered."

I jump out of my seat and get Del a glass of water as she slides onto a stool and places onto the island the three-ring binder she's been gripping. I'm almost worried about her. It is so unusual to see her flustered.

"Okay, so when I was looking into the Alfred and Brenson Oakes connection, I stumbled across something weird about Tom."

"The graduate student who worked at Bookcourt?" Mimi asks.

"Tom was a new hire and the instigator of the union discussion among employees," Mom says matter-of-factly, but she's looking at Del with rapt attention now.

I remember that Mom interviewed Tom on her show at the start of the whole debacle.

"Well, it turns out Tom was writing his dissertation on unions. He'd been working on it for years," Del says, handing my mom a stack of papers from the binder. Mom starts to scan them as Del continues. "But the proposal for his final project, dated six months before he started working at Bookcourt, details a sociological field study in which he planned to rouse union interest among employees."

"Is this a draft of his final paper?" Mom asks, paging through a lengthy document and looking at Del with surprise.

"Yes," she says, avoiding eye contact.

"And how did you get this?"

"Do you really want to know?"

"Probably not." Lilly's eyes round as she reads through more material. "So Tom, having realized he couldn't go after Ms. Adler or the store finances since it was barely making a profit, then zeroed in on Alfred?"

"Exactly," Del confirms.

I shake my head. "So Tom was manipulating everyone?"

"It looks like it." Mom frowns. "Del, if we can find a way to get this information in a more legitimate way, I could have you on the show."

Del's jaw drops. "Are you serious? That would be amazing."

I smile, happy for my friend, but I feel uneasy. "Shouldn't someone talk to Ms. Adler about this?" I say. "Between Alfred and Tom and Senator Delgado's campaign, her business is kind of being used as a prop. That seems really awful."

"It's really quite upsetting," Mimi agrees.

"Interestingly, even if Tom manipulated his way into the store, I think he did expose some real vulnerabilities for the workers there," Mom adds.

"But, Mom, even if that's true, essentially what is happening is that three men are trying to control a business owned by a woman. A woman who put her blood, sweat, and tears into it."

Mom looks at me thoughtfully. "That's an excellent point, Anna."

"So what should we do about it?"

"I'll talk to Ms. Adler, explain to her what we found out, and see what she wants to do with the information," Mimi says.

My mom and Del both nod. "I think that's a great idea."

I'm beyond relieved Mimi is taking charge of the conversation. But I'm conflicted about the Bookcourt situation. My mind spins as I try to figure out what Del's revelation means for the bigger issues at play—the attempts at unionizing, the machinations of a mercenary law firm, the future of independent bookstores. I feel further away than ever from figuring out my feelings about the boycott. But as Del and my moms continue to talk, I wonder if Gabe had a point after all. Maybe being unsure is the most sensible way to feel on such a thorny issue.

# CHAPTER
## 37

After a truly miserable weekend, filled with missing Gabe, and just generally feeling suck-y, I wake up Monday with a bit of a lift. I tell myself it's not because I know that I'll see him. I feel optimistic as I sit down to breakfast, a yogurt parfait with berries and a fresh mint sprig on top. Mimi gives me a kiss on the head as she heads out for an early surgery. This means Mom is making my lunch, which won't be half as good as Mimi's, but I don't bother to say so since I'm in such a good mood.

Mimi walks back into the kitchen a moment later.

"Forget something?" Mom asks.

"No, Anna has a visitor."

Is it Gabe? My heart beats wildly as mom and I both turn to find ourselves staring at the tear-stained face of Beatriz Delgado. Her brown hair is in two pigtails, which somehow make the tears even sadder.

"Bea," I say, alarmed. "Are you okay?"

"She's probably just overwhelmed by living with the patriarchy," Mom suggests under her breath. Mimi and I both glare at her.

"It was a joke," Mom insists.

"I'm late for work and have to go. Lilly, I take it you'll remember the age of your current audience."

Mom sends a somewhat mocking two thumbs up, then adds more somberly, "Yes, of course."

Mimi hurries out.

"What does patriarchy mean?" Bea asks as she slides onto the stool next to me, eyes still teary.

My mom winces, obviously feeling bad that Bea overhead the dig.

She looks at my drink. "Is that coffee? Can I have one?" She looks hopefully toward my mom, who shoots her a genuine smile.

"Think we're a little young for that, but can I offer you steamed milk with some chocolate powder on top?"

Bea smiles through her tears. "Deal. Thank you." She looks around and nods approvingly. "This is a really cool place."

"Oh, thanks," my mom says, now biting her lip to keep from laughing. Seems like Bea, despite her parentage, has already done the impossible and charmed Lilly Morningstar.

"So, Bea," I say once she seems relatively calmed down. "What exactly are you doing here?"

"Oh, right." Bea straightens her shoulders bravely, but her chin quivers. "I need your help with a big problem."

"What sort of big problem, honey?" My mom looks concerned and softens her voice.

"A boy problem!"

"Any boy in particular, or all of them in general?" Mom asks.

"One in particular!" Bea exclaims with a fresh round of tears. "But I think he hates me."

Mom and I look at each other, concerned and uncertain. We are out of practice at dealing with the emotions of twelve-year-old girls.

"I'm sure he doesn't hate you," Mom says, again in a surprisingly gentle tone.

"Yeah, he does!"

"That's hard to imagine. You seem pretty awesome to me." I grin.

"What exactly happened, Bea?" my mom presses.

"Noah happened."

"Noah Brent?" I realize she's likely referring to Mason's little brother.

"Yeah! That's why I came here. Gabe told me that Mason was once your bestie, which is beyond cool, so I thought you could help." She smiles at me before her face falls in another glum expression. Even her pigtails seem to sag with sadness.

"I'm sure he thinks you're pretty neat too!" I insist.

"He definitely does not." Bea's voice trails off as more hiccupping sobs are heard.

My mom places a cup of water in front of Bea and instructs her to breathe.

"In one, out one." Bea closes her eyes and exhales with exaggerated focus.

My mom and I both press the back of our hands to our mouths to stop ourselves from laughing.

She eventually gets to ten and clasps her hands in front of her, resting them on the kitchen island, and slowly, deliberately, opens her eyes. "Something happened. Something awful." She pauses dramatically.

Mom motions for her to go on.

"I've thought for so long that he's the cutest boy in my class, but he never seems to notice me! Which is beyond awful, you know?"

"It's always hard to feel ignored," Mom sympathizes.

"So you want us to help you get him to notice you more?" I ask, hoping that's not it.

Bea puts her head in her hands. "I wish! I tried that on my own, and it was a disaster. See, I pulled out his chair as he was sitting down for Social Studies yesterday. You know, as a joke, but he fell super-hard, and he started crying really hard, and everyone started teasing him for being a wimp!"

I wince. "Okay, not ideal. But I'm sure he knows it was an accident."

"No! He definitely does not! He turned to me and said, 'I'm never talking to you again,' and I told him, 'You never talked to me in the first place!' And then he just ran out of the room still crying! I really didn't think he'd fall *that* hard."

"Yeah, well, Mason is just as annoying as Noah. His girlfriend is always so mean to me, and Mason does nothing!" I realize I'm stooping to the level of a sixth grader, so I pull myself back. "I'm sorry, Bea. That sucks."

"I don't even want to go to school today."

"Honey, in this case, a simple apology would go a long way," Mom insists.

"Really? He seemed super upset," Bea says doubtfully.

"Well, look on the bright side. He definitely knows who you are now," I point out.

"That's true!" She beams at me. "So, knowing what you do about Brent boys, do you think he'll forgive me?"

I smile. "I do. They're sensitive souls, those Brents, but they have big hearts."

"Yay!" Bea beams. "Okay, I think I can go to school after all."

"So glad to hear that, and just in time, too." Mom looks at the clock on the microwave. "Let's get going, ladies. We've got hearts and minds to change." She sails out of the kitchen, and Bea and I walk quickly in her wake. She pauses in the foyer. "Wait, Bea. Do your parents know where you are?"

Bea twirls her hair. "I left them a note, but I snuck out before anyone was up. Didn't think they'd agree that me biking here before school was the emergency it absolutely was." She scratches her head. "I doubt they'll even notice because Gabe and my dad have been too busy fighting to even listen to me."

Mom looks caught between humor and alarm. "Okay, well, let's take you home, sweetheart. We'll fix the rest later."

As we head out, I ask Bea, "Do you know what the fighting is all about?"

She shrugs. "I don't really know. I just heard all the yelling, which is weird because Gabe never yells at my parents. He's quite the boring teenager. Right?"

I open my mouth to ask her another question, but my mom hurries us along, and the moment is lost.

# CHAPTER
## 38

"Thank you so much for bringing her back, Lilly. I'd like to wring her neck for this, but I'm so darn happy to see her." Mrs. Delgado is still hugging Bea even though we've been having the same awkward conversation in their front hall for five minutes.

Senator Delgado is shaking his head, his relief palpable. "Our Bea, always keeping us on our toes! All of this over some boy. I thought I had another few years before I had to worry about that." He turns to me. "Annabelle, how is school going for you? Studying hard?"

"Yes, sir," I say with a nod.

My mom gives me a glance at my use of "sir." I return a look that I hope says, "When in Rome…"

"And track? Big meet on Friday, Gabe tells me."

My eyes round. "Ah, yes, that's right." I couldn't believe Gabe knew about the girl's meet, much less told his dad about it.

"Well, if you make as big an impact on the track as you do on my son, I'd say Edgartown's running team is in great shape."

I'm startled by Senator's Delgado's comment.

For another moment, we all stand around in awkward silence. Then Bea asks, "Mom, Dad: Can they come over to dinner sometime? You know, to thank them for taking such good care of me when I ran away."

"I don't know if an hour-long absence with a detailed note saying where you were going and why counts as 'running away,' but of course," the Senator says.

Mom laughs at this.

"She left out that part, didn't she?" Mrs. Delgado smiles at my mom. "Not that we love you leaving the house without telling us, young lady."

"But we'd be honored to have the whole Morningstar family join us for a meal … no matter what you say about me on TV." Senator Delgado laughs good-humoredly.

I can tell my mom is on the verge of saying something most unfriendly.

Before she has the chance, Bea claps her hands and jumps up and down. "Great! So you'll come? Can we do it tomorrow?"

We all laugh at her enthusiasm.

"Tomorrow might be a little soon. But would Friday the 30th work? Lilly, we're actually having the head of Edgartown College over. That might be enjoyable for everyone."

My mom remains silent a beat longer than is comfortable. I can't read her expression, and then it dawns on me. She's feeling awkward! She's not sure what to do. I stare at her. So that's what social discomfort on Lilly Morningstar looks like.

Before she can answer, Gabe comes through the door. My heart leaps to my throat. He's back from a run, wearing a black sleeveless shirt and matching Nike shorts. His skin is slicked with sweat that makes his dark hair curl.

Gabe smiles when he sees his sister. "Bea, you've come back," he says in a mocking relieved tone. He gives her a sweaty hug before she shoves him off. "I actually ran to your house to see if she was still there." He flashes me a smile that has my insides curling.

I realize that if I keep looking at Gabe in his running clothes, I might spontaneously combust or otherwise humiliate myself. "Whoa, look at the time, Mom. School, work… shouldn't we all get going?"

She raises a brow at my strained tone. "You're right. I have a meeting in thirty minutes, and you've got to get to school."

I'm relieved at her all-business tone. It means we're about to go into super-speed mode.

"I can take you to school," Gabe offers.

I gulp. This is the last thing I need.

Mom looks conflicted. I know my friendship with Gabe makes her a little uneasy, but after a look at her watch, she says to him, "That would be a huge help."

I glare at my mom. Can't she tell I'm in distress? She looks at me, confused. "Is that okay, Anna?"

All eyes turn to me. Why do parents do this? Asking me if "it's okay" in such a public fashion is not in any way helpful! It's like I'm being abducted at gunpoint, and she's asking my kidnapper if I mind getting in the unmarked black car with the male abductor. Yes, I do mind! But of course what I actually say is, "Totally fine. Thanks, Gabe."

Mom nods and glances at her watch again. "Okay, well, what an exciting morning. Bea, it was a true pleasure."

"And we can brainstorm more ideas on Friday about how to handle Noah."

"Those Brents are such pains in the asses." Gabe glowers.

"Language," his mom reminds him.

He gives her a thousand-watt smile in response.

Is anyone going to make him shower? I wonder somewhat desperately. I'm unsure what I might do if I have to keep looking at sweat glistening all over his insane body.

"Friday?" Mom looks confused for a second, then remembers the accepted dinner invitation she has conveniently blocked from memory.

"For the dinner. You're coming, right?" Bea's eyes grow huge, as if she's horrified at the idea that we might not join them.

"Right, of course. Thanks so much for the invitation. Just let us know the time and what we can bring," Mom says in a strained tone.

Senator Delgado smiles knowingly at my mom. "It could be worse, Lilly. We could have invited the Peters family over too."

Lilly's eyes narrow. "But, you see, then we just wouldn't come at all," she says.

The Senator's eyes narrow even more than my mom's. He opens his mouth as if he's about to respond in kind.

His wife jumps in. "Hold it, sweetheart." She turns to my mom. "Please just bring yourselves and tell Mimi I'm looking forward to having you all over."

Mom nods again, and Bea says, "I'll walk you out!"

Gabe turns to me. "I'll be down in ten." He gives me a smile, and I find myself completely flustered.

Gabe heads upstairs and Senator Delgado excuses himself to return a call.

Mrs. Delgado pats me on the arm. "Don't worry, honey. The Delgado men tend to have that effect on ladies. It's terribly frustrating."

I smile weakly, beyond embarrassed that Gabe's mom seems to have noticed I have the serious hots for her son.

# CHAPTER

## 39

$A$fter Mrs. Delgado leaves to take Bea to school, I find myself alone. Before leaving, she offered me tea and the choice of enjoying it in the kitchen or on the commodious outdoor loveseat on the side of the house—apparently it remains a favorite thinking place of her children. I settle into the seat (it's really quite cozy) and let my mind drift to the image of Gabe sweaty in his sleeveless workout ensemble. What makes that look so sexy? I wonder as I remember the shape of his arms, the cut of his cheekbones, the intensity of his golden-brown eyes. Am I really so helpless before the sight of raw masculinity?

"Ready to go?"

Gabe's voice makes me jump out of my seat.

"Startled you," Gabe laughs, gently reaching out to steady my hands so I don't spill my tea. I am now standing before him. He slowly drops his hands from mine. Gabe's close enough for me to breathe in his woodsy smell. Damn it. "Ugh," I say out loud, feeling my pulse race. "I still have the hots for you. It's completely uncomfortable."

Gabe lifts a brow. "I thought I was too much of a Northsider for you?"

"I thought you were too." I look him squarely in the eye. "Speaking of that, Bea made it sound like you were fighting with your dad about something?"

"She's such a big mouth. But yes, I did get into it with him."

"Can I ask about what?" I give him a sheepish look. "I know I'm being unforgivably nosy, but I'm dying of curiosity."

The corner of Gabe's mouth twitches in humor. "Well, we can't have you die, now can we?"

"So…" I prompt.

The smile falls from Gabe's face. "I tried to talk to him about how important I think it is to fully support gay marriage, and the conversation escalated quickly."

My heart thuds in my chest. "Wow, Gabe. What did he say?"

"He basically let me know he disagrees and thinks I've been brainwashed, likely by you."

"Oh, hmm." I look down, not sure how to feel about all of this. "It means a lot to me that you tried."

Gabe moves his shoulders like he feels an itch between his shoulder blades. "Well, what you said kind of stuck."

"Annoying, isn't it?"

"Yeah, super annoying."

"I can relate."

"You can?"

"Yeah, this surprisingly insightful guy I know told me I have a problem with nuance, and I've spent the last week basically thinking about all the times that's actually true. Especially with this Bookcourt craziness, and even how I pretended to like that dumb play at the college. I just assumed I was missing something, like I do any time my moms, Del, or Mason think something is a good or worthy cause."

"Hard to have parents like ours. They're pretty convincing."

"They sure are."

Silence spins out between us.

"I really missed you this week," I finally say.

Gabe's expression softens. "Me too. I've missed your hot-headed comments. No one sees the world quite like you." He pushes a curl behind my ear, takes a step closer to me, then pauses as if seeking my permission to do or say more.

"I've really missed seeing all the small, sweet things you do

216

and hearing your ideas—you're always so steady and wise. It's comforting."

Gabe eliminates more of the distance between us.

I feel like my heart is going to thump out of my chest. My mind scrambles with anticipation and concern about the state of my coffee breath.

He pauses and drops his hand. I see what I think looks like fear in his eyes.

"What's wrong?" I ask a little breathlessly.

"It's just occurring to me how complicated this could be." His voice sounds uneven.

"Isn't it already?"

We're still standing close. I can feel his gentle exhale on my skin.

"We did this once and ended up in a huge fight."

"True," I acknowledge, but I'm so distracted by all my swirling desires, I can't focus.

"I think we should go on a proper date." He nods his head as if convinced by his own words. He takes a step back. His smile grows more confident. "We haven't really done that yet."

I tilt my head, confused. "You think that will make things less complicated? I was thinking we could just keep hooking up and going on runs together until we figure this out."

"Well, as appealing and romantic as that sounds… are you free Saturday?"

"Romantic?" I say, startled.

"You don't want a date to be romantic?"

"Can't it be casual?"

Gabe laughs. "Is that supposed to keep you from falling for me?"

I grimace. "Something like that."

He smiles. "If you say so."

"Wait, I can't come on Saturday. I'm grounded," I groan. "Long story short, but it's totally our fault."

"Alright, so we wait a week. Next Saturday?"

"For a *casual* date next Saturday?"

"Whatever the lady wishes."

"Okay." My heart starts beating excitedly again. Damn it.

"Your chariot awaits," he says, pointing to his Jeep.

I stare at the gas guzzler. "Just to be clear," I say, "my chariot would have much friendlier carbon emission standards."

He laughs again. "Duly noted."

He opens the car door for me, and I slide by him, bumping my head as I'm distracted by his smell. He laughs again.

"Whoops." I smile sheepishly.

He closes his door and puts his arm around the back of my seat as he pulls his car out. For the first time all week, I find myself truly smiling.

# CHAPTER

## 40

It's Saturday night, and I can't for the life of me figure out what to wear on our first actual date. Everything feels wrong—too fancy, too casual, too alluring, not alluring enough. My room looks like a tornado tore through my closet. Clothes are strewn across every inch.

"Anna, honey, it's 7:15. You're going to be late!" Mom shouts, the sound reverberating off the hardwood stairs. "Not that I mind you making him wait, of course."

"Lilly," I hear Mimi scold. "We discussed this."

"I knew it! You're secretly mad that I'm going on a date with a Delgado!" I yell down the steps. Why is she bringing this up now? Unfortunately, I really need my mom's help getting dressed. Ugh, if I were just a little more fashion-savvy, I could slam the door and, like any self-respecting teen, tell her I hate her. "Mom, I need you!"

"If she's calling me, must be a fashion emergency, not an emotional emergency," I hear Mom say to Mimi.

"That's for sure!" I call down. "Mom, hurry!"

After what feels like forever, but is really only a few minutes, Mom comes through the door and gives me a look.

"No politics. Please, Mom, I'm nervous enough! This is my first date ever."

"I come in peace." She holds up her hands. "How about when that nice Spencer boy took you out last year?"

"We split a root beer outside of Green and Shop. I'm not sure that counts."

I look at my mom, feeling both proud and envious that she's so glamorous in her casual night-at-home outfit of black slacks and a silk turtleneck. Tiny gold earrings and a delicate gold necklace complete her look. I find myself wishing I could possess such easy elegance. I look critically in the mirror at my shorter frame and wild curls.

Shoot, I catch myself. Now I'm being body un-positive and going on a date with a Northsider. How the mighty have fallen.

I glance at my phone and note it's now (eek!) 7:30. "What should I wear?" I demand.

"What look are we going for here?"

"Hmm. Del suggested hip with a dash of sexy."

Mom lifts her brows. "Don't let Mimi hear you say 'a dash of sexy,' or she'll forbid you from leaving."

I roll my eyes. "It's a dinner date. He said somewhere nice."

"I bet you my primetime spot on Rachel Maddow tomorrow that you're going to Billington's—a generic steakhouse that's bad for the environment."

"Mom!"

"Okay, okay, so go preppy. Wear the gray sweater dress and your leather loafers. Hair down."

"But it's so frizzy."

"It's curly and cool. Embrace it."

"Fine, fine." I look in the mirror and smile, suddenly seeing myself through Mom's eyes. She's right. My hair is pretty cool.

"And add a little more lip gloss," she commands, pulling out my jean jacket.

I comply, eyeing the discarded outfit pile I look in the mirror and let out a sigh of relief. "So much better. Thanks, Mom."

"Here." She takes her necklace off and clasps it around my neck.

A knock at the front door has me jumping. "He's here!" My heart gallops wildly in my chest.

"You look beautiful, honey. Have fun, but not *too* much fun."

We walk down the stairs side by side. A show of support.

# CHAPTER 41

As Gabe and I walk down the stone steps of my house, I wipe my sweaty hands on my jacket. Illuminating the flagstone driveway are small, circular ground lights. I'm relieved to see that Gabe has borrowed his father's stately sedan and left his Jeep at home. The last thing I need is to drive off into the sunset with a Northsider in an SUV.

"So where are we going?" I ask, pulling my jean jacket tighter around me. I can't tell if it's the cool November air or looking at Gabe in a fitted black cashmere sweater that's giving me goosebumps. "Del and Mom both bet Billington's Steakhouse, but Mimi thinks you'll stay East to make me more comfortable."

Gabe looks at me winningly. "Well, I'm glad to say I'm not predictable."

"Oh really?" Why does his smugness turn me on? What is wrong with me? I really need to start seeing Dr. Maggie twice a week.

"Really. We aren't eating either on the Eastside or on the Northside. I figured we could use some neutral territory. So you won't have to face too many carnivores or linen napkins, and I'll be spared an over-decorated plate of microgreens."

I want to laugh and quip back, but I'm too nervous. "Are we really doing this? Like going out on an actual date? By the way, I really like your sweater. You look uncomfortably handsome in black."

Gabe stares at me and bursts out laughing. "Thanks." His expression turns almost shy as he adds, "You look uncomfortably pretty too." Then his cocky expression is back in place. "And I guess since you can't keep your mind out of the gutter, yeah, we're really doing this."

"Right." I exhale a deep breath. "We're doing this." How long until I get to kiss Gabe again? God, I hope soon. I think of placing my hands anywhere on his black sweater, and my insides smoke. I shake my head. I've got to get myself under control. "So where are we going?"

"To the Mountain Pies pop-up."

"Very cool," I say, genuinely impressed. "Del's been talking about that place nonstop." It's an artisanal pizza pop-up at the foot of the Blue Ridge Mountains. "How long is it going to take us to get there?"

"Google Maps says forty-five minutes, so get comfortable." Gabe switches on the engine and pulls out of the driveway with the speed of a careless high schooler who believes nothing bad will ever happen to him.

"So, what are we going to do for the next forty-five minutes?"

"Well, I thought we'd talk." He shoots me his trademark boyish grin. "Crazy idea, I know, since we never do that."

I shake my head and laugh. "But this feels really different."

"Because it's a date, and not just me, you, and Sam stuffing our faces or working out?"

"Yeah, pretty much. And I'm really nervous." I look at him. "Are you nervous?"

"I was, but I'm not now."

"What changed?"

"Seeing you. Or more accurately, hearing you talk."

"What does that mean?"

"You really put it all out there. The nerves, the excitement… you always do. It calms me down."

"My anxiety calms you down?"

Gabe laughs. "Yes."

"That's weird," I say, and he laughs harder. I glance at his profile and sigh.

"What?" He looks at me quickly before his eyes land back on the road.

"I just realized you calm me down too."

Gabe smiles softly. "I do?"

"Yeah, you're just so level-headed and reasonable. And you're also so freaking good at everything."

"Come on, I am not."

"No, you really are! It's actually unfair."

"Unfair?"

"Yeah, talent should be more spread out. But it's my curse in life to be surrounded by people who are good at everything, I guess. Del, Mason, my moms, and now you."

"And you're not?"

"Not what?"

"Good at everything."

I snort. "Not even a little."

He's about to say something when his phone rings. Scottie Peters' name flashes on the car's dashboard. Gabe cancels the call.

"I have a burning question for you."

"Yes?"

"How can you stand to be friends with Scottie Peters? He seems like the actual worst."

"That's probably a little harsh, but he's definitely a little narrow-minded and a little misogynistic and a little full of shit."

I laugh. "Then why do you hang out with him?"

"I grew up with him. He's like that annoying cousin you can't stand but also love. The Peters family really stepped in for Mateo when he was having a hard time while my parents were campaigning. I'll never forget that." Gabe shrugs. "Plus his dad is a huge donor to the party. Huge. He really helped my dad get elected. Smoothed the way for those who weren't thrilled to have him on the ticket."

He frowns. "It's weird. On the one hand, both Scottie and his dad are super protective of my family, but on the other, you

223

should see Scottie's face when my mom serves ropa vieja at formal dinners."

"And not just because beef is one of the worst things for the environment, I assume?"

Gabe rolls his eyes at me. "I'm definitely not sharing pizza with you. God knows what topping restrictions you have."

"Worst comeback I've ever heard."

Gabe laughs.

"Wow, look at all those stars." Suddenly I realize we're off the interstate and driving on country roads. I gaze up through the sun roof.

Gabe looks up and grins. "It's going to be an awesome view for our pizza picnic."

I smile back at him. "You really know how to elevate experiences. I like that about you."

He smiles back. "What a great compliment," he says.

# CHAPTER

---◆——— 42 ——◆———

W e pull onto a dirt road. The sight of twinkling string lights and the sound of bluegrass music pop against the mountain landscape. Gabe parks on the grass. I open the door, charmed by the scene in front of me, and pull my jacket over me. The air is cool and sharp. I breathe in the mountain smell. My loafers sink into the grass as we walk toward the wood patio where picnic benches are decorated with daisies in mason jars and tea light candles. The savory smells of bread and sauce perfume the air. In the darkness of the night, I can barely make out the peaks and valleys of Mount Mitchell.

"Okay, this is kind of amazing." I smile at Gabe. We walk side by side, and I feel hyperaware of his presence. I sneak a look at him, and my heart thuds in my chest. I'm way out of my depth.

A large, tattooed host, sporting an impressive beard, seats us with a smile and places a menu in front of us.

Gabe looks around, pleased with himself. "I love the feeling of nailing it."

"We haven't even tried the pizza yet," I remind him.

He snaps a picture of me and taps his iPhone.

"What did you just do?"

"I sent a picture to your mom of you here."

I don't know whether to laugh or wince. "Why would you do that?"

The waiter places a jug of water and two house-made ginger root sodas in front of us, garnished with a paper straw and ginger cubes on a tooth pick.

"To assure her I didn't take you to a Northside steakhouse. I thought it would endear me to her."

I laugh. "It won't work. If you wanted that outcome, you should have sent it to Mimi."

"Really?" Gabe's lip turns slightly as if he's disappointed that his charm offensive might fail.

"Really. She's much more of a sucker."

"I'll keep that in mind."

Since Gabe looks sweet when I burst his bubble, I offer a toast.

"Cheers."

We clink glasses.

Looking at the menu, the pizza offerings are all exotic. There's honey, cured meats, whipped ricotta, and plenty of vegan options, too. We select a few, and Gabe adds a few more at the last minute. The variety feels decadent, but also fun.

We start talking about Edgartown High, and soon enough we're laughing over our competing impersonations of our ninth-grade English teacher, a failed Broadway star, who made each class a theatrical experience. We argue over whose impression is better and end up recording each other's attempts and sending them to Del and Sam to vote. We decide that the winner owes the other a hot chocolate and a triple pancake stack at Floppies.

Did we just schedule our next date? I wonder as the waiter arranges our elaborate pizza order across the table.

I wonder if Gabe is thinking the same thing as I am. He looks a little unsure.

We turn our attention to the pizzas that look like edible art. I say how lovely they are and Gabe laughs.

He looks so cute when he laughs.

Gabe, catching me staring, looks at me curiously. He grabs a plate and loads it up with an impressive number of slices.

I heap quite a few on my own plate.

He smiles at me, then looks lost in thought.

"What?"

"I don't get what you said in the car."

"What did I say?"

"That it's your plight to be surrounded by people who are good at everything. It seems to me that you're just as good at everything."

I smile because it's nice he sees me that way. "Okay, let me explain, but I already know you won't get it, and you'll ask me weird questions."

"Thanks for the all the faith you so clearly have in me."

I ignore him and continue. "I'm from a smart family."

"I know."

"Both my moms are academic stars, amazing test scorers, called brilliant by all who cross their path. Ivy Leaguers. But not just Ivy Leaguers. Like, Ivy Leaguers who only think Princeton, Harvard, or Yale count as Ivies."

"They're total snobs. Got it."

"Intellectual snobs."

"How is that different from other types?"

"It just is."

"We'll debate that one later because I want to hear the rest of this." He pushes at his dark waves. "So, brilliant family. Got it. Ivy League or bust."

"And brilliant friends. Del just got a perfect SAT score. Her parents are throwing her a party."

"That seems kind of tacky."

I shrug. "Yeah, but it's still perfect, and I'm sure Mason got pretty close to a perfect score, too."

"I'm sure," he says, barely suppressing an eye roll.

"Well, I scored pretty far from perfect, and it's not the first time. In elementary school, I was diagnosed with a Language Processing Disorder."

Gabe nods. "I remember from that day I had to chase you down in the woods after your History exam."

"That's a little dramatic," I object. "You *caught up* to me in the woods."

227

Gabe gives me a look that says, "Oh really?".

"What I do remember is you freaking out with concern over my wellbeing. You clearly had the major hots for me even then." I wink.

Gabe's eyes crinkle as he smiles. "You sure talk a lot for someone with language problems."

I glare at him, but note with internal glee that he didn't refute my claim. "That's not what it means."

"So you had to be taken out of class for one-on-ones and stuff like that?"

"Yeah, I was taken out once or twice but not regularly. My parents got me incredible tutors. Homework was always a struggle, and I didn't really get grammar or spelling for a long time. Still don't, honestly."

"Okay, then why didn't you have to go to The Lab school like Cara or Dexter?"

"I guess because my LD issues weren't as serious, or maybe I just got better help."

"But aren't you in AP English?"

"Yes."

"And AP History?"

"Yup."

"Then—"

"Did you know Albert Einstein had a learning disorder?"

"He did?"

"Yes! And so did lots of other brilliant people. Trust me, my parents learned the whole list." I take another bite of pizza while I pause. It always feels a little embarrassing to say this aloud, to realize the person I'm talking to will likely not understand, or will assume I'm just not that smart. But I keep thinking of that day in the woods when I was feeling so low and Gabe made it clear he thinks I'm smart, no matter what my grade suggested. "Look, it's hard to explain, but high school is actually easier for me than elementary school or middle school, and I think college will be even easier. Like the fundamentals are kind of hard, but I'm super good at abstract reasoning and coming up with interesting thesis statements and stuff like that. Does that make sense?"

Gabe looks at me blankly. "Kind of?"

"So do you think of me differently now?"

"Whoa, no. I think you're saying you had a hard time understanding things that are easy for others, and an easier time understanding things that are hard for most people?"

"Yes! Pretty much." I love how he phrased that.

"Okay."

"Anyway, I thought I was kind of over the learning disorder stuff that made me feel like a total outsider among my friends and family. I stupidly thought that maybe I, too, could get into an Ivy, but the SATs reminded me that I'm still just that LD kid— despite having tutors and the best genes possible."

Gabe looks at me, opens his mouth, then closes it.

"What were you going to say?" I ask, suspicious of his reaction.

"Just," he starts, but then pauses nervously before continuing. "I wonder if you really care that much about going to a name brand school? Maybe you just want to go there because your moms did and your friends would think it's cool?"

My jaw drops so fast that half a pizza crust escapes my mouth. "What's that supposed to mean?"

Gabe winces, as if what he'd said sounded harsher than he meant. "Look, of course going to an Ivy would be amazing, but you get in your head that there's only one right way to do things." He makes a rolling motion with his hands. "This just seems like another example of that."

Anger courses through my blood. I just bared my soul to this guy, and this is his response? "And where do you plan to go? Bet it's Dartmouth, just like your dad, and bet you'll get in no matter what."

Now Gabe bristles. "I know I have an advantage, which is why I've worked my ass off both academically and with sports to try to accomplish admission on strictly my own merits."

"Doesn't make you any less entitled," I spit back but immediately feel guilty saying. I know Gabe practically kills himself to do well at all the stuff he shines at. Why am I being so mean? I start to apologize, but before I have a chance, Gabe starts speaking.

"I'm entitled? Well, you're elitist. You basically just claimed that not getting into Yale, Harvard, or Princeton would be a catastrophe for you. Besides, we both have a well-known parent and have been given nothing but top opportunities. Not so different."

"But at least I'm aware of my privilege, and I fight to make things equal for people with less."

Gabe looks at me like I'm from outer space. "Yeah, if you ask me, you fight in a kind of lofty way. If the Liaisons spent less time on shit like demanding we say our preferred pronouns at the start of every class and more time helping actual people, Edgartown would be better off."

I fold my arms. "Helping people feel comfortable in their identity is extremely important!"

"I'm not saying it's not! People should be able to use whatever pronoun they want! But what is starting every single class by going around the room accomplishing?"

"It's accomplishing acceptance!" I raise my voice.

"What about … I don't know, volunteering to feed the homeless like the Young Republicans do every Sunday? Or finding out which janitors at our school don't have enough to eat for Christmas dinner, instead of protesting Starbucks for selling coffee cups that say 'Merry Christmas' like you all did last year?"

"Those janitors wouldn't be struggling if we had a higher minimum wage! The Liaisons organized a protest for that last May."

"Yeah, sure, picketing around town while chanting dumb slogans is a lot more helpful than putting an actual hot meal in front of someone. Great logic."

The waiter appears and clears his throat to get our attention. He looks at us with annoyance. "Excuse me. We're getting complaints from our other guests about the volume level at this table."

Gabe and I both look around and cringe. Several diners are either staring or glaring at us.

"Sorry," I whisper.

Gabe looks ashamed. "Won't happen again."

The waiter leaves. Gabe and I wince at each other.

"Should I buy everyone a round of ginger soda?" he asks.

"I guess that wouldn't hurt, but they'd probably prefer alcohol."

"Am I allowed to do that?"

"We can try."

Gabe nods and goes and talks to the waiter.

When he comes back, he sits down and looks at me sadly. "This isn't really how I was hoping tonight would go."

"Me either." I look down at my food, my shoulders feeling heavy. "Does this mean we aren't compatible?"

Gabe holds my gaze. "I don't know. I hope it doesn't mean that."

We finish the rest of our dinner in awkward silence. From everything we just said to each other, my head is spinning. Have I really been elitist? Does Gabe have a point?

# CHAPTER

## 43

Ten minutes into a silent car ride home, Gabe hits the turn signal and pulls over to the side of the road.

"What's wrong?"

"I don't want our night to end this way."

I turn to look at him. "Me either," I say in a rush. "I feel like my insides are eating me up."

Gabe turns on the car radio and country music plays. "Me too."

"What do we do about how different we are?"

"I think we have two choices."

"What?" I ask.

Gabe stops fiddling with the radio and looks at me. "We can decide our differences are either a strength or a weakness. If it's a strength, we keep trying and if not, we end it." Gabe pops a piece of spearmint gum into his mouth and plays with the wrapper. I have never seen him fidget like this. He's nervous.

Sitting this close to him, catching the familiar minty scent as his gum releases its distinctive flavor, I want nothing more than to be in his arms and hear him assure me that we can do this, that we can make our relationship work. "I'm really hoping it's a strength," I say, emotion straining my voice.

Gabe looks at me with hope in his eyes. "Me too." He takes

my hand. "I really want to make this work."

"Even with the most elitist girl in town?" I joke.

"Yes, even with her." His face gets more somber. "Really, Anna, it can't be all bad that we think in different ways. It forces us to get out of our bubbles."

I nod. "I think that's right. Even what you said about college—at some level, I know you're right. Everyone else lets me wallow, but you're kicking my butt about it. And it does sort of resonate—how sometimes the Liaisons get caught up in loftier, impractical ideas."

He kisses my hand. "Yeah, since getting to know you better, I'm constantly reconsidering things. It's hard, but I feel like you make me really think."

My heart leaps. "Does this mean we get to kiss now? I've been wanting to do that the whole night," I admit.

Gabe laughs. "Yes, please."

I smile at him, unbuckle my seatbelt, and launch myself in his direction, not even minding that I bump my leg roughly on the gear stick.

Between passionate kisses, Gabe says softly, "I really do admire your enthusiasm in all areas, Morningstar."

I laugh, but as my lips meet his again and again, I don't bother to respond.

I get to kiss Gabe several more times that night. On the drive home, we pull over one more time near a wide stretch of farmland. We get out so we can make out unencumbered by the confinements of the car. Later, as I close the passenger door in front of my house, Gabe approaches and spins me into him, which steals my breath and makes me feel weightless.

We kiss again as he walks me to my front door. I melt into him, and he laughs and tells me I'm cute. Our kiss doesn't last long, as either Mom or Mimi turns on the porch lights. I feel like I can't stand the kissing to be over, and at the same time, I'm relieved that it has to end. It feels dangerous to be so far removed from my wits.

Gabe waves to me as he gets in his car and shyly says goodnight.

Something has shifted in the universe, I think, as I walk upstairs in a daze and answer the moms' rapid-fire questions. Then I realize I'm being dramatic. The universe is the same. It's me who's different.

After I throw my hair in a bun, wash up, and change into my pancake pajamas, I settle in beneath my fluffy comforter.

I look down at my phone. I have new texts on the group thread. Sam and Del have finally weighed in on our impersonation contest. It's been such a long night, I had almost forgotten our competition.

Gabe, Anna, Del, Sam

Del: Sorry, Anna. You win for enthusiasm but Gabe wins for accuracy

Sam: I have to second that

Me: Although I maintain my artistic integrity, I concede

Gabe: I'm a born winner. What can I say?

Del: I just vomited in my mouth a little. I change my vote.

Gabe: Hey! Not fair

Del: My vote is for Annabelle. Final answer.

Sam: Lol. Even though I agree he's a sore winner, I keep my vote for Gabe

Me: A tie!

Gabe: We'll have to think of a tiebreaker

Del: This is getting too kinky for me. Goodnight, kids

Sam: Agreed

Del, Anna

Me: How could you say 'too kinky'? I am dyinggg

Del: Just calling it as I see it. If you can't take the heat, get out of the kitchen

Me: Oh, I can take it. I just might never recover!!!

Del: It was that good??

Me: Better. I got the full-on spins

Del: Sounds hot

Me: It was. And he is so hottt

Del: So do you really like him or is this a lust thing?

Me: I think I really like him?!?

Del: Really like him or really, really like himmm

Me: TBD I guess. But I'm pretty sure it's really, really

Del: This feels complicated but exciting

Me: Yeah, I guess that's a good way to describe it


Gabe, Anna

Gabe: Tonight was pretty great

Me: Yeah, it really was

Gabe: I'm really excited to see you Monday at school

Me: Me too


Anna, Mason

Mason: Can we talk sometime this week? Alone

Me: Yes, of course

# CHAPTER

## 44

As I walk up the stone steps to school, my pulse races. I can't wait to see Gabe. I'm relieved that Del has an early newspaper meeting this morning and therefore won't bear witness to my current state of anxious anticipation. Every time I close my eyes, I remember the warm, firm feeling of Gabe's lips on mine. I think of the wave of his hair and how I plan to run my hands through it the next time I see him.

And then my thoughts go back to the time at his party when I saw him shirtless, and I wonder, almost painfully, what it would be like to run my hands across his abs. I feel drunk on these thoughts. I chew on my lips—the very lips I carefully placed fresh lip gloss on thirty minutes ago.

"Anna." I whip around hopefully when I hear my name, but my face drops in disappointment when I see it's Mason.

"Ah, hi to you too?" He looks at me strangely. "Were you expecting someone else?"

I look into his green eyes and see he looks confused but not upset. Realizing he doesn't know about my date with Gabe, I shift uncomfortably. As far as he's concerned, I'd called it off. Mason has told me how much he approves of that decision several times over the past week, so I've shied away from telling him that Gabe and I are giving it another shot.

Mason pushes his dirty-blond hair off his forehead. It's easy to see how he has all the Eastside girls swooning.

"Eh, well, funny you should ask…"

"Anna!" I hear my name called with enthusiasm. I turn to see Gabe. His eyes light up, and he grins at me in a way that has my heart whirling. I want to whisk him away to a hidden corner. I grin stupidly back at him.

"Hi," I say.

"Hi." He loops his hands in his belt loops and stands closer to me than is totally appropriate.

Mason looks between us uneasily.

To my shock, Mason steps in between us. "What's up, Gabe?"

Gabe looks at me. I realize he's asking me what I want him to do.

I blankly look between Mason and Gabe.

Luckily for me, Zoe appears out of nowhere. I've never been happier to see her in my whole life. She walks up to us and greets me with some warmth, ignores Gabe, and says, "Mason, can you walk me to homeroom? I really need to talk through this composting idea before I present it to Principal Jenkins."

Gabe snorts with laughter, and all three of us glare at him.

"It's an important project, Gabe. It could lower our footprint four-fold in just this academic year alone," I point out.

"Sounds very noble to me." He holds his hands up as if to say, "I come in peace." "It's just Jenkins isn't exactly sympathetic to the environmental cause."

"Or any cause," Mason says under his breath.

"Exactly." Gabe nods.

"But we still have to try," I encourage.

"I'm not saying you shouldn't try. I'm saying you need to be smart about it. He can be bargained with."

Zoe assesses Gabe. "You might be right." She taps a pen to her chin. "Okay, Gabe, come walk with us too."

I laugh a little as Gabe looks startled by her demand.

"Eh, I was hoping to talk to Anna."

Mason's head snaps up. "About what?"

"That's between me and Anna, buddy."

Before Mason can retort, Zoe says, "We don't have time for this back and forth. My meeting is in an hour. Let's go, boys."

Gabe looks at me. I gesture for him to text me. He nods and, as Zoe pulls him away, shoots me a WTF look.

My phone buzzes.

Gabe, Anna

Gabe: Meet me at that student garden after first period?

Me: By the tomatoes or cucumbers?

Gabe: Is that some weird vegetarian joke?

Me: Yeah, I guess it is.

Gabe: It's a good thing you're so adorable.

My heart somersaults as I read that. I'm too overwhelmed to respond with words, so I just send an emoji with a halo on it.

# CHAPTER
## 45

For five magical minutes, we make out on the stone bench in the student garden, then jump apart as a group of freshmen girls walks by. I'm breathless and clasping the bench. I look at Gabe. His hair is disheveled from my searching hands. I feel giddy.

We smile at each other.

"Wow," he finally says.

I laugh because it feels so accurate.

"Is this what it's always like for you?"

He laughs. "No. Why, is it for you?"

He looks nervous when I don't answer.

I smile and shake my head.

"Well, to be fair, I'm probably the first person you've made out with who doesn't have an iron deficiency."

I roll my eyes. "Well, to be fair, I'm probably the first person you've made out with who has a soul, so…"

"Harsh." He smiles. "I like it when you get a little fired up."

I look down for a moment.

He lifts my chin. "You okay?"

I nod. "It's just I'm still a little worried about how different our views are."

Gabe acknowledges this with a slow nod, then grins. "We are a modern-day Romeo and Juliet, I guess."

I laugh, and without totally realizing it, let my head drift toward his chest. I breathe in his clean scent. "I guess we kind of are."

"How romantic of us."

He takes my hand gently in his. The bell rings. He kisses my hand tenderly. My insides melt just a little. "Till next time, Juliet."

I laugh as we part ways and I head off to History wondering how I'm supposed to focus on anything else today.

# CHAPTER

## 46

O ver the next week, we continue to meet at the student garden whenever we can.

Gabe, Anna

Gabe: I'll never look at a vegetable garden the same way again…

My smile extends to my ears as I read his text.

Me: Tomatoes are ruined forever for me.

Gabe: Lol. Want to hang out after school? I'm done with practice around 4 pm.

Me: Yeah, that works. I'm done around the same time :)

Was that weird to text a smiley face? I panic. I look up, wanting to ask Del if I've forever ruined my sex appeal by continuously using basic emoticons. I see she's busy talking to Kyle, the layout editor, at the drafting table several feet from me with the paper in front of them. My phone buzzes again. It's Gabe texting me back. "Great:). I promise not to serve you any BLTs… I'll meet you outside of the gym."

I feel nervous and excited and scared and I need to interrupt Del's meeting. This can't wait!

But just as I fly out of my seat, Mason enters the room carrying a towering pile of pizza boxes.

His thick hair is mussed like he and Zoe were similarly occupied. "Pizza is here."

The aroma of freshly-baked dough and melted mozzarella floods the room. It's our Thursday tradition to order pies from Pete's and eat in the newspaper room while Del rushes to get the paper ready for its 1 pm deadline.

Mason looks at Del, who's still deep in conversation with Kyle. "Let's dig in."

My mouth waters. Del perks up and signals for me to get her and Kyle a slice. I dutifully comply.

"So good." She takes a huge bite. "They have the best pies."

"You know it's only the best because it's the one time a week we eat dairy, right? Same reason Claudette's has the best dessert. It's the only *other* time in the week we eat dairy."

Mason laughs. "Shh. Don't say it out loud. Golden rule, Anna."

Kyle shakes his head. "Mase, what if I take a picture of you and send it to Zoe? I could caption it *Moooo*."

Mason looks genuinely panicked, and we all laugh.

Del looks down at her phone and groans. "Uh-oh, the printer is jammed again. Kyle, let's go. Of course this happens with twenty minutes until deadline."

Del marches off, and Kyle follows behind.

Mason shrugs, his mouth full of pizza. "Glad my only job is the column."

I smile. Mason's weekly humor column is wildly popular.

"So, we still on for movie night? I think we're doing *Rear Window* tonight. I can swing by at 5ish."

I grimace. Since sixth grade, Mason and I have had a tradition: Every third Thursday of the month, we work through some sort of best-of list. For the last few months, we've been doing the top 100 movies of all time. "I totally forgot!"

He looks at me. "What are you doing instead? Can't you cancel?"

"Uh, well... can we do it Friday?" I plead.

A flicker of hurt passes through his eyes. "Yeah, sure."

"I'm sorry, Mase. I love List Night." I suddenly feel sad, like I'm breaking some sacred bond of friendship. I'm about to offer to cancel my plans with Gabe when I remember that Mason has also flaked on me to hang with Zoe. "Hey, you did the same thing to me when you and Zoe first started dating."

Mason's head snaps up. "Wait! Are you seeing Gabe after school? Are you guys back on?"

I fidget in my seat and make a big show of biting my pizza.

I nod, resenting Mason for making me feel guilty. "Can you not overreact, please?"

"What's next? Internship at the NRA?"

"Very funny. He's not that bad. Even you used to be friends with him."

"That was like a million years ago."

"It's not like Zoe is my favorite person, but I accept her because she's important to you."

Mason's eyes flash. "Now Gabe's important to you?"

"Why are you mad at me?"

"What do you even really know about him?" Mason snaps.

"Why are you yelling?"

Mason runs a hand through his hair, disheveling it further. "Because I don't understand you right now, and that really fucking scares me."

"It scares you? Dramatic much?" I turn to stalk off, feeling tears well in my eyes.

He grabs my arm. "Wait."

I wrench my arm away. "You're being such an asshole."

Mason shrugs sullenly. "Maybe I am, but I'm just looking out for you."

"You are? Because it feels like you're just mad at me."

Mason's eyes latch onto mine. "I am."

"Why?"

"Because I don't understand what you see in him."

"Do you have to understand that to support me? We're supposed to be best friends. I like him. I want to see where this goes."

"Supporting you doesn't mean turning my cheek while you fall into bed with the enemy."

"He's not the enemy, Mason. That's insane. He's a teenage boy with a good heart. You're being so extreme... and so unfair!"

Mason blinks. "You don't even sound like yourself!"

"Things are more complicated than 'He's wrong, we're right.' And yes, I'm learning that. I wish his views were closer to ours, I do, but that doesn't mean everything he thinks and feels is animated by evil."

"Wow. So now conservative policies are suddenly acceptable to you?"

"This is exactly what you did when you started dating Zoe. Don't you see that? Having someone you care about and respect challenge your beliefs is part of falling—" I break off because I am not sure how to end the sentence. "Part of this whole dating thing."

"I just don't get it. I didn't think he was your type. I thought you'd be with someone like me."

"What does that mean?"

Mason looks like he wants to say more, but shakes his head as if deciding whether to hold back. "I don't even know." He looks at me sadly. "It just feels like everything is changing a little too much and a little too fast."

"I'm still me, your best friend. That will never change."

Mason nods, but his eyes are troubled.

I can practically feel the thick wall of tension go up between us.

# CHAPTER

## 47

Mason's words weigh heavily on me. In fact, I'm so distracted that I drop the relay stick twice during practice. Mary Sue, a senior, scolds me, "Anna, get your head in the game! We have the Perchot meet this weekend." She pushes her ever-present headband into place and gives me a firm look.

"I know, I know," I grumble. Her words help me focus on practice during the final thirty minutes.

Coach Erin looks disappointed. She arches a brow at me during our cool-down stretches. "We all need to clear our heads and really focus. You girls have worked hard—too hard—to throw it all away now. If we give it our best on Saturday, we may end up with one of our best seasons ever."

Angie, our star mile runner, walks with me to the locker room. "You okay?"

"I will be by Saturday," I promise, ashamed I let boy problems affect my teammates.

Angie smiles knowingly at me. "Hey, if I were hooking up with Gabe Delgado, I'd have focus problems too."

My cheeks flush. I laugh at the twinkle in her eyes. "Thanks for understanding, Angie."

Mary Sue joins our circle. "So, it's true? You and Gabe?"

I shrug. "Kinda."

"Hmm, I can see it actually." Mary Sue slips off her workout sweatband and pulls a purple velvet headband over her straw-blonde hair, popping it into place. She's only 5'1," so she has to look up to see me and Angie. "He is indeed quite handsome…and distracting apparently."

"Mary Sue, let's try and not be too pushy. Anna is allowed to have an off day," Angie scolds. Angie and Mary Sue are somehow one of the school's only Eastside-Northside best-friend duos. Their friendship began on the track team and blossomed through Bible study; they are two of the more religious people at our school. Angie pulls her hair into a low ponytail.

"I don't know how not to push. It's why I'm such a good 200-meter sprinter," Mary Sue says matter-of-factly.

Both Angie and I laugh, and I feel tension roll off my shoulders. "I'm more worried about his politics than his appearance."

Angie looks sympathetic. "It's hard. He's so hot, but his dad is so closed-minded."

"Senator Delgado has done many wonderful things for our community, I'll have you know," Mary Sue huffs.

"I don't consider closing down two Planned Parenthood sites good for the community."

Mary Sue glares at me. "Let's not get into your anti-life antics. I think we all know it's not productive for team spirit."

Angie laughs. "Don't you admire how she brings up politics and then makes you feel bad for doing the same?"

"I don't know what you're talking about," Mary Sue objects, all innocence.

Angie and I smile.

Mary Sue rolls her eyes. "Even though you're antagonizing me intentionally, I do need to warn you about something."

"What?"

"Be very careful around Caroline Loran. Don't think she's out of your way just because they caught her for with her little driveway artwork. Bless her soul, but I don't trust that girl for a second."

I sigh. "Agreed. She's so, so…"

"Two-faced?" Mary Sue supplies sweetly.

Angie laughs again. "She definitely seems to think Gabe is hers."

I shrug. "What's the worst she can do?"

"Let's hope we never find out."

I look at my phone and yelp. "It's 3:50! I'm meeting Gabe at 4."

"Where?"

"Here!"

Both Angie and Mary Sue clap their hands in excitement as they rush me into the shower.

With their help, I'm clean, relatively made up, and dressed in no time.

When we exit the locker room, Gabe is sitting on the bleachers looking freshly showered. He wears a long-sleeved tech shirt and a gray Patagonia jacket. I secretly celebrate his wearing such an environmentally conscious brand.

All three of us draw in our breaths at the sight of him.

"It must be a sin to look that good," Angie sighs.

Mary Sue links arms with her. "I couldn't agree more."

"Go get him, girl."

"But not too much of him!"

I laugh again. "Thanks, guys."

As I walk over to Gabe, he grants me a huge smile. "Good practice, I take it." He dips his hand to do a cool boy version of a wave toward Angie and Mary Sue. They nod back.

"Not really. I was pretty off my run today."

"Oh, but you look so happy."

"I was just thinking how awesome it is to have good teammates."

Gabe smiles. "Totally. It's the best."

"How was your practice?"

"It was okay."

"Just okay?"

"Yeah, Scottie was being a real dick."

"Even more so than usual?"

Gabe holds open the gym door and we step outside. The

fresh fall air cools my cheeks.

"Maybe, a little. He seems bent out of shape."

"What do you mean?"

Gabe tenses his jaw. "He was saying some real fucked-up stuff today. If I did anything that one-upped him, he retaliated by making jokes about my background."

"So that's his way of what? Putting you in your place?"

"I guess so. He does it a lot, but today was especially bad."

"That's really awful. I'm sorry. What are you going to do about it?"

He shrugs. "There's a lot of history. Shared experience. Also, as I told you, his dad has done a lot for my family."

"But that doesn't give him the right to be an asshole."

Gabe looks annoyed. "Of course not. But what's the price of getting into it with him? I don't see how defunding one of the only Cuban Republicans in high national office is helpful."

"You really think that would happen?"

"I'm not sure." He lets out a breath. "Can we talk about something else?"

We're facing each other now. The parking lot is far from full, but students are trickling out from various extracurriculars.

I look at the pain in his eyes, and all I want to do is soothe him. I smile and say, "All my teammates think you're a major cutie."

A wicked gleam lights his eyes. He puts his hands on my waist and guides me to the side of his car, stepping so close to me that I can feel his warm breath on my cheek. He flicks a gentle finger over my nose. "I bet my teammates are thinking the same about you."

"Yeah, right. I don't think I'm really the talk of the men's locker room. Not that I want to be. I mean, gross."

"What do you mean? Just look at your rocking body."

I feel stunned. Sure, I'm in shape from sports, but I always carry a bit too much weight at my midsection.

He runs his hands up my sides, and I feel like my body is melting. "Then there's your awesome hair and big eyes."

I feel like I'm going to die if he doesn't kiss me soon. I stand on my tippy toes, ready to be swooped into the head-spinning feeling of being kissed by Gabe, but he pulls back abruptly.

Gabe smiles, then looks uncertain for a moment. "As nice as it is for you to constantly remind me of my movie star good looks, you know that I'm also fun and smart, right?"

"Well, actually, I don't know that for sure."

Gabe crosses his arms at his chest. "What does that mean?"

"I suspect you have those qualities from our recent hangs, but you're still a Northsider, so...."

"Very funny."

I grimace. "If it only it was."

Gabe leans forward and brushes his lips against mine with a surprising tenderness.

I breathe in sharply. He leads me around the car and opens the door for me.

Once we're both buckled in, and he's pulling the car out, he begins to grin ear to ear. "I'm really happy I get to spend the afternoon with you."

I smile because his statement is so simple and cute. "The truth is, I've known for a while now that you're fun, sweet, and smart. The sweet part is my favorite."

Gabe puts his fingers over his lips. "Shh! Don't tell anyone." He winks and takes my hand with his free one.

I squeeze his hand, and stare in wonder at his profile.

# CHAPTER
## 48

What is more liberating than enjoying sex? Or, in my case, sex-related activities, because I'm still extremely virginal.

If you really think about it, though, having a robust sex life, even if it's with a Republican-in-training, is very feminist of me. Indeed, you could say I've never been more liberal.

So on Tuesday, when I pull Gabe into the janitor's closet at school, and his shock turns to enjoyment when I jump into his arms and press my lips to his, I feel like I'm basically Susan B. Anthony. On Saturday, when he again takes me out to dinner (this time to an annoyingly stuffy place on the Northside), I make him blush by playing footsie with him under the table, and I feel like Jane Fonda.

On the following Friday, I finally attend another one of his lacrosse games. As Gabe locks eyes with me from the field and fumbles a pass from Sam, I'm practically Alex Cooper.

I share this train of thought with Del on a lazy Sunday morning walk, and she bursts out laughing. "If anything, it sounds like you're Danielle Steel."

"What does that mean?"

She looks at me skeptically. "I don't think you need to justify your sexual escapades with Gabe as some sort of feminist revolution. That's a little much."

"And extremely inaccurate," Mason adds, despite doing his best to tune out our conversation, which is what he does whenever we talk about guys we're dating. Not that he'll ever admit to filtering out girl talk. He glares at me. "Can we please talk about something else? Anything else?"

"Fine," I agree.

Del looks at Mason's face keenly. He does look pretty pissed. I shrug.

Del changes the subject, attempting to persuade us to try out her new yoga class at 3pm. She and Mason start bickering about whether blacklight yoga is culturally insensitive. I tune them out and think about what Del said about Danielle Steel. During our make-outs, I've been feeling a little inexperienced compared to Gabe. Sure, I haven't had as much actual experience as him, but I have read a ridiculous number of romance novels! Maybe I'll look over some of those sex scenes this afternoon and, when I see him tonight, I'll absolutely wow him with a move!

# CHAPTER

## 49

To: Gabriel.Delgado@edgartownhigh.edu
From: Annabanana@edgartownhigh.edu
Subject: Kissing and other thoughts


Hi Gabe!

You're probably wondering why I'm awake and emailing you at 3 am. It's actually kind of annoying that they time-stamp emails. Am I right? Like, can't Google respect our right to email a boy without letting him know just how late into the night we're obsessing over him? Stop blush-ing—even though I find it rather endearing that you blush so often given how sure of yourself you always seem. I re-ally am jealous of that. Effortlessly cool, always making tough stuff look easy. Even the way you walk. It projects the right amount of swagger without being a full-on strut.

And then there's me. I'm really embarrassed that I tried that sucking-your-finger move during our make-out sesh to-night. I got it from my romance novel reading. Every time I am about to fall asleep, I replay it in my mind, and I shoot up into a sitting position cringing. It makes me feel gross and weird when I so badly wanted to be attractive, desirable, and sexually knowledgeable. Fingers do so many gross things … wipe things, pick things… Why would it ever be a good idea to suck someone's finger? Sigh. Anyway, just wanted to let you know that your fingers will be safe tomorrow.

I have no idea how to sign off an email to you.

Confusingly,

Anna

------------------------------------------------------

To: Annabanana@edgartownhigh.edu
From: Gabriel.Delgado@edgartownhigh.edu
Subject RE: Kissing and other thoughts


Anna!

What a delight to wake up for my 6 am run and see this email. I am not mocking you, I promise. It's just that I haven't laughed so hard this early in the morning since… well, maybe ever :) I will assure you that even though the sudden, abrupt finger-sucking was a little, eh, surprising, nothing about the "sesh" was gross or weird. To be totally honest, it blew my mind.

Gabe

------------------------------------------------------

To: Gabriel.Delgado@edgartownhigh.edu
From: Annabanana@edgartownhigh.edu
Subject: Re Kissing and other thoughts


:):):)!!!! That is how your email makes me feel. It also

makes me feel like I can't wait to kiss you in school again (in a non-PDA way of course!). It also makes me think about what a great kisser you are. So passionate. And that makes me think what a great activist you'd be once you join Team Good. Because passion equals activism, ya know.

Can't wait for school,

A

P.S.

By that I meant I can't wait to *kiss* you at school!

------------------------------------------------------

To: Annabanana@edgartownhigh.edu
From: Gabriel.Delgado@edgartownhigh.edu
Subject RE: Kissing and other thoughts


Let's not hold our breaths about me switching teams, much less becoming a left-wing activist (what a nightmare). But I do appreciate the nod to my passion. I also can't wait for school.

G

# CHAPTER

## 50

"Where are you taking me?" Gabe asks, amused as I lead him up the one-mile section of the Greenway that usually only families with young children traverse. There's a waterfall at the top that the under-five set finds particularly exciting.

"I want to show you what I do when I'm really upset," I explain. I'm pretty sure what I'm about to demonstrate will cement my status as an emotional loose cannon, but after witnessing just how much Gabe keeps bottled up, I decide he really needs to try my method.

"You mean besides telling Mason and Del, your therapist, your moms, and your entire social media following…oh, and now me and Sam too?"

I elbow him in the ribs. "Very funny. I'm trying to help you here!"

Gabe swings his arms around my waist from behind and leans over to give me a kiss on my cheek that is so soft I nearly melt into the rocks. I'm obsessed with how my back feels against his strong chest.

"And I appreciate that, Morningstar," he says in my ear, which sends shivers down my spine.

He releases his arms and takes my hand. I pull him to one side of the waterfall, scaling a few rocks until we reach a small inlet that looks like a mini cave.

"I thought we learned our lessons about bears," Gabe says doubtfully when I crouch at the opening in the rocks.

I roll my eyes. "No one will ever let me live that down."

"Probably with good reason."

I ignore him. "Okay, ready? Here's my hot tip of the day for emotional release and regulation."

Gabe starts to scoff, but when I shoot him a look, he composes himself and nods somberly.

I inch back further into the rocky inlet and then yell, at the top of my lungs, "I am Annabelle Morningstar, and I'm scared of a few things!" My voice ricochets off the rocks and echoes three times.

Gabe's jaw drops a little. He looks around, clearly embarrassed, as a few kids at another waterfall several yards away whip around in confusion. "Whoa, that is some echo."

I continue shouting to maximize the sound. "I'm scared I won't get into any good schools, and I'll be left behind!"

Gabe's face turns beet red. "Anna, everyone can hear you."

"Who cares?"

"What is the purpose of this exactly? Public humiliation?"

"No, no, something about hearing your worries echoed back to you makes them seem less bad. Like hearing yourself say something aloud kind of reveals how much you should worry or not worry about something."

"Huh? Not following."

I crawl out of the cave. "Try it. Yell something you're worried or mad about. If it still bothers you after you hear it echoed back all three times, then you know you need to deal with it."

Gabe looks highly skeptical. "I don't know about this one, Anna."

"Come on, just give it a try! No one can see us from here. It's really a wonderfully healthy release."

He looks at my pleading face and sighs. "Okay, one time." He changes places with me and shakes his head as if he can't believe he's about to do this. "I have such a huge crush on Annabelle Morningstar that I'm risking public humiliation!" he yells into the cave.

I listen to the echoes and, as much as I love hearing that Gabe is crushing on me, I glare at him. "You're not taking this seriously!"

He shrugs sheepishly. "I just feel so silly."

"Okay, then close your eyes and do it." When he doesn't reply, I urge him, "Come on, trust me here. Let it go!"

"Are you quoting *Frozen* to me now?"

"So full of jokes today, aren't we?" Looking around, I notice we're now alone. Maybe I scared off all the kids. "Look, no one is even up here now. It's the perfect time."

"Okay, okay." He rolls his shoulders. "I shout anything I'm feeling?"

"Yes, anything."

Gabe lets out a breath, closes his eyes, and shouts. "I am so tired of having to be perfect all the damn time!"

I hear Gabe's deep voice echo three times, and the power of it moves me.

He opens his eyes and looks at me.

"So?"

"That did feel pretty good."

"Want to do another one?"

"Ladies, first."

I switch with him, but instead of closing my eyes, I stare directly at him and shout, "I'm afraid we're so different that this won't work, and I'll get crushed!"

Gabe looks at me sadly. Crouching down, he crawls to sit next to me in the cave. He takes my hand and kisses it. "Let's try not to let that happen because I'd be pretty fucking crushed myself."

We gaze at each other, the tenderness of the moment almost making me cry.

"I kind of want to just scream in here. Is that weird?" Gabe asks.

"Not at all. I think it's a great idea."

He takes my hand again. We sit cross-legged next to each other, close our eyes, and let out huge, frustrated screams, listening as our fears and resentments echo back to us.

# CHAPTER
## 51

"Look what the cat dragged in," Mason drawls. He's in the corner of Kyle's basement, swirling a brandy in his hand.

It's Friday night, and I feel disoriented. I spent all of last week with Gabe, blowing off almost everything else, and now I'm back on the Eastside and feeling lost.

"Anna, you're here!" Del, beer in hand and looking impossibly chic in ripped jeans and a blue silk top, rushes over to hug me.

I remind myself that Gabe and I agreed to spend tonight with our separate set of friends. Thankfully, Kyle was hosting a party for *The Red and Blue* staff.

I felt grumpy as I was getting dressed, but now that I'm here, I'm happy to see Mason and Del. I hug Del and open my arms to include Mason. He reluctantly joins us.

Del lifts an eyebrow at me. "So? Tell us everything."

Mason shakes his sandy hair. I observe a few Eastside girls in the room tracking his moves, and I smile.

"Well, guys, I'm officially in deep. I'm so into Gabe!"

Del smacks her head good-naturedly.

Mason glowers. "Seems risky."

"Can't you be happy for your oldest friend, Mase?"

"The age-old conundrum—friendship or societal downfall."

"That seems a little exaggerated."

"Does it?"

"Del, help me out here."

"Tell her she's lost it," Mason counters.

"I'm not telling either of you anything. I have to run actually."

"But I just got here," I whine.

"I have a date."

"With whom?" Mason asks.

"Sam."

"Not you too!" Mason exclaims as I say, "You do?"

"Guys, this is literally no big deal."

"What is happening?" Mason looks genuinely distraught.

"Don't worry. I have zero risk of catching actual feelings, unlike our friend Anna over here."

"Hey!"

"It's true. Ta-ta, friends." She blows an airy kiss over her shoulder, leaving us standing there.

We watch her depart.

"I'm not in the mood for a lecture, Mase."

"Okay, fine." He shoves his hands in his pockets and asks, "Want to go to the backyard? I left my guitar out there and wanted to play you some new lyrics I wrote."

I smile. "Sure. By the way, I loved your new song about second chances. I think we need to use it Sunday at the prison reform rally."

"Yeah. I was really proud of that one. Did you see it got, like, 20 thousand views?"

"That's so cool! It's humbling to be besties with a rising celeb."

Mason blushes. "Come on, Anna. Maybe one day."

We walk out to the empty backyard. It's cold, and I pull my coat tighter around my body. Mason's guitar is leaning against the deck steps. He picks it up, and I sit a couple steps down from him.

I smile. Listening to Mason's new music is always so special.

Mason warms up by strumming the guitar. His hands move artfully on the strings. He starts singing, his voice distinctive and beautiful. He looks directly at me as he starts to belt out his new song, which unnerves me. Normally, he only looks at his guitar when he plays.

"Who has she become?" Mason sings. "My best girl, the one I knew so well, I see her and she's somehow gone. The one who always made me laugh, the one I always leaned on. Who has she become? An empty shell of her former self, a self I miss—"

"Hey!" I interrupt as it dawns on me. "Not cool, Mason! Is this about me?"

I'm startled to see his eyes are wet. I can remember seeing Mason cry twice before. Once in third grade, when he learned of the horrors of factory farming, and then again in sixth grade when his aunt died. I held his hand during the entire funeral.

Mason closes his eyes slowly and opens them. "I guess it is about you."

"Some of those lyrics are beyond mean, Mase. It's like you're trying to hurt me."

He turns for a moment, putting his hand to his forehead in a defeated fashion. "Maybe I am." He looks at the sky and yells, "Damn it!"

I jump back. "What was that?"

Mason shakes his head and steps closer to me, his green eyes shining into mine. "I don't know." He presses his hands into his temples.

I look at him but feel scared and lost, like a precious relationship is slipping away.

"I'm jealous, okay? Jealous and disappointed and so many other things, and it's making me act terribly, which I know is shitty."

I'm so shocked by his words, I can't even process them. "You're what?"

Mason sighs deeply. "It literally drives me crazy to think about you with Gabe."

I shake my head, trying to clear it. "What are you saying?" I ask slowly. I feel chilled. I look at my beautiful best friend—the nerdy boy turned love object of all the Eastside girls. I remember how annoyed I was when he started dating Zoe. "I guess I know what you mean. It wasn't easy for me when you took up with Zoe."

Mason's face softens and he smiles. "I do remember you being a little, eh, snappish with me that first month."

I laugh because I had all but taken his head off over the smallest of things. "I know you've felt let down by me. Questioned my moral purity. It's hard for me not to resent you for that, Mase."

"These times are just so awful. It's going to take a lot to fight all that's wrong in this country, and I wanted you there with me."

I let out a breath. "I'm with you on most of it, and I will be when it really counts."

"I hope that's true."

"It is," I promise.

He leans forward, placing his forehead against mine. I lean in. I let myself enjoy the closeness, the security of our bond.

We stay like that for several beats, then compose ourselves.

When we break apart, we smile.

I hear a strangled gasp. We turn to see Zoe at the back door looking shattered. She turns and runs.

Mason looks at me quizzically. "What was that about?"

"Do you think she thought…?" I let the words hang in the air because saying them aloud feels too awkward.

Mason looks startled. "I hope not."

"Maybe you better go find her."

"Right, I better." But he doesn't move right away. "Are we okay?"

"Yes." I smile.

"Can we do List Night this week?"

"I'd love that." I beam at him. He beams back.

"Okay," he says reluctantly. "I better go find her."

"Yeah, you probably should."

He stands for another moment, as if still unsure we're really okay.

"Go," I say with a laugh.

He laughs too and hurries off to locate Zoe.

I'm left alone in Kyle's backyard. I turn my face to the sky, looking at the stars and letting the cool air wash over me. I shake my head, not wanting to think about what just happened.

My phone buzzes in my pocket. I pull it out.

Gabe: Is it weird that I miss you?

Me: I hope not. Because I really loved getting this text

Gabe: How's the party?

Me: Dramatic

Gabe: What happened? Did someone not recycle their beer can?

Me: Haha…

Gabe: I can hear the sarcasm all the way here in the Northside

Me: Lol. Mason and I got into a weird fight

Gabe: Oh. Are you okay?

Me: Yes… we made up

Gabe: That's good

Me: Yeah, it's just weird how much we've been fighting lately.

Gabe: Well, he's self-important and humorless, so you have every right to be annoyed at him

Me: Gabe!

Gabe: Okay, okay. But, come on. You know it's true.

Me: I'm ignoring this. What are you up to?

Gabe: At Drew's party. I'm bored

Me: Come get me?

Gabe: On my way

# CHAPTER

## 52

"Mason likes you," Gabe says.

"What?" I shake my head. "No, trust me," I say. "He's super into Zoe, and we've been best friends most of our lives."

"Okay, so he's probably in love with you." Gabe's face looks stoic, which is disappointing because it must mean he's not jealous.

"You don't get it. He's a really passionate guy. This is just how he is."

"Sounds high maintenance," Gabe grumbles.

I laugh.

Gabe looks at me. "What's with the smile there, Morning-star?"

"You sounded kind of jealous just now, and I really like it."

Gabe grins. "God, you're cute."

My heart flutters as he leans closer to me and brushes his lips against mine. I fall into the kiss happily. "Why are you such a good kisser?" I pull back, suddenly suspicious. "How many girls have you kissed?" It occurs to me how juvenile that question is and my voice rises as I say, "And how many have you had sex with?" My cheeks flush. "I am definitely not ready to do that, FYI!"

Gabe throws back his head and laughs even harder. "Noted." He leans in to kiss me again, but I pull back.

"Nuh-uh, not till you give me numbers."

Gabe rolls his eyes and puts his hands behind his head. "I have only had sex with one girl. I don't know how many girls I've kissed. I haven't counted."

"Ugh. That is the worst possible answer. It means you've kissed a lot. I've kissed two boys, and never had sex."

"Which two?"

I ignore him and say, "I am majorly judging you for being with Caroline."

"Didn't you used to be friends with her?"

"Yes," I grumble.

"What happened there?"

"She dropped me and left the Northside. There are a lot more social climbing opportunities on your side of the fence, and that's her thing, as you know."

"Hey now. But, ouch. Getting dumped by your friend must have sucked."

I look at him and he looks back with golden eyes full of compassion. He gives me a gentle smile. My heart flips in my chest. He's so wonderful.

I must be staring because Gabe asks, "What? You have that look."

"What look?"

"Your 'I can't believe I'm making out with a Northsider' look."

I giggle and decide to go along with it instead of telling him the truth. "Caught me. You're just lucky I don't have it in me to argue with anyone else tonight."

He laughs again, and I cuddle into him as he places his arm around me. I rest my cheek in between his shoulder and neck, which is where I like it best.

# CHAPTER

## —— 53 ——

The following week, I'm at another Northsider party, this one hosted by Sam, which should make it better, but somehow doesn't. I'm standing in the corner of Sam's ginormous living room while Mary Sue keeps me company. I'm enjoying myself. Mary Sue is always an entertaining conversationalist. But then she announces, "I'm leaving. Too much drinking! Besides, nothing good happens after 9:30." She fixes her sparkly "party" headband and sails off to say goodbye to Sam.

As soon as she leaves, Caroline moves to join me. Caroline's walk is purposeful and slow. Her hair swings around her oval face. "Wow. Look at you at another one of our parties. Must be so exciting for you."

"Hey, Caroline. Yeah, it's a real thrill."

"Sarcasm." She narrows her eyes. "So you don't want to be here?"

I sense I'm walking into a trap and backpedal. "No, not the case at all. I love Sam. Happy to be at his party."

"But you don't really have anyone to talk to here. It must be awkward."

I glare at her. "My boyfriend is here, so I'm more than fine. But thanks *so* much for your concern." I regret my words almost as soon as they leave my mouth. *Boyfriend?* Why did I have to say that?

Gabe and I haven't discussed labels.

Caroline's eyes light up at my obvious discomfort. "'Boyfriend.' Really? I didn't know it was so serious between you two."

"Oh, well, I wouldn't say serious."

Caroline smiles at me narrowly. "With Gabe, 'boyfriend' is definitely serious. Trust me." She flips her hair again. "He didn't call me his girlfriend until forever. And that was about the same time he told me he loved me. So, you see what I mean."

I've never wanted to punch someone so badly. But I smile tightly and say, "I really don't, but—"

Before I can finish, Gabe walks up and swings an arm around my shoulders. Caroline stiffens.

"Gabe," she acknowledges.

"Caroline." Gabe matches her curt tone.

"Anna was just telling me how you two are official."

Gabe looks blank. I want the ground to open up and swallow me whole. He sends Caroline an easy smile and kisses me on the cheek. I appreciate the show of support but would like nothing more than to safely escape this situation.

"So glad you're taking such an interest in our dating lives, Caroline. Really means a lot."

I try to restrain my smile. There's an edge to Gabe's voice, but his posture is still relaxed.

Caroline's mouth drops open. "So it's true? You're together now?"

Gabe gives her a cold look that scares me a little. The thought of being on the receiving end of Gabe's disdain is heartbreaking. "Yes, it is."

You'd never know he'd never actually agreed to what he's affirming.

He takes my hand and says, "Let's go say hi to Sam."

Gabe leads me to where Sam is talking to some lacrosse guys. I puff out my shoulders to boost my confidence. Gabe notices and laughs. "Later tonight, make sure you tell me what's going on in your head right now."

I look at him. "Why?"

"Because I know it'll make me laugh."

I give him a look, but he bends down and brushes another affectionate kiss on my cheek. I grin up at him, feeling happy and light. I have a strong desire to pull him in for a proper kiss. I settle for stealing a quick peck.

We join Sam and their teammates. I find them easier to speak to than I imagined. I try not to feel too self-conscious about how many tall, in-shape guys are surrounding me. I groan internally when Scottie joins the circle. Pretending he's not there, I angle my body so I don't have to look at him.

All is well until Scottie zeroes in on me, and his glance flickers over my hand, which is brushing the back of Gabe's. Scottie's gaze settles just as our pinkies momentarily link and unlink. Aware of his interest, I move my hand from Gabe's and grip it more firmly around my cup.

"So, you two are a whole thing. Who'd have thunk it?" Scottie observes sharply. "Not me. But that's the thing about our Gabe-y here. He keeps us guessing."

"So glad to hear that, buddy. Would hate to think of you sitting home bored by all our other lame, predictable friends," Gabe teases. He slings an arm around my shoulder.

Everyone laughs. Scottie smiles, but he remains keenly focused on us. "Hey, guys, just thought of something in honor of Gabe and our new friend Anna."

Sam rolls his eyes. "Great. Can't wait to hear your pearl of wisdom."

"What happens if you put a Cuban and Jew together?"

"Scottie—" Sam warns.

I tense looking at Gabe, but his face remains neutral, relaxed even, as he looks at Scottie.

"A cheap cigar!" Scottie laughs and a few of the others follow suit.

Sam looks at me. I flash him a look, then turn back to Scottie.

I'm opening my mouth to tell Scottie off when Gabe spins me away to the makeshift dance floor where a few people are jumping along to a Today's Top Hits Spotify mix.

"Why'd you do that?" I ask.

"Would you believe it's because I badly wanted to dance with you?"

"No."

"Look, I'm at my best friend's party with my best girl. I don't want to waste energy on getting into it with Scottie."

I narrow my eyes. "That's insanely avoidant, Gabe. Someone needs to put him in his place."

"But does it have to be us, and does it have to be tonight?"

I look into his glittering eyes and at his handsome face, and think. Someone has to give Scottie a proper come-uppance. But then Gabe dips me with such finesse that I laugh.

Gabe is a fun dancer. Unlike most boys I know, he's not afraid to try big moves. I, myself, am a slightly awkward but very enthusiastic dancer. We make each other giggle with ridiculous moves. At some point when the music slows, he pulls me in close. He takes my beer and puts it down, so I can wrap my arms around his neck. My head spins pleasantly as I breathe in the smell of cheap beer mixed with Gabe's usual scent of spearmint and musk. His lips find mine, and I melt into him dreamily.

\* \* \* \*

Later that night, I'm lying in bed, mentally replaying the super steamy car make-out session I had with Gabe after the party. I guess SUVs do serve a certain purpose. But a nagging thought disrupts my reverie: What does it say about Gabe that he chooses to overlook Scottie's bigoted comments? What does it say about me that I let him? When we ignore Scottie's racist jokes, don't we give him tacit approval to keep making them? I turn to my side, troubled. Wasn't that everything I'd been raised not to do?

# CHAPTER

## 54

**G**abe: Checking in on my girl. Everything ok?

I stare at the text for the fourth time that morning. Conflicting emotions course through me: glee that he is calling me "his," and stomach-churning anxiety from another source. I can't get Scottie's "cheap cigar" comment out of my head. Or, more accurately, I can't forget the way Gabe totally ignored it. I don't know how to justify his passivity. I've tried to speak to him about it twice. First, asking him if it bothered him as much as it troubled me. Gabe just shrugged it off, claiming, "Scottie is an insecure dick." Then again when I asked Gabe if he'd consider confronting Scottie. He'd totally shut down and asked me to drop it.

I look at my phone trying to think how to reply, when the phone starts vibrating and Gabe's name and his (heart-thump inducing) picture appear on my screen. My whole body tenses up. The temptation to just answer is almost overwhelming, but I'm afraid that once I hear his soothing voice I might forget why I'm so upset in the first place. And I can't do that. This feels too important to just let go. I quickly send the call to voicemail.

Ugh, I realize, he might think something is really wrong with me. I usually respond to any contact from him in less than two seconds flat.

Me: Hey! Cramming for my math exam.

I type out my lie quickly.

Gabe: If you're up for a study break later, hit me
up. Good luck!

I send him a picture of my desk.

Me: Unlikely, will probably be here all day!

Gabe: Go get them, Banana! Also, love that pic.

Tears instantly well up in my eyes. I hadn't realized my screen-shot captured the picture of me and Gabe I recently tacked front and center on the bulletin board over my desk—the one Sam had taken of us after a recent Coach Farmer session. Gabe's arm is around my shoulder and we are staring adoringly at each other. I flop backwards on my bed, feeling like the lowest of the low for having lied to Gabe. I throw my phone to the side and bury my head under my pillow, wanting to escape myself and the day.

\* \* \* \*

A hours later, I'm sitting with Del outside The Scoop, our favorite ice cream shop in town. We're on a white wooden bench in front of the peach-painted store. Del is eating one scoop of mint chocolate chip in a cup. I'm eating an ice cream sundae, known as The Chocolate Death, in a bowl. We both shiver despite our hats and scarfs. It's a tad chilly to be eating ice cream outdoors.

"It's not helping," I whine, again feeling emotions bubble to my throat.

Del eyes me skeptically. "Did you really think you'd find clarity through The Chocolate Death?"

"Yes," I respond emphatically. "Chocolate really clears things up for me." I grumble and shove another bite in my mouth. It's starting to melt a little and my lips are sticky.

"I think you should talk to him," Del says again.

"I know, but I've tried and he won't hear it. I don't want to be disappointed again." I wave my spoon in the air, this way and that, matching my frenzied feelings. "I like him so much it hurts."

Del sighs. "I hope I feel that way about someone one day."

"You will, and it won't be this morally gray for you," I say, longing for the same imagined simplicity. "My mom wouldn't put up with this nonsense for a second," I whisper, stabbing my spoon into my ice cream, then downing another large bite.

"Yeah, but you're not your mom. Isn't that what this whole thing with Gabe has taught you?"

I nod as her words sink in, my mouth too full of ice cream to respond. "Yeah, but right now, I don't remember if that is a good thing or a bad thing."

Del puts her ice cream down and turns to face me.

I eagerly turn to face her, scooping another chocolate bite into my mouth. She has that calm, ethereal "I'm about to dispense super wisdom to you" expression on her face. But, just as she starts to say, "I think—"

"Anna," a shocked voice interrupts from behind me. I know who it is even before the faint scent of spearmint reaches my nose. My heart drops to my feet. I jump up and turn to face Gabe.

As I find myself, ice cream in hand, staring into his beautiful, bewildered face, intense shame washes over me.

He looks at the ice cream I'm clutching and Del, then back at me.

"Study break already?" His voice is emotionless, but his eyes are filled with hurt.

"I... uh ..." He's holding what appears to be the Tessa Bailey romance novel that comes out next month and a bouquet of tulips.

"How did you get that?" I ask, dumbfounded, pointing at the book.

"I found this website that releases early copies in exchange for a review." His posture his rigid and his voice is cold as ice.

"That's amazing, I've been dying to read it."

"I know." His eyes refuse to meet mine.

I feel as though someone punched me in the gut. Unable to find the right words, I breathe in sharply, prepared to apologize. But then I think of how he let Scottie spew that lovely mix of anti-Semitism and xenophobia and my mood rapidly shifts. "I lied about studying because I'm really mad at you!"

Gabe blinks, taken totally aback. "Mad about what?"

"The party. You just let Scottie say that crap to us and you didn't do anything." My hands form a death grip on the ice cream bowl.

Gabe's jaw goes rigid. "Well, Anna, next time try being honest."

"I tried talking to you about this and you dismissed me!"

"What about letting something go for once. Novel concept, I know."

"What happened at the party was a huge deal and you're ignoring it." Furious tears fill my eyes.

"So you lied to me? Grow up." He drops the book in my hands and turns, throwing the tulips into the cow-shaped trash can next to the bench and starts to walk away.

"Gabe, wait!" I start to run after him, tossing my ice cream in the trash, where it plonks on top of my flowers. "Let's talk about this."

He turns and holds his hands up in front of him. "I need some space right now."

I nod, but I'm surprised by his cold expression. "Okay."

As he watches a tear roll down my cheek, he hesitates for a brief moment, but then the angry glint returns to his eye and frustration emanates from his body. "I thought we'd come farther than this." And with that he turns around and leaves me. I walk over to the trash and fish out the tulips, which are now splattered with chocolate ice cream.

Del hands me a napkin and winces. "Well, it was super sweet that he was going to bring you a book."

I groan and rest my head on her shoulder.

\* \* \* \*

After returning from town and a nauseating run (ice cream sundaes and runs do not mix!), I step out of the shower and slip into my silk olive-green robe. I'd begged for it after my sweet-sixteen trip to New York, where we stayed at a boutique hotel in Nolita. I discovered the robe at the hotel gift shop and thought it would be so romantic and mature to have a silk robe. Now I feel like an imposter wearing it.

My mind turns to Gabe for the hundredth time since he left me on the street. I wonder if he's read yet any of my quite lengthy explanatory texts or emails. Sure, I definitely shouldn't have lied. But he should have been stronger the other night!

I check my phone again. Still nothing. My anxiety is shooting through the roof.

Me: When can we just talk about this??

I gnaw nervously on my lips after I hit send. Am I over-texting just a bit? But then my phone dings. I eagerly grab it.

Gabe: Look, we both need to cool off. We'll talk soon.

I stare at my phone, and blink several times, before sinking to the ground and burying my face in my knees. Gabe has never before put this type of distance between us.

Eventually, I force myself to stand up. I find the Tessa Bailey book and, clutching it in my hands, take it to bed with me. I fall asleep reading.

# CHAPTER

## 55

On Tuesday at school, Caroline saunters over to where I'm sitting with Del and Mason. She gives me a smug, cat-that-ate-the-canary smile. "How quickly young love fizzles."

Mason and Del both look at me, confused.

My stomach sinks, even though I don't know exactly what Caroline is talking about. I look down at my veggie sushi roll and push it around on my plate. I would love to reply acerbically, but the huge lump in my throat prevents me from saying anything at all.

"Can we help you with anything, Caroline?" Del finally says. "Or is this just a friendly lunchtime visit?" Del looks at her expectantly.

Caroline gives a hard look at Del. "I like your sweater. Too bad your taste in friends is so disappointing."

Mason rolls his eyes. He thinks Caroline is too ridiculous to respond to.

"Wow, Caroline. What a burn," Del responds sarcastically.

"Whatever. If the shoe fits." Caroline finally turns to me. She gives me another self-satisfied smirk. "I knew you couldn't possibly be Gabe's girlfriend for long."

"Just spit out whatever lovely thing you came to tell Anna and get on with it," Mason says, shooting me a worried look.

"That's really all I had to say. This morning Gabe practically announced to all of us that you two were barely even seeing each other anymore." Caroline looks thrilled with herself. "Well, enjoy your little lunch." She waves her fingers in a goodbye and flits off.

My stomach shoots to the ground. I glance over to where Gabe is sitting with his lacrosse friends. He isn't facing me, so all I can see is the back of his head. I slump further in my seat. I haven't exchanged one word with him in more than twenty-four hours. I cross my arms over my chest. "Do you guys think he really said that?"

Mason rubs the bridge of his nose as if he has a brewing headache. "No way. Look, I don't like the guy, but he's way too much of a 'gentleman' to talk about you with his ex-girlfriend."

"Yeah, I agree, Anna. Doesn't sound like Gabe."

I nod. Their words ring true, which softens, but doesn't remove the pit in my stomach.

But then Gabe glances over at our table. Our eyes meet for a moment. I can't read his expression. He nods at me, then quickly turns back to his group.

"Ouch," I mumble. "That was pretty frosty." I look anxiously at Del and Mason. "What should I do?"

"Have you thought about what you want to say when you talk?" Del asks.

"I kind of want to apologize for lying and then talk about why I was so upset in the first place."

Del smiles. "That seems like a solid jumping-off point."

Mason looks at Del as if she's lost her mind. "I totally disagree. You're making completely valid points, Anna. He needs to start standing up for what is right. Not just with Scottie, but in the larger sense too."

"I think you've been spending too much time with Zoe," Del replies. "They're in a relationship. It can't be all politics."

"But how can she be in a relationship with someone who doesn't care about anything important?"

"How do you know he doesn't care?" Del argues.

"Well, he doesn't care enough to do anything about it. So that really says it all right there."

282

As Mason and Del continue to go back and forth on this point, my mind turns from the anxiety generated by getting Gabe's cold shoulder to outright anger. Mason is right. All I did was tell a tiny fib. He's the one sitting casually by and not fighting for what's right. How dare he get mad at me?

"You okay there, champ?" Del eyes me critically. "You have a scary look on your face."

I watch as Gabe gets up from the table to throw something in the trash. He turns around again and glances at me, and this time I full-on glare at him. He has the audacity to look annoyed. He shakes his head and returns to his table.

"Anna, I don't think scowling at Gabe is the way to handle this," Del says. "You need to talk to him."

"Del is totally right. Talk to him and find out if he's capable of grasping how much his dad contributes to the downfall of society."

"That's not what I meant." Del sounds exasperated.

I nod again. I stare at Gabe, hoping he'll turn back so I can give him a kinder look. But, for the rest of lunch, he doesn't so much as peek over at our table.

Beethoven starts to play over the loudspeakers. We gather our trash and dump it, carefully scraping our food scraps in the compost bin that Zoe recently set up.

As I walk to fifth period, I finally get the nerve to text Gabe and ask if we can talk after school. He responds quickly with "That's a good idea." Tears prick my eyes. I hope he doesn't break up with me. I'd be devastated.

# CHAPTER 56

After school, Gabe and I meet in his car. I feel nervous and unsure of myself. I look at him. His handsome profile, which usually excites me, doesn't. He seems intimidating and unreachable.

"So, are you breaking up with me?" I demand. "Your girlfriend already told me. So, don't worry, I'm not surprised."

Gabe turns his head towards me. He searches my face. "I thought *you* were my girlfriend."

My mouth falls open a little. "I thought so too, but we never made it official, so I didn't know."

Gabe smiles, looking more like his normal self. "Not that it stopped you from telling certain people that."

I flush. "Well, I called it like I saw it, and I was right. At least then."

Gabe reaches over and, as is his habit, tucks a stray curl behind my ear. "Hey, I still want you to be my girlfriend. I'm just mad at you. There is a difference, you know."

I smile. "Okay, good." My smile gets wider. "I've never had a boyfriend before." I close my eyes to see how it feels.

"What are you doing?"

"I'm seeing if I feel any different."

"Because we're in our first fight?"

"No, because I have a boyfriend."

He laughs. "Okay. So do you?"

I lift one eye. "I'm not sure. I guess I thought our first fight would be more throwing stuff, less cold shoulder."

"Throwing stuff at each other?" Gabe sounds alarmed.

"Not in a way that, like, actually hits each other. Just, you know, in a fit of passion."

"Is this another romance novel thing?"

"Maybe. But there would be blatant sexual tension even in our fights. Which is way more fun and sexy than being ignored at lunch."

Gabe looks a little guilty. "Sorry about that." He gives me a sheepish smile. "I was just so pissed."

"Why exactly were you so mad? Because I lied?"

"No, it's the constant pressure to think about things the way you do."

I blink. "Oh."

Gabe looks at me with intensity. "And I guess I felt kind of foolish buying you flowers and that book, only to catch you avoiding me."

I wince. "Yeah, not my finest moment." I exhale. "Look, Gabe, I was upset that you didn't stand up to Scottie at the party, and I kind of freaked out. I just really need you to be able to confront stuff like that."

Gabe nods slowly. "Part of why I'm upset is because I have been doing more of that. I've been arguing with my dad, and I've been processing the Scottie stuff differently, so it sucked having it thrown back in my face."

"I get that. I do. But I've been seeing things more through your eyes, too, and it freaked me out when I just enjoyed dancing with you after what Scottie said to us. I can't ignore that stuff, Gabe. It's too ugly, and I don't want you to ignore it either."

As he often does in tense moments, Gabe runs his hand through his thick, tousled hair.

The gesture normally makes me lustful, since something about his tousled hair really gets to me, but my heart is too in flux to feel romantic right now.

"Anna, you need to understand this. When it comes to standing up to my dad, and even in a way, Scottie, I'm only going to go so far. I'm not getting bogged down in what I can't control, and I'm not willing to risk putting my dad's reputation on the line. And whenever possible, I'm going to enjoy my life, enjoy my family."

"At any cost?" I push.

Gabe shakes his head in disbelief. "For the purposes of this conversation, yes." He looks tired, and all of a sudden, he seems less like the arrogant, suave boy I've spent the last month with. "I care about you, Anna. A lot. But you need to figure out if you can be with me as I am, because if not, we should call this off now." He leans over and gently kisses the side of my forehead. "Think about it, and let me know." When he gives me a final intense look, I realize he's waiting for me to get out of the car. I move slowly, reluctantly, but finally open the door and step out.

I watch as he drives off, more confused than ever.

# CHAPTER

## 57

I don't hear from Gabe for the rest of the night. I feel lonely and agitated as I replay our conversation in the car.

I miss him desperately. And not just his perfect bod and handsome face either. I miss talking with him, laughing with him, and the wonderfulness I feel from being in his presence.

"It sounds like you're saying you're in love with him," Del says when I share my distress. She's sitting on the carpeted floor of my bedroom applying navy nail polish to her toes. Her messy topknot spills over her face as she states what she clearly thinks is oh-so obvious.

"Love?" Mason looks up from *the New Yorker* he's perusing. He's lying on his stomach at the foot of my bed. "That's a little dramatic, Del," Mason says with a laugh, but his eyes look a little panicked. "Right, Anna?"

I'm too dumbstruck to answer. "Oh my god." I sit up, my hair sticking to my face. "Is that what this is?" I look at my two best friends in shock.

Del looks amused and Mason seems annoyed.

"Are you in love with Zoe, Mason?" I ask, wanting someone who's familiar with the sensation to explain it to me.

Mason flushes and tugs at his scarf. "Um, I think I love her. I mean, I really admire her."

Del looks at him thoughtfully. "You love her, but you're not in love with her?"

"I—" He breaks off and looks down. "I think so." He lets out a whoosh of breath. "That feels crappy to say. I'm not even sure if it's true. I admire her so much, and I'm attracted to her because I think she's amazing. So I don't know. Maybe I am in love with her, right?" He looks at me, then Del, as if we have the answer.

I feel concerned by the increasing paleness of Mason's face. "It sounds like there's something there," I encourage him.

Del looks doubtful, then shrugs. "I mean, sure, I think admiring someone and feeling attracted to them are pretty major. Maybe you're falling in love."

Mason's face relaxes. "Yeah, maybe I am."

"It's funny, right? Love? Like there are certain people we love because they're our parents or our oldest friends, and then there are people we love for reasons we can't label, and I guess you can also love the idea of someone," I ramble.

"I guess the question is: Is it better to love someone emotionally or because you like who they are?" Del asks.

Mason looks at us, and a calmness settles on his face. "Ideally, you'd have both, right?"

Del and I nod. Of course that's true.

A wave of sadness falls over me. How do I fit Gabe into any of this?

# CHAPTER
## 58

$A$ few days later, still confused over what to say to Gabe, I take refuge at Bookcourt. I make a beeline for the romance section, where I spot Ms. Adler. She's on the phone in her little glass office off the back of the store. Her face looks uncharacteristically agitated. A moment later, she slams down the phone and rests her forehead in her hands. She looks up and sees me staring. I wave tentatively, giving her what I hope is an encouraging smile.

She stands up and exits her office. As the glass door shuts, I catch a snippet of the Joni Mitchell track she's playing from her office.

"Anna." Ms. Adler's expression softens. "I've been meaning to reach out to you."

"You have?"

"Yes, of course, sweetie." She walks over to me and squeezes my shoulder. "I'll forever be grateful for all you did to help uncover what Tom and Alfred were up to." Her expression darkens as she mentions her son's name.

"Well, it was really Del who figured all that out," I say, shifting my stance from one foot to the other.

"Yes, but your mom told me how it was you who pushed everyone to help." She sighs wearily. "As shocking as it all was, it's so important to know the truth now."

I look at Ms. Adler. "So, is it true what they say?"

"What's that, dear?" she asks.

"Does the truth really set you free?"

She lets out a tired laugh. "I'm not sure. The truth tends to be pretty darn complicated."

My stomach turns. "So what happens now?"

"Well, now I have some apologies to make, some answers to demand, and I have to figure out how to return the special spirit to this place."

We both look around the store. The floors are still gleaming and the walls are still blue and pink. "Maybe it can come back even better than before," I suggest.

"Maybe." Ms. Adler looks at me, pondering. "What made you keep fighting to figure out what was happening at the store?"

"For one, you really changed my life when I was younger and struggling with reading. You gave me such a gift—the love of books. It really set me free from something."

"Oh honey—if nothing else, that's what we're here for at Bookcourt." She embraces me.

"And then I guess someone important to me reminded me to trust my own instincts and not to rush to conclusions; to ask questions rather than come up with quick answers. That's really what led to me realize something was awry." My mind flashes to Gabe and all the times he reminded me not to get mired in doubt and to stay true to myself and the process.

"I love that," Ms. Adler says softly. "You know what? You're my good-luck charm."

I smile. "Really?"

"Yes. I am about to meet with the store staff."

"The whole staff?"

Ms. Adler nods. "Yes, everyone, even Terry and the others."

"Wow! Quite a big deal"

"Sure is." She taps her chin. "I wasn't quite sure what I was going to say to them, but I'm going to keep what you just said in mind. It seems like a really wonderful blueprint for figuring things out."

I stand up a little taller. "You're right. It totally is."

We smile at each other and say goodbye. Twenty minutes later, I leave the store with two books in hand. I reach into my pocket for my phone and call Gabe. He answers on the second ring.

"Hey there." His tone is warm but a bit hesitant.

I suck in my breath. "Hey."

A brief silence spins out.

"Is everything okay?" he finally asks.

"Yes, um, I just had a really great talk with Ms. Adler, and I wanted to thank you." I'm standing at the corner of Main and Cranberry. Foot traffic and street cars swoosh around me.

"Thank me?" he says.

«Without you, I don't think I'd ever have figured out what was really going on at Bookcourt."

"I don't know about that, Anna. I think you would have. It just might have taken you a little longer."

"Knowing you has made such an impact on me." I feel choked up but try to disguise it. Things feel so fragile between us.

"Same, " he says gently. "I miss you."

"I miss you too. So much."

Another silence spins out.

"Can we talk after your game tomorrow?" I ask, finally feeling ready.

"Yes, of course."

"Ok, well, I know you'll be great."

I hear Gabe exhale. "I don't know about that."

"You always are."

"Not always," he says, sounding down on himself. I hear his father call him from another room. "I've got to go, but I'll see you tomorrow?" He sounds uncertain.

"Yes!" I say exuberantly even though I feel overwhelmed.

Gabe chuckles lightly and says another goodbye before hanging up.

I stare at my phone for a minute and then shove it in my pocket. I take a winding route home, walking by all my favorite streets in town as I anticipate tomorrow.

# CHAPTER
## 59

The next day, I drag Del to Gabe's Thursday evening lacrosse game. It's a fairly big deal since they're playing our biggest rivals, Pencoast. We sit in what have become my usual seats—the middle of the third row.

At the start of the game, I make eye contact with Gabe, his white shoulder pads making him appear broader than usual. He nods at me, but then quickly looks away. His game face is on.

The first ten minutes of the game are largely uneventful except for a brilliant pass by Gabe and a fumble by Scottie.

Senator Delgado, who's sitting in the row ahead of us along with his security detail, turns to greet me.

I reply with a friendly "Hi."

Del smiles weakly, looking as if she'd rather be anywhere else.

The senator turns to talk to the man next to him, who has slicked-back hair and wears a blue button-down shirt. When I catch the man's profile, I have no doubt he's Scottie's dad. The resemblance is overwhelming—the thin, pencil-like face and the light brown hair.

We all cheer as Sam blocks a shot in goal. I whoop and jump up and down and even Del claps loudly. A few minutes later, Edgartown's offense is running toward Pencoast's goal.

I can hear Caroline, who's in the first row, cheer loudly for

Gabe. She even holds up a sign she's made for him with his number, "38." I want to murder her. As she calls out Gabe's name, I see Scottie—who lacks Gabe's game focus—look up, and I'm a little startled by the look of pure hatred on Scottie's face as he takes in Caroline's sign.

A minute later, with some graceful footwork, Gabe breaks free of the Pencoast defenders and is wide open. Scottie has the ball and is struggling to get past a defender. I hear his teammates shout to pass it to Gabe, but Scottie doesn't. The coach is getting increasingly angry. Gabe continues to outmaneuver his opponents and to get free, but Scottie refuses to pass to him.

The whistle blows. Edgartown's coach calls a timeout.

I look at Gabe. I can see the tension in his jawline as he purposefully walks over to Scottie. My heart is in my throat. I want to run down to the field to offer my support. It's unusual to see Gabe looking so tense.

"What the fuck was that, bro?" I hear Gabe say as he angrily confronts Scottie.

I'm relieved when Sam stands next to Gabe and lays a hand on his shoulder. "Let's all cool off, guys."

Senator Delgado freezes in front of me. He looks disapproving but doesn't move.

Scottie's dad also looks a little uncomfortable.

Gabe shrugs off Sam's hand. "I'm not cooling off until this asshole tells me what that was all about."

The crowd on our side goes very quiet, as if they sense that a fight is brewing.

Scottie crosses his arms at his chest. "Ah, here's the famous Latin temper. I knew Gabe couldn't hide his natural state forever."

I'm seeing red. Del looks around to see how she can help. I hold my breath.

Gabe pauses. He looks up to the stands and finds me. Our eyes briefly meet, and I try to communicate that I want him to do what is best for him.

Scottie follows Gabe's gaze and laughs. "You're looking to dykes-for-moms up there for help? I thought you were more of a man than that?"

I feel like someone has drenched me in ice water. Del goes totally still. Finally, we exchange purposeful looks and move to go down. Before we make it more than a step, we hear Gabe yell, "You racist, homophobic fuck" before he lands a hard punch right on Scottie's face. Blood splatters. The team goes toward them, but not before Scottie knees Gabe in the groin and head-butts him. Gabe lands another punch. Scottie's nose and mouth are bleeding, and Gabe's cheeks look inflamed as their teammates rush to drag the two apart. "If you ever fucking talk to me or my girlfriend or anyone else like that again, you're done," Gabe finally says.

Scottie's dad looks at the senator with disapproval. "Gabe's gone way too far this time."

The senator doesn't respond but walks in a clipped gait toward the field.

"Did you all hear that? He basically threatened to kill me. I hope everyone heard that—" But before Scottie can finish, Sam walks over to Scottie and empties the contents of his water bottle onto his face.

# CHAPTER

## 60

Before I can talk to him, Senator Delgado rushes Gabe off the field. An hour later, I approach the Delgados' home on my bike and let out a sigh of relief that I'm almost there. I want to see Gabe with my own eyes and make sure he's okay. Despite the cool air, sweat trickles down my cheek.

"Anna!" Someone calls me as I approach the Delgados' long driveway.

I look up to see Mason running toward me. He crosses the street and reaches the Delgados' property at the same moment I do.

Mason, like me, is out of breath. He's wearing a white t-shirt, his blond hair windswept. "I saw you from my porch. Are you okay?" Gabe and Mason live across the street from each other on Cranberry Road, the dividing line between the East and North sides.

"Yes, sorry, Mase. I have to get to Gabe's. There was this whole shit show at the game today."

"What happened?"

I shake my head. Anxious to keep pedaling up the driveway, I get back on my bike. "I'll fill you in later, but there was a big fight between Gabe and Scottie. Del was there. She can tell you."

"A fight?" Mason repeats with a shake of his head. He looks

toward Gabe's house and then back at me. "Okay, well…" He hesitates.

"I'm sorry, Mase, but I really need to talk to Gabe." I'm about to pedal off, but he grabs my arm. I'm surprised. I look at his hand on my forearm, then back at him.

He shakes his head again. "Yes, right."

"I'll let you know what happens."

I'm about to speed off when he says, "Wait."

"What?" I shimmer with impatience.

"Can you stop by my place after? I want to talk to you, um, about some stuff."

"Yeah, sure." I give him a rushed smile and pedal off.

"See you then!" he calls behind me.

"Yup!" I call back without turning around.

I pedal up the long driveway, throw my bike to the side of the flagstaff steps, rush past the two stone lions that flank the door, and knock.

* * * *

The Delgados' housekeeper, Marla, lets me in. She looks concerned and frenzied. I greet her, and I'm about to run up the grand staircase to Gabe's room when I hear my name being called. I want to scream in frustration. But I swallow my attitude when I find myself face to face with Senator Delgado.

He's wearing the same shirt and khakis that he wore to the game. "Annabelle, hello. You look a little flushed, young lady. Are you here to see Gabe?" He narrows his eyes. "I take it today was your influence."

I smile weakly. "Hmm, I can't take all the credit, Senator." I bite my lip. "I hope you're not too mad at him. You know he'd do anything for you."

The senator nods. "Yes, like attack the son of my biggest donor."

I grimace. "Well, Scottie was being a real jerk," I say, "but, yes, violence is never the answer. There was a lot of blood, which is highly unfortunate."

"Scottie was being quite the prick, but he comes from a long line of pricks, so I'm not sure he can help himself."

A loud laugh escapes me. The senator smiles, then looks sober. "Not that I want this repeated by either of you. You and your mom are hotheads, and that's not how we do business here."

I bristle but force myself to be polite. "But, sir, Scottie insulted not only you and your son, but also me and my parents, and I'm..." I break off.

"Yes?" The senator asks with playful innocence.

"Eh, his good friend, so what was he supposed to do?"

Senator Delgado laughs heartily. "'Good friend'? Is that what you kids are calling it? Well, if I ever mope the way Gabe has this week over a 'good friend,' God help me."

My eyes light up. "He's been moping all week? Because of me?" My smile widens.

"Your poker face betrays you, Annabelle. Perhaps not the most strategic move." He laughs again when he sees how mortified I look. "I'm just teasing you, my dear. Let's try and not be too serious now. We've had enough of that today, and I'm afraid all this won't end so easily."

My stomach swishes nervously. I hope Gabe doesn't get into too much trouble. "Yes, sir."

"Well, remind Bea and Gabe we're here if they need us."

"Will do!" I assure him before I bound up the spiral staircase, past the urns and plants on the landing, up another flight, and down a long hall toward Gabe's room.

"Gabe!" I exclaim as I throw open the door and see his disheveled and bloody face.

"Did you bring more ice?" Bea asks anxiously.

I say yes and close the door with my foot, pulling multiple ice packs and bandages out of my backpack.

Gabe winces. "Who else are you planning to bandage up?"

"Very funny." At the front of his bed, I sit next to where his head is propped up on pillows. I put an ice pack on his lip, guiding his hands to hold it in place as I apply Neosporin to the cuts above his eyebrows and those on his cheek, even though I can tell they've already been tended to.

"You didn't have to come." He holds my gaze. "What a complete mess."

He looks so vulnerable on his bed that my heart melts a little. I want to cuddle up next to him and rest my hand on his uncut cheek, but instead I ask, "Are you okay? That was awful."

"I don't know." His expression is unreadable. "The whole thing got out of hand so fast."

Now Bea and I exchange looks. Gabe looks blankly out the window.

"What Scottie said was so repulsive. Breaking someone's nose isn't the most productive way to handle it, but—"

"He deserved it!" Bea interrupts. "Gabe was protecting your honor just like in the movies."

"I'm pretty sure the damsel in distress motif is passé, but anything can make a comeback."

"What does that mean?" Bea asks, looking at me with interest.

"Don't encourage her, Anna. It's dangerous."

Bea scoffs. "Dangerous? I wish. I would love to be dangerous."

"So would I. I would love to be able to intimidate people."

"Exactly."

Gabe looks between us and shakes his head. "Anna, when you're agreeing with a twelve-year-old, it's time to re-examine your position."

I smile at Bea. "I guess it depends."

"On what?"

"On how smart the twelve-year-old is."

Bea beams. "Well, I'm very smart. So you don't ever have to worry about agreeing with me."

I smile indulgently. "Good to know."

"Okay, Bea. Mind giving me and Anna some privacy?"

Bea pouts, in a manner so much like her brother that it startles me. "Why can't I hear too?"

Gabe looks at her kindly. My heart flutters again when I think about what a great big brother he is.

"If you give us ten minutes, I'll sneak you some Fruit Roll-Ups later."

"An entire box and you have a deal."

I laugh. "Very skillful, Bea."

She shrugs arrogantly. "When you got it, you know it."

I laugh again.

"Okay, fine," Gabe grumbles. He throws a small pillow at Bea that misses as she walks out of the room.

We watch her leave. I turn back toward Gabe. "How are you really?"

With Bea gone, Gabe's expression further sours. Gone is any humor. He was just protecting her, I realize. He looks ashen. "I don't know who I'm more disgusted with, Scottie or myself."

I go to his side and take his hand. "Gabe, I agree it got extreme, but what he said was unforgivable."

Gabe closes his eyes. "Yeah, hard to unhear that. I couldn't stand it when he went after you like that. It was so hateful, so public…" He trails off as if his mind is far away.

I take his chin and gently bring his face back to mine. "It'll be okay."

"Will it? I'm sure I'll at least be suspended for a handful of games, and my relationship with Scottie will never be the same, which is fine, but we share a lot of the same friends. And I'm sure his dad hates me now, which I'm almost relieved by, except if it messes anything up for my dad. If that happens, I don't know what I'll do. But what I really can't get over is how I acted, what I risked out there. I totally lost control."

"It was an impossible situation."

"Nothing is impossible, Anna. I can see it on your face too. We both know I could have tried to get him thrown out of the game. Anything but what I did. My dad would never have done anything like that."

"Gabe, you're hurting. It's an emotional day. Dr. Maggie always says when you bottle too much up, you'll blow. And he's been making so many digs for so long that you never…" I break off, realizing finishing my statement would be far from helpful.

Gabe's eyes darken. "What were you going to say? That if I had just listened to you and stood up to him all those other times, today would never have happened? Great. Helpful as always, Anna." His voice is like ice. Fury pulsates through his jawline.

"That's not what I meant at all. I just meant today was a long time coming."

Gabe shakes his head. "It's so unlike me to act that way." He looks at me like I'm a stranger. My heart cracks.

Gabe's phone rings just then. I hear him greet his coach in a low, controlled tone. The call is brief, but Gabe's eyes grow more and more cold. Finally, he hangs up.

"What did Coach say?"

"Scottie's off the team for the rest of season. I'm sitting out the next three games."

I close my eyes, feeling awful. "But the semifinals?"

"Yeah, I'll miss 'em," he sighs. "I doubt the team has much of a chance without me or Scottie... This was supposed to be our year, too." The boys' lacrosse team had been a favorite for making it to the all-state championship. I think of all of Gabe's hard work, all his extra conditioning. I hope this setback doesn't mess up his chances at college recruitment.

"I'm so sorry. I wish there was something I could do."

"I think I want you to leave."

"W—what?" I say, stricken.

"I don't like who I am right now, and I need to think."

"And that's my fault?"

"No." His tone softens. "Of course not, but I've changed since knowing you."

"I've changed too."

"Have you? How? I kind of feel like I've been taking all the risks lately. Starting fights with my dad ... and now this." He lays a hand on his head, and I can tell he's in pain.

I move closer to him, wanting to grab his hand to get him to listen. But then he looks up at me and I see a rigidity that chills me. "I'll go, Gabe. I don't think what you're saying is totally fair, but I can see you're hurting."

He nods and closes his eyes. I see a tear escape down his cheek.

I walk out of his room, feeling like my heart is cracked into two. I race out of the house and burst into wild sobs as soon as the Delgados' front door closes behind me.

# CHAPTER
## 61

Coach Farmer decides that Gabe's suspension includes Monday conditioning practices for the rest of the month. By the time the weekend rolls around, it's been ten excruciating days since I last spoke to Gabe. I'm beyond hurt. With all the chaos, I totally forgot that this Friday is the date for the notorious Morningstar-Delgado dinner that Bea arranged what seems like a lifetime ago.

"Mom, you've got to be joking. There's no way I can go to this!"

"Honey, if I can go, you can go." Mom pauses at the door. "Although maybe you have a point. Especially now that Dean Pedrow isn't even coming," she says, referring to the head of Edgartown College. Mom looks to Mimi. "We could say we all came down with a sudden, horrible stomach bug"

Mimi shoots us both reproving looks. "Ladies, get up. We're going. We aren't disappointing a twelve-year-old girl because you're in a fight with her brother, and you don't like her father's politics. It's called class, and I insist that my family have it."

Mom and I exchange looks. When Mimi gets like this, which she rarely does, it means business. We stand up.

"How do I look?" I ask.

"Beautiful, honey." Mom fluffs out my hair from behind my ears, reapplies her own lipstick, and we're off to the Delgado mansion for dinner.

****

My stomach is in knots as we approach the Delgado front door. I think of all the times over the past month that I've been at this house, all under such different circumstances. Just three weeks ago, I had bounded to the door, impossibly excited to see Gabe. He had been waiting for me, opening the grand door before I could even knock and swept me in his arms, off my feet, and into a passionate kiss. I remember that feeling of exploding happiness as I watch Mimi knock on the door now. I steel myself to see him.

Mrs. Delgado and Senator Delgado open the door together, which in my experience is quite rare.

"Lilly, Mimi, so wonderful to see you both." Mrs. Delgado gives them each a warm smile.

The senator, with a more reserved smile, takes their coats and offers them wine.

"We also have excellent brandy. I find it takes the edge and awkwardness off most things," Mrs. Delgado counters, earning a smile from my mom.

Mimi looks embarrassed at the mention of the obvious discomfort and Senator Delgado bristles. "There's nothing for anyone to feel awkward about. Just because Lilly insists on slandering me on TV every night doesn't mean this evening will be anything but a delight."

Lilly's face turns stony. "And just because the senator here insists on championing archaic and harmful bills—"

"Enough," Mimi hisses at Mom as Mrs. Delgado elbows her husband none-too-subtly in the gut.

Bea comes into the foyer, followed by Gabe, who looks as handsome as ever in a hunter green sweater and khakis. I try not to stare at him and find myself completely unsure how to greet him.

"I thought you were going to bring them into the living room right away!" Bea complains. She turns and gives me and Mimi a quick hello before beaming at my mom. "Look! I wore this sweatshirt for you." Bea points to the black top she's wearing with the word "Feminist" in white scrawl.

Senator and Mrs. Delgado roll their eyes in good humor while

308

Gabe's morose expression transforms momentarily into a small smile.

"Come on!" Bea takes my moms' hands and drags them toward one of the two living rooms in the house. "We have awesome appetizers! Wait until you see this spread. They def pulled out the best for you guys."

"Don't give away all our trade secrets, darling," Mrs. Delgado jokes and follows them in. "Oscar," she says to her husband, "why don't you get our guests some drinks?" She looks at me and smiles sympathetically, patting my shoulder. "Always a pleasure to see you, Annabelle."

I smile but can't quite manage to get any words out. I'm watching Gabe, who seems intent on avoiding eye contact with me.

Senator Delgado gives me a somewhat comforting smile before turning to his wife and complaining, "How did we raise such a Lilly Morningstar fangirl?"

"The world is a true mystery," Mrs. Delgado says as they walk into the living room, leaving me alone with Gabe in the foyer.

Several beats of silence pass.

Frustrated by the stiltedness between us, I force myself to look at him. I wait for him to finally lift his head and meet my eyes. He holds my gaze for a moment, and my heart sticks in my throat. Before he breaks eye-contact, I see a flash of torment pass over his face.

"I guess we should head in with the others," he says in a formal tone.

I want to scream at him to act normal. He turns to head into the living room.

"Wait, Gabe," I say, stepping forward.

He pauses and turns slowly. "Look, I'm not really ready to get into anything."

Stung, I fold my arms protectively around myself. "What does that mean? What did I even do to deserve the full-on silent treatment?"

Gabe's expression softens for a split second. "I'm not doing this to punish you. I'm doing this because I'm not sure how I feel

309

about anything right now."

"Meaning…?"

"Meaning that I need to figure out if I like who I am right now… if I like who I am when I'm with you."

I step back. "And what am I supposed to do? Just sit around and twiddle my thumbs while you figure this out? It doesn't feel fair! We've both had to compromise a lot to be together."

"Anna, I'm not saying this is fair, but I'm still not ready to have this discussion with you." His voice falters for a second. "Because of that, I hate that you're here right now."

My eyes burn with tears. "I'm so sorry my presence is such a burden to you, Gabe. Let's just go in and get this over with." I stalk past him, but he touches my arm to stop me.

"That was harsher than I meant it to be. It's really hard for me to see you. I want a clear head right now, and I can't have that when I'm near you." His arms fall back by his side. "Let's just make the best of tonight."

I nod slowly. I want to demand to know when he'll be ready to truly talk, but instead I gulp down my avalanche of feelings and follow him into the living room.

Thirty minutes later, we're seated at dinner, and the only people who aren't in high spirits are me and Gabe.

Everyone else is laughing and having what appears to be an actual good time. Bea is holding court, Mrs. Delgado is re-filling everyone's drinks, and Mimi and Senator Delgado are bonding over having "headstrong" wives.

Gabe's eyes meet mine in a bit of wonder. Neither of us can believe the night is going so well.

We're just cutting into the main course when Marla comes in the room, flustered.

She leans down to the senator and says, in a low voice, "Mr. Peters is here."

Mom and Mimi share a sharp glance. Gabe and Bea both look a bit worried, and he lays a comforting hand on her shoulder.

Mrs. Delgado is the only one who seems calm.

"Excuse my rudeness, but it appears I have an unexpected

visitor," Senator Delgado says.

We watch him leave.

Mrs. Delgado smiles at us as if she doesn't have a care in the world. "Marla, let's top off everyone's drinks, shall we?" She turns to Mimi to ask a question about the hospital where she works when loud voices from the other room startle us into silence.

We hear Mr. Peters bark, "After everything I've done for you, you're just going to stand by and let them unionize? Do you know what that'll mean for every other business in Edgartown?"

"I'm not playing dirty, Jeff. I told you that from the get-go. I don't appreciate all the details you left out when you originally approached me about this. Turning a son and a mother against each other? It's beneath even you."

I'm so shocked by what I'm hearing that I drop my fork, which clinks loudly on my plate.

The sound appears to catch Mr. Peters' attention because he asks, "And just who are you entertaining tonight? I swear I saw a car with some interesting bumper stickers out front."

Before we know it, the dining room door swings open and Mr. Peters is standing there in shock. "How cozy," he seethes. "First your son punches mine, and now you're entertaining the Morningstar family. I don't even know you anymore." Mr. Peters strides out.

We all watch him leave. The senator is stoic, but tension seems to radiate off him, and the rest of the night, a stilted, odd air lingers.

# CHAPTER

## 62

Over the next few days, the strain between Mr. Peters and Senator Delgado intensifies. Mr. Peters goes on a slew of talk shows hinting that the senator has lost his conservative "values," causing wild rumors to start swirling about the senator's future in politics. To top off the media backlash, a video of Gabe punching Scottie makes its way onto the internet, and Twitter has a field day when an old story resurfaces about Senator Delgado spending a night in jail after a bar fight his junior year of college.

To make matters even more complicated, Ms. Adler and the Bookcourt employees finally reach an agreement. The union is approved, and the boycott is over. Unfortunately, the huge loss in profits over the past few months cut deep, and Ms. Adler decides to put The Bookery up for sale to keep the store afloat. I'm devastated for Kim and mourn all our great bookstore memories. Who knows what the new owners will do?

Losing the Bookery isn't the only consequence. As customers cautiously return, a shift in the store's atmosphere becomes apparent. Lingering distrust between the customers and Ms. Adler taints the air with a strange heaviness. I hope the tension passes. Increasing numbers of protesters start to arrive at the Delgados' house, with pro-union activists celebrating on one side. On the other is a crowd angry about the senator's "failure" to keep unions out of

Edgartown. Both sides are pissed at him.

The only upside is Ms. Adler finally fires Alfred from Bookcourt. She doesn't explain why, only saying mixing family and business isn't always a good idea. She rehires Terry, and nearly every employee returns to work, except Tom, of course.

Meanwhile, Gabe ignores my calls for two days when I attempt to check on him. Del and my moms try to console me, but I'm a mess.

When I wake up on Sunday morning, I feel increasingly frustrated that Gabe is taking this out on me, and decide he's has had enough time to wallow. As gather for morning bagels, I announce to my moms and Del that I'm going to go to the Delgados' house to have it out with Gabe today.

"I think you should give him some more space," Del advises. "Did you see the footage of what's happening in front of his house? It looks wild."

"It must be so upsetting for all of them. They're facing a barrage of protests from all sorts of people with unconventional beliefs." Mimi shakes her head as she sips orange juice. "It's no longer just about unions. It's taxes and individual liberty and who even knows what."

"I hope little Bea is okay," Mom worries.

We all look at her in surprise.

"What?" she asks.

I groan. "But I can't wait one more second. This is insane! Gabe's being irrational, and he's never irrational. It's annoying! If we're over, fine, but I can't have it end like this."

"Is it really fine?" Mimi asks sympathetically.

A new round of tears forms in my eyes.

Mimi, Mom, and Del simultaneously push toward me the individual packs of tissues they've been carrying around since the lacrosse game. I take a tissue from Del and blow my nose heartily. "No, it would be awful."

"I don't understand how Gabe can't see how much you've changed since knowing him," Mom comments.

We all turn to her in surprise again.

"What do you mean, Mom?"

"Before Gabe, when you had any doubts about what I was saying or what your friends were saying, you suppressed them. You never trusted your own judgment. But how you handled the Bookcourt boycott was entirely different. I doubt you'd have been able to stick to your guns the same way if you hadn't started spending time with him." Mom pauses before adding, "He gave you a reprieve from all of us."

"That's totally true," Del agrees. "Falling for Gabe gave you room to see what you really cared about."

I look at my moms, love filling my heart. "Thanks for seeing that and for understanding me so well. I didn't fully realize you did."

"Honey, no matter what, you're my daughter. I always see you."

Mimi is holding back tears.

"I'm going to go get him back!" I say. After a hug from each of them, I hop on my bike and pedal toward the Delgados.

As I ride up to their house, my heart drops. The sight before me is utterly chaotic. Various groups of people are shouting about everything, from wild claims that Senator Delgado is heading an extreme left movement in the Senate, to support for worker's rights, to predictions of the demise of capitalism. Amidst the clamor, I even hear a call of "Gabe is our hero!"

The scene on Gabe's front lawn humbles me. Realizing that there's no way for me to push through the throngs of people to reach the front door, I step away from the crowd. I call Gabe's cell again, but he doesn't answer. I leave yet another heartfelt message, this time adding that I've had some really important realizations of late, and that if he would just give me five minutes, I'd leave him alone afterward.

I cross the street and find myself in front of Mason's house. I wonder if he's home. He's been weirdly absent this weekend. I get the sense he doesn't want to hear me wail about Gabe. I text him and ask if he's around. He says he will be right out.

I feel a weird sense of déjà vu, and I realize I never complied with Mason's request to stop by after I saw Gabe the day of the fight.

When Mason meets me on his front lawn, he looks alarmed. "Are you okay? This is all pretty intense. Between this and the Bookcourt news, what a strange few days. How is Gabe doing with it all?"

I'm confused. "Gabe's not speaking to me. I thought you knew that."

"I didn't. Wow." He glances at my face again. "You seem really upset."

I blink, my confusion growing. "Of course I'm upset. I just told you he's not speaking to me." My mind wanders. I again see the expression on Gabe's face as I was leaving his house after our family dinner. My voice breaks again. "He could barely look at me," I whisper as a new onslaught of tears cascades down my face.

Mason looks stricken. "You really care about him, don't you?"

I look into Mason's eyes, and suddenly it feels essential that he understand. "I'm in love with him, Mase."

"You're what?" Mason holds a hand over his chest as if he's in pain.

"Why are you so shocked? We kind of talked about this last week."

Mason stares angrily at me and gives me a tortured look. "I feel like I'm losing you."

"You're not losing me. I'm right here." I let my watery gaze meet his. I smile to show him my conviction. I raise my hand to reach for his.

But he just stands there, staring at my outstretched hand. I struggle to keep a smile on my face.

When Mason lifts his head, I see his eyes are wet as well. "It's funny. When I see your hand reaching for mine, a million memories come to mind." He gives me a sad, quiet smile. "I remember in first grade when you picked me up after Scottie used my scarf to swing me in the air and drop me on the ground. I remember when we were eight years old at summer camp and held hands when we jumped off that frightening high dive. I remember lifting you off the grass at Lizzy's party freshman year when you got drunk for the first time and felt nauseated."

I can't make complete sense of his nostalgic wanderings, but as I look at my open hand and his hands clenched into fists at his sides, I feel a sense of despair. "Then why won't you take my hand now?"

Mason's green eyes pierce mine. "Do you really love Gabe?"

I shake my head in distress. "Why are you asking me in that tone? What's this really about, Mase?"

"Just answer the question, Anna!"

"Stop!" I reach up to grab his shoulders. "What's wrong with you? Why are you acting like this?"

"You know why." He looks infuriated.

"I really don't." Tears spill down my cheeks.

"When you first started this Gabe thing, I thought it was some weird rebellion. But it's not that at all. I'm so dumb."

"You're not making any sense, Mason!" I'm yelling now too. I drop my hands from his shoulders and turn away in frustration.

"How's this for clarification?"

Before I know what's happening, Mason spins me around and presses his lips to mine. The feeling is warm and nice, but I pull away in shock. "What are you doing?"

His eyes are over-bright. "I thought the reason we weren't together was because of Del. I understood that. But do you love Gabe more than you love me?"

I shake my head again, not able to make sense of what's unfolding. I desperately wish it were a dream I could wake up from. "I'm not answering that. It's ridiculous."

"He doesn't have any morals."

I'm incensed. "Oh yeah? Gabe's not the one who has a girl-friend and yet is kissing other girls. Or have you forgotten about Zoe?"

Mason looks ashamed. "Of course I haven't."

Suddenly a voice interrupts. "I'm so glad to hear that," says the voice. "Funny how I just keep finding you two in these special moments."

We whip around to find Zoe on the steps, ten feet from us. Her face is stony, but her eyes show such stark betrayal that I recoil.

Mason looks horrified. He steps away from me, staring at Zoe. "Zoe," he begins haltingly. "I don't know what to say. I'm so ashamed and sorry and—"

Zoe cuts him off. "Why don't you save it? This sucks, Mason. Really. I'm so into you, but..." She shakes her head. "I'd rather talk to you alone." She looks at me. I'm frozen like a statue.

"Of course," I finally say and scramble to leave, but as I'm passing Zoe, she calls out: "Wait."

I brace myself. With a deep breath, I turn around. "Yes?"

"I actually should tell you that I heard the Delgados' cell phone reception is all messed up because of the protesters. No one can get through. I thought you'd want to know that."

I digest what Zoe said, and I look into her eyes. We've caused each other so much pain, but at the end of the day, I know Zoe is a good person—a good person who I just hurt in the worst possible way, even though I never meant to.

"Thank you for telling me." I smile sadly and walk away.

As I cross the street back toward the Delgado house, past the protesters, the weight of all this hits me. I pull out my phone but, realizing it's useless to try and reach Gabe, I head home.

# CHAPTER

## 63

As I ride back to my house with a heavy chest, my mind is in loops. How did everything get so screwed up? I think of Zoe and wish the ground would swallow me whole.

"Anna."

I'm so focused on my thoughts that it takes me a moment to realize a stately black car is pulling up beside me.

It's Gabe. My jaw goes slack.

"I've been calling your name and honking at you for like ten minutes." Gabe's eyes look guarded.

I'm so relieved to see him that I fall off my bike. I yelp as the frame tumbles on top of me.

Before I know it, Gabe jumps out of his car and pulls me up.

"Are you okay?" He adjusts my wobbly helmet, then quickly removes his hands and shoves them in his pockets.

"Yes, I—" I brush off the dirt from my now-torn jeans, wincing as I feel what is definitely a gash at my knee.

"Are you sure?" Gabe looks down at my knee. "You're bleeding," he says, looking alarmed. "We need to wash this right away." He turns back toward the car, but I grab onto him.

"I'm fine. I am. I have so much to tell you. But first, how did you escape the house?"

"We have a passageway from the basement that leads to a garage across the street."

"You do?"

"Yeah, we all thought my mom was crazy when she insisted on it, but as usual, she was right."

"It's funny how moms seem to have superpowers."

"Yeah, it is."

"I've been trying to reach you non-stop. Did you get any of my messages?" Hurt washes over me.

"I got a few, but by your expression, I don't think I got them all. I haven't been responding to anyone."

I look into his face. "Zoe just told me the cell signal in your house has been off because of everything."

He nods. "Yeah, it has been. How did she know that, though?"

"Er." My cheeks feel hot. "I wasn't really able to ask her any follow-up questions."

Gabe tilts his head, clearly noting my discomfort. "Why not?"

"Well, uh, I didn't think it was great timing given that she'd just caught Mason kissing me."

I watch with anxiety as rage settles over Gabe's face. He clenches his fists into tight balls, and his jawline goes rigid. "You kissed Mason? What the hell, Anna? I'm out of here."

"No! Wait!" I step in front of him. "He kissed me, and I immediately pulled away and yelled at him."

Gabe's body relaxes a fraction. "Are you okay?" He searches my face for answers, and I assure him I'm fine. "Okay," he exhales. "I know how close you two are. That must have been awkward."

It feels so weird to be standing here with Gabe after days of agonizing.

I let out a shaky breath. "He's in pain." My voice hiccups. I hate to picture Mason in pain, and I especially hate knowing I may have caused some of it.

"You can't blame yourself, Anna. It's not your fault you don't have those type of feelings for him. Besides, it was pretty scummy of him, considering you're both with other people. I mean, I don't really know what our status is right now, but the point stands."

His words pierce my heart. Suddenly, I feel furious. "Fuck you, Gabe. You're being so mean to me. I've been beside myself for days. Do you know what it is like for me to be totally cut out by you?"

Gabe studies my face quietly. "I'm sorry, Anna. I know that was hard. It was hard for me too, but I had to sort through some stuff on my own. I can't believe I caused this whole mess for my dad." He looks at me, eyes wide and vulnerable. "I think you know how much I'd feared doing just that."

"I know," I say. Gabe seems more like himself than he's been since the lacrosse game, but I'm not sure what it all means. Part of me wants to step toward him, but I'm too unsure of myself. "How is your family doing?"

"They're taking it in stride. My dad thinks it will blow over, but I can tell it's taking a toll on him. I swear he has more grays than he did last week."

"And your mom and Bea?"

"My mom's trying to make it a festive lockdown experience. She says she'll take any excuse for family bonding, but she's stressed. Bea seems to be over that little crush she had on Mason's brother, but she's still in full-drama mode. But when is she not?"

I nod, my eyes brimming with tears. "I hate that this is happening to you." I want to take him into my arms, but I'm not ready for another rejection, so I stay still.

He looks into my eyes. "I've realized something the past couple days. In a weird way, the protesters helped, especially the really crazy ones."

"They have?"

"Yeah, it's like watching all my worst fears come true, and it sucks, but I'm still me. I'm still okay, and I wouldn't have traded for a different situation. You were right. Standing up to Scottie was a long time coming. And even though it created a mess, maybe for the first time since my dad came into office, I was just acting for myself, making mistakes, and growing from them. It feels important." He looks me directly in the eye. "And I know I have you to thank for that."

I stare at him, dumbstruck.

"Wow, I've silenced you. I didn't really think that was possible," Gabe jokes, but he looks a little worried.

"Very funny, but no one will ever do that." I try and smile back, but too many feelings are warring inside me. Finally, I manage to put some words to my internal tornado. "I want you to know it's the same for me. This whole time, liking you and then being with you, I was so afraid of losing myself and my moral edge. But really, I found it. I finally can sit in the gray, not knowing the answers, not assuming the people around me are automatically right. It's so powerful to feel that. To feel like my own separate person."

Gabe's smile ticks up to a full beam, but he looks nervous as he says, "I know it sucked that I iced you out these last two weeks, but I'm hoping you can forgive me because I could really use a hug right now."

I let out a big breath I hadn't realized I'd been holding. I step toward him and into his arms. He pulls me tightly into his chest and murmurs he's sorry again. "I care about you so much. I hope you know that."

I turn my head upward and kiss his cheek and then work my way down his jawline and toward his lips.

Gabe lets out a laugh, and I notice that his eyes are shining with emotion.

He places his hands on either side of my cheeks. I luxuriate in his warm touch. He leans toward me, but I step back.

"What? I thought we just had a moment there?"

"We did, but one more problem." I stare at him intently.

"Yes, Annabelle?" he asks with amusement and exasperation that feels so familiar I want to sing from a rooftop.

"You said you care a lot about me?"

"Yes, and I stand by that."

"Well, that's not really good enough, considering I told Mason just thirty minutes ago that I'm in love with you."

Gabe breaks into a smile so wide that I laugh.

"I have to say, darling, you sure upped me in the romance department."

"Is that all you have to say?"

"No." His smile fades as he pulls me close. He rests his forehead on mine for a moment before pulling my chin up gently and I'm looking straight into his eyes. "I love you, Annabelle Morningstar. You drive me crazy half the time, but I really do love you."

I leap into his arms with a whoop. He laughs and stumbles, trying to maintain our balance. He pulls my face to his, and our lips meet again.

# CHAPTER
## 64

One Month Later

I pull my car behind ten others lined up on the dirt path near the Greenway's main trail. My heart swells with pride as I get out and see twenty of our classmates with bags in their hands.

Gabe, who looks adorable in a "Clean Up the Greens" baseball cap, is directing people to different areas. He came early to help Zoe set up.

Del and Mason approach me. Del has the same hat on, her wavy hair lopped through the back of the baseball cap. "I have to say, this is pretty cool."

Mason looks at me, and we exchange awkward smiles. We've tried our best to rebalance our friendship over the last month, but we're still hesitant to hang out without Del. The awkwardness still beats loudly between us, but I continue to hope it will retreat one day.

"I have to admit Zoe did well with this," I say.

Mason emphatically agrees that she did a "fantastic job." His eagerness to praise Zoe seems tinged with his usual guilt. She broke up with him the night after she caught him kissing me. Zoe acted pretty heartbroken at first, but now mainly seems to relish bossing him around at Liaison meetings.

After funding for the parks was slashed in a recent budget cut, Zoe organized an ongoing trail cleanup. She has had a minimum of fifteen volunteers out here every weekend to keep up trail maintenance and remove any trash.

Gabe walks over to us. He greets Del with a smile and flicks her hat teasingly. He nods coolly at Mason and places an arm around my shoulder. Gabe and Mason are still extremely tense around each other.

One of the best things about Zoe's latest project is that it's a cause Gabe and I completely agree on.

Gabe takes the extra trash bags I just picked up at the store. "Great. Thanks, babe."

I can see Mason narrow his eyes at "babe."

I can also tell by the twinkle in Gabe's eyes that he was intentionally trying to piss off Mason. I roll my eyes and elbow Gabe in the stomach, which makes him grin.

Mason heads over to help Lizzy, who's struggling to fish out some plastic bottles from a large, muddy stretch of the trail.

"Okay, let's get to work, team," Gabe enthuses to me and Del. He's team captain today.

Del takes a handful of bags. "Where do you want us to start, Gabe?" she asks as a yawning Sam walks up to join us. He projects his usual good-natured attitude.

"Would you and Sam mind going to the southside of the trail about a mile up? Looks like some hikers left their lunch wrappers there."

"You got it, boss." She tips her hat and tugs Sam behind her.

I link my arm with Gabe's as we start walking behind them. I kiss his cheek.

"What was that for?"

"For being an awesome Greenway team captain."

He kisses me quickly on the lips. "I have to say it feels pretty good."

I beam at him, thinking how much more relaxed I've felt in the last month. I'm back on the Liberal Liaisons executive team, championing the pro-choice movement and gay rights. I'm still fig-

326

uring out how to balance all my feelings about what happened with Bookcourt, but I'm giving myself space to do it. Zoe agreed to let me back on the Liaison executive team as long as I let her send me weekly articles on the subject of worker's rights.

Meanwhile, my running times continue to improve thanks to Coach Farmer's rigorous trainings and I'm loving it. I've even found myself caring a little less about exactly what college I attend. I just want to find the right fit for me, whatever school that might be.

"Where did they go?" Gabe says, looking around.

"Isn't that Sam?" I point to a tall tree, which Sam seems to be leaning on with his face pressed against the trunk.

"What's he doing?"

We take a step closer. "Oh my god!" I exclaim.

Gabe's jaw drops open. "No way."

Sam and Del are full-on making out against the tree.

Gabe and I look at each other and start laughing.

"Well, that explains why she's been busy the past few weeks. Guess we know what she's been up to."

Gabe shrugs and shakes his head in disbelief. "Sometimes it's better not to know." He turns away from Sam and Del, who are still wrapped in each other's arms. "I think we better work on their area for them. Seems like they'll be indisposed for a while."

I laugh, slightly taken aback at their display of passion. As I follow Gabe toward the clearing, a thought occurs to me: "Do you think we've started a trend?"

Gabe looks over his shoulder with a smile. "You mean like Republicans and Democrats hooking up?"

"No, I mean like Republicans and Democrats falling in love."

He takes my hand, tugs me toward him, and gives me a long, mind-bending kiss. "Crazier things have happened."

I sigh happily. "Yes, they have. Now let's go save the planet."

Gabe laughs. "What else would we be doing on a Saturday?"

Hand in hand, we walk up the mountain, stopping to pick up litter, refreshing the trail markers, and sneaking kisses whenever possible.

# ACKNOWLEDGEMENTS

It truly takes a village—especially in my case.

Thank you to my world-class agents, Jane Startz and Dorothy Vickery, for your faith in me, your wisdom, and your brilliance from start to finish. What a pleasure to be shepherded by two such formidable women!

To Bruce Bortz, my amazing publisher, thank you for seeing the potential in this book, for your contagious enthusiasm, and for giving me this opportunity.

Thank you to my wonderful, all-knowing publicist Kathleen Carter.

To my dear friend Julie Nusbaum—how lucky are we to have met at a summer program in our teens? Thank you for seeing me so clearly, for all the late-night texts, calls, thoughts, edits, and reassurance through this novel and the last twenty-plus years of friendship.

To Chris Wlach, my wise literary buddy: You were one of the first and last readers of the book and your edits and comments shaped it immeasurably.

To Giselle Barcia and Anna Kadyshevich—thank you for your unending care and patience in navigating this process.

I've been blessed with strong, female friendships. I'd like to thank Alison Bowen, Ariel Cherkasky, Rebecca Chubak, Kate Meek, and Rachael Sussman for loving me through all my hopes and dreams (and as you know, that requires a lot of zany conversations).

Thank you to my wonderful in-laws, aunts, uncles, and cousins for their encouragement.

To Jessie Roberts, Kate Skolnick, and Marc Williams, thank you for dotting my i's and crossing my t's.

Thank you to my Brooklyn moms, my NCRC moms, and my Mann moms for sharing this experience with me.

To Margot Locker, my wonderful sister, the first victim of my imagination: Thank you for always being there for me!

Thank you again (and again and again) to my mom and dad, to whom this book is dedicated and without whom I'd never be here for so many reasons. You're simply the best.

Last but not least, thank you to my three boys: my husband, Daniel Bernstein, and our sons, Alex and Theo, who have been by my side (whether they wanted to be or not) through all the twists and turns of the writing and publishing process. The joy and humor you bring to my life makes this all the more meaningful.

## ABOUT THE AUTHOR

Emily Locker spent most of fourth grade persuading her friends to reenact scenes from Sweet Valley High. She was raised in Washington, D.C., by two psychotherapists, who often caught her reading well past midnight and who inspired her early interest in the human psyche and relationship dynamics.

Emily moved to New York City after graduating from the University of Rochester to complete a Social Work graduate program at New York University. Her first job was at The World Trade Center Program, where she provided individual and group psychotherapy to first responders.

She recently returned to Washington, D.C., where she lives with her husband and two young sons.

When Emily is not writing or chasing after her "lively" boys, she works as a therapist in private practice.

Running Mates is her first novel.